5/22

Murder at an
Irish Christmas

MURDER AT AN
IRISH CHRISTMAS

CARLENE O'CONNOR

THORNDIKE PRESS
A part of Gale, a Cengage Company

Copyright © 2020 by Mary Carter.
An Irish Village Mystery.
Thorndike Press, a part of Gale, a Cengage Company.

**LIBRARY OF CONGRESS CIP DATA ON FILE.
CATALOGUING IN PUBLICATION FOR THIS BOOK
IS AVAILABLE FROM THE LIBRARY OF CONGRESS.**

ISBN-13: 978-1-4328-9245-6 (hardcover alk. paper)

Published in 2021 by arrangement with Kensington Books, an imprint
of Kensington Publishing Corp.

Printed in Mexico
Print Number: 01   Print Year: 2022

This novel is dedicated to both sets of my grandparents: paternal grandparents, Vernon and Virginia Carter, and maternal grandparents, Howard George and Mary Cunningham-George. There's nothing like the love of a grandparent. I was lucky to know and cherish all of mine. Gone, but never forgotten.

ACKNOWLEDGMENTS

Thank you to the usual suspects: My editor, John Scognamiglio; my agent, Evan Marshall; publicist Larissa Ackerman; and all the editors, and copy editors, and book cover artists, and hardworking Kensington staff. We all know it takes a village to make a book. Many, many thanks. Thank you to friends and family for cheering me on, especially during the gray winter months. And thank you, readers. I wouldn't keep doing it without you. Cheers!

CHAPTER 1

Siobhán O'Sullivan and her brood were here, in a rocky pasture in front of an old stone whiskey mill in a colorful village in West Cork. Dubbed the "Wild West" of Ireland, and running from Kinsale to the Beara Peninsula, West Cork was known for its rugged coastline, unique peninsulas, and mountains, with villages spread out along the Wild Atlantic Way. The region attracted adventure seekers, water enthusiasts, and hikers alike. For Siobhán, the only thing on the agenda this year was peace, joy, and a little holiday fun. James, the eldest of the O'Sullivan Six, had yet to arrive. He and his fiancé, Elise, were due any minute. With the wind whipping around them, the O'Sullivans stood in the middle of a crowd, waiting for the doors to the mill to open. Siobhán wished the old stone walls could talk. Or pour her a drink. In the distance the field ended in a rocky cliff with the

Atlantic Ocean churning below it. What a magical setting to celebrate the holidays. Even if this one did come with strings. An entire orchestra of them.

This holiday would be all about music and fun. *Craic agus ceol.* James was engaged to be married to Elise Elliot, and they had new family members to embrace. (*Or kick in the arse.*) Thoughts like the latter made Siobhán fear she wasn't dealing with it very well. When it came to family, change didn't come easy. At least he was marrying into a musical family. Hadn't she always wanted them to be more musical?

A colorful banner strung above old wooden doors marked the entrance to the old mill:

WELCOME ORCHESTRA MEMBERS!

In front of the mill, an excited crowd had gathered. A sea of gloved hands clutched instruments and held boxes overflowing with wreaths, tinsel, and fat red bows. An enormous pine tree leaned against the front of the building, as if it had grown tired of waiting to be let in and adorned. A pair of donkeys brayed from the top of the nearest hill, browned off that they hadn't received an invite. And neither man nor beast could blame them. This is where the holiday concert would take place, six days from now on Christmas Eve, with their own private orchestra. Members of the RTÈ National Symphony Orchestra and a few musicians from London would be in attendance. It was all in honor of renowned conductor Enda Elliot. And Elise just happened to be his granddaughter. How exciting.

Christmas Eve was one week away, and musicians and villagers alike had volunteered to help decorate the old whiskey mill for the concert. A sense of excitement thrummed through the crowd despite that howling wind whipping Siobhán's auburn locks into her eyes. She tucked the errant strands into the back of her cap, then tightened her scarf. Rumors of snow had been dancing around, and she could smell it in the air.

"Why are they standing out in the cold?" Her jittery brother Eoin bounced beside her. Although he had safely driven them here from Kilbane, he'd been fueled by large mugs of tea and he was eager to get inside and use the jax. Ciarán, Ann, and Gráinne had yet to get out of the car; they were still in the back seat huddled over *Miracle on 34th Street* playing on the family iPad. Given they'd grumbled about watching a black-and-white film in the first place, Siobhán was over the moon that they'd fallen in love with it just as she had so many years ago. She remembered watching it with James and her mam and da, when it was just the four of them cuddled by a peat fire. Every Christmas that came and went brought those memories back into sharp focus, sweeter than any shiny wrapped gift.

"I'll see what's going on." Siobhán nudged, and then elbowed, her way through padded winter coats, and flutes, and trumpets, and cellos (or so she was guessing based on the sizes of their cases), wondering which of these folks were related to Elise. She lamented that the lovebirds were traveling separately, but no doubt they wanted some romantic alone time before being bombarded with family. A longing for her own fiancé, Macdara Flannery, rose in her, but she tamped it down. He needed to spend his holiday with his mam. He would arrive the day after Christmas, and they would at least have New Year's Eve together before heading back home.

In front of the doors to the mill stood a tall black man and a Korean Irish woman. Of course Siobhán recognized them immediately from her recent internet searches. She elbowed her brother. "Harry Williams and Leah Elliot," she whispered.

He grunted. "Don't talk to them, I can't hold it much longer."

Siobhán couldn't talk to them if she wanted to, as her admiration rendered her mute. Leah Elliot, a world-class violinist, was born in South Korea, moved to Dublin with her family when she was barely a year old, declared a musical prodigy by two years of age, was performing solos by age ten, joined the RTÈ National Orchestra three years ago as first chair, and five years ago became Enda Elliot's third wife. That was a lot of dates and ages for Siobhán to keep in her poor head, but she couldn't help it — the violin virtuoso had officially turned Siobhán O'Sullivan into a cyberstalker. And now here she was, so close Siobhán could reach out and touch her.

Leah Elliot was a striking woman wearing a faux-fur purple coat with matching purple streaks running through her silky hair. The man beside her, Harry Williams, was another famous conductor from London and if the rumors were true, he was somewhat of a rival of Enda Elliot. His nemesis? Did such a thing even exist these days? There had definitely been some chin-wagging about it online. The buzz was that he was trying to lure Leah to London. Siobhán could imagine that didn't sit well with Enda. It probably didn't help that Mr. Williams was younger and extremely handsome. Not to mention stylish in a suede golden coat. It looked so soft Siobhán imagined running her hands down the sleeves, which brought a flash of heat to her cheeks. Siobhán knew she was staring, her eyes ping-ponging between the renowned musicians as if trying to memorize the moment. Leah had a string of garland draped around her neck like a scarf. In her right hand she held a violin case, whereas Harry Williams gripped folding chairs.

Were they waiting for Enda Elliot? Siobhán did a quick scan of the crowd, wondering if he was standing in their midst, but there were too many old men to choose from. If he was here, he wasn't standing by his gorgeous wife. It was hard not to gawp at the age difference between them. Leah Elliot was clearly only in her early thirties, and Enda Elliot was seventy-five. Siobhán knew she shouldn't judge — perhaps a love forged by music knew no age. "It's dire straits," Eoin croaked. "I'm going to have to find a tree." He glanced at the Christmas tree propped up against the mill. Siobhán shot him a look — *Don't you dare* — then turned to Harry and Leah, smiled broadly,

14

and pointed to the door.

"Is it locked?"

Harry and Leah turned to her in unison and blinked. *Of course it's locked, you eejit, that's why everyone's standing out in the cold.*

"Unless you have a key?" Harry Williams asked. He had a smooth, deep voice and an English accent.

"Sorry, no." Everything Siobhán wanted to say was stuck in her throat.

"Catherine Healy was supposed to be here already," Leah said. She had a lovely Irish accent and was even more beautiful up close than in all her glamour shots online. "Moira should have known better than to let her take charge of the key."

"I hear it's going to snow," Siobhán said. *Eeejit, eejit, eejit. Say something intelligent. Or witty.* "Happy Christmas!" Something festive would have to do.

"Happy Christmas," Leah echoed. "We're certainly going to remember this year."

"Happy Christmas indeed," Harry Williams said.

Eoin, who had apparently reached his threshold, bolted for the back of the building. Harry raised an eyebrow, and Leah tilted her head. Siobhán continued to smile as if she hadn't noticed. She prayed no one was around the back of the building to witness him watering the landscape, or her brother could be hauled off to the drunk tank despite being perfectly sober.

"There's Moira," Harry said, scanning the crowed. "Moira!"

Moira. Elise's mother. Siobhán turned to see.

An older woman brushed past the crowd in a black fur coat. The ends of her stylish gray hair fluttered beneath a soft pink hat. Siobhán suddenly wished she had worn something other than denims, a black jumper, and her bulky winter coat. These people were dressed to impress. "I can't get ahold of Catherine," Moira said as she neared. "She swore she'd be here bright and early to get a start on painting the mural." Moira Elliot was petite, like her daughter, with similar Bambi brown eyes. The pink hat matched her rosy cheeks. "Moira Elliot?" Siobhán asked.

"Yes?" Her tone was friendly but guarded.

"I'm Siobhán O'Sullivan. James is my brother."

"Right. Lovely." Her rigid smile betrayed her words, making it quite obvious the engagement wasn't exactly welcome news. Despite feeling the exact same way, Siobhán couldn't help but feel a bit stung. *You're lucky to have us,* she wanted to say. *We're the O'Sullivan Six. Flawed, but adorable. And whatever you do, don't venture to the back of the building.* Moira turned to the crowd. "I'm afraid we're locked out."

"James?" Leah said, flashing Siobhán a bright smile. "As in Elise's fiancé?"

"Yes," Siobhán said. "The very same."

Leah reached out and squeezed Siobhán's hand. Even though they were both wearing gloves, the thought flittered through Siobhán's head that she was never going to wash her hand again. "We can't wait to meet the man behind her cow eyes," Leah said, fluttering her eyelashes. Then she let out a sound that was too pretty to be called a laugh. Perhaps she was trying to moo. She was a delight.

Moira's mouth disagreed. It twitched in annoyance.

"We're thrilled to meet Elise's family as well," Siobhán said. *I mean you. I'm thrilled to meet you.* "We're not very musical ourselves." *Now why did she go and say that?* "But I do a bit of whittling." Another eejit remark. Maybe she could whittle Leah a violin. It had been too long since she'd practiced the craft taught to her by her grandfather as an attempt to keep her temper in check. Then again, she could never craft a violin that Leah wouldn't be

17

able to play. *Useless.*

"Everyone is musical to some degree," Leah said with a grin.

Harry Williams leaned in. "The rhythm of life."

Leah nodded enthusiastically. "Exactly. If you stopped to listen now, what do you hear?"

Siobhán waited with rapt attention, realizing too late it wasn't a rhetorical question. She forced herself to listen. "I hear voices and the wind."

"Good," Leah said, her eyes bright and attentive. "What else?"

"Birds. Footsteps." *Why doesn't she know the names of birds? She could sound sophisticated. I hear the ascending call of the curlew.* But she wasn't sure what kind of bird it was, so she kept her gob shut. "I heard a donkey earlier, and it feels like I can hear the ocean."

"You're musical after all," Harry Williams said.

"Indeed," Leah chimed in. "Music is all around us, all the time, you'll be grand." She toyed with the garland around her neck. "Although you might find the Elliot family gift exchange a bit of a challenge."

"The what now?" Siobhán blurted out.

"Secret Santa," Harry Williams said, rubbing his hands. "I can't wait."

"Secret Santa?" Siobhán felt like a stunned parrot, just repeating everyone around her.

Leah held up a hand as if she didn't want to be blamed. "It's Elise's idea. We're all going to draw a name from a hat. Whoever you pick, you become his or her Secret Santa."

"And the gift you choose must be music related," Harry chimed in.

"Oh," Siobhán said. "Lovely." *Horrible, horrible, horrible idea.* How on earth could any of the O'Sullivans choose a musical gift for orchestra members? And in this tiny village in West Cork? What would they be able to find? Elise hadn't even arrived yet and she was already giving Siobhán a pain in the head. Did she even bring her headache tablets?

"You don't look too pleased," Leah said.

"It certainly looks like you struck a wrong note with that news," Harry agreed with a hearty laugh. Before Siobhán could think of anything else to say, a white lorry splattered with mud screeched into the drive, throwing up gravel, and all heads turned.

"Catherine," Moira said. "At least we know why she's late." Siobhán glanced at the driver of the lorry, a youngish man with an old-fashioned mustache and a wide grin.

19

"Theodore Baskins." Moira spit the name out as if it were something distasteful. "I can't believe he has the nerve to show his face." There was a story there, but Siobhán didn't know them well enough to pry. *Yet.*

"Don't forget," Leah said in a singsong tone. "It's Christmas."

"Of course," Moira said. "What's a little theft between neighbors when it's Christmas?"

Ouch. There was so much water under that bridge it was floating. "Theft?" Siobhán couldn't help but ask.

Moira turned to Siobhán. "My father won a very important award last year, and a month ago yer one stole it right off his fireplace mantle."

"Catherine brought it back with her apologies," Leah said softly. "A drunken joke, apparently."

Moira's eyes said *Bah humbug,* and they didn't leave Theodore Baskins for a second, even as a middle-aged woman in the passenger seat got out of the lorry and headed for them. Baskins beeped his horn with a grin, making Moira and many others in the crowd jump. He threw his head back and roared with laughter.

"One of these days," Moira said under her breath.

20

"Where's Enda?" Harry asked, scanning the crowd and looking as if he wanted to change the subject.

Moira frowned, then glanced at Leah. "Didn't he meet you at the airport?"

Leah shook her head. "We had to rent a car."

Moira tilted her head. "That's odd. Did you call him?"

"Voice mail," Leah said. "You know your father." It was jarring, hearing Leah say *Your father* to the older woman. But of course, he was Moira's father. *Younger wife. Older daughter.* Did Moira resent the much younger wife? How could you resent someone as talented and beautiful as Leah Elliot? She was warm and had style. Anyone who wore purple faux fur with matching streaks in her lovely hair had to be fun to be around. Gráinne was going to like her based on the hair alone. Siobhán's younger sister was a personal stylist. But as wonderful as Siobhán found Leah, she could feel the tension between these nonblood relatives. No matter how different the village, family drama was always the same. And since it wasn't her family drama for once, Siobhán was glued to every word.

Catherine Healy trudged toward them in work boots, flannel, and denims as a wad of keys jingled by her side. Her long salt-and-pepper hair was so tangled, Siobhán found herself imagining a giant brush, combing it out. Wasn't she freezing without a winter coat? Siobhán was getting frostbite just looking at her. "I started a practice mural at home, and before I knew it night turned into morning," she said. A paintbrush was tucked above her ear, and specks of green shone from her hands and cheek. The keys continued to jingle like Santa's sleigh.

"The musicians are going to get frostbite," Moira said. She threw a look to Theodore, who still lingered in his lorry. "I hope they'll still be able to play."

"Sorry, sorry, sorry," Catherine said. "I told you it's my fault. There's no need to blame Theodore."

"I would never," said Moira. Leah gave her a look and shook her head.

Theodore leaned out the driver's window. "My fault." He too had an English accent, but not the same smooth baritone as Harry Williams.

"We know," Moira yelled back.

"Still a grudge, I see," Catherine said with a friendly lilt.

"Still shacked up with a thief," Moira replied, her tone equally as friendly.

Fascinating.

22

Despite the cold, beads of sweat gathered on Catherine's forehead, and she wiped it with the back of her hand, transferring the specks of paint to her face. Harry and Leah parted as Catherine stuck a key into the massive wooden door, jiggling it several times before the door finally groaned open. She turned to Moira and handed her the keys. "You should think about doing the Polar Bear Swim on Christmas morning."

Moira took the keys and frowned. "Me?"

"A shock of cold can do wonders for one's perspective."

"My perspective is quite clear, I assure you."

Just as Siobhán was about to push past the bickering women and enter, a yell rang out from behind the building. Siobhán recognized the voice immediately. *Eoin.* "What in the world?" Moira said.

"Eoin?" Siobhán called, heading for the back of the building. "What's wrong?"

An old man emerged, holding Eoin by his ear and dragging him along. Mother Bear instincts kicked in as Siobhán's adrenaline surged and she hurried toward them. "Unhand him right now."

Startled by her tone, the old man dropped his grip on her brother. "Caught him wetting me tree!"

Oh no. "An honest mistake," Siobhán said.

"Me Christmas tree!" he bellowed, drawing attention from those who had not yet wandered inside.

Siobhán glared at Eoin. Why on earth would he choose a pine tree?

Eoin's face reflected his embarrassment; nevertheless he shrugged. "To be fair I had no idea it was a Christmas tree." He pointed. "It's still planted, and it's not decorated."

"I was just about to cut it down!" Spittle flew from the old man's mouth. Siobhán knew she had better turn the heat down on this argument before the poor man worked himself into a lather. Before he could snatch Eoin's ear again, Siobhán took her brother by the arm and tugged him along. "Sorry! It will never happen again."

The old man was still incensed. "What about me tree?"

"I'm sure it will dry just fine," Siobhán said. She fumbled in her purse, found twenty euro, and held it out to him.

"That beauty is worth a lot more," he said, eyeing the money.

"He didn't kill the tree," Siobhán said. "Give it a little spray of water, and it'll be grand."

He took the twenty with a shake of his

24

head. Siobhán hurried away before he could argue for more. Money was always tight around the holidays.

"Sorry I embarrassed you," Eoin said. From his red face, she knew he was mortified.

"We'll laugh at it someday," she said. *Definitely not today.* "Check on the young ones?"

He nodded. "Whatever you do, avoid the pine tree on the left," he said as he ambled back for the car, whistling as he went. Siobhán was headed for the entrance once more when a woman's scream rang out. The next thing she knew, the crowd had shifted directions, voices raised in panicked. "Call the guards," she heard a voice shout. "Call an ambulance."

"I'm a guard," Siobhán said, moving sideways to get clear of the stampede, getting jostled left and right. When she finally stumbled her way into the building, she encountered a large open space with a timber floor and stone walls. A second-floor gallery with a railing was situated just above their heads, and a spotlight shone on the space below. Harry, Moira, and Leah were huddled near the area in the center that was lit by the spotlight. Siobhán followed their gaze to a broken railing above, then to a felled ebony harp below. Why were they all so panicked about a harp? Was it that valuable? *A harp doesn't need an ambulance.* It took another second to see that the harp had a pair of wellies sticking out from its base.

"It's Enda," Leah called out. "He's not moving." Siobhán drew closer and took in the older man's face beneath the harp. He looked as if he was sleeping, but not quite peacefully.

"Oh no." She drew closer, and knew, from his thousand-yard-stare and the faint blue coloring of his lips, that he was gone. Nevertheless, she knelt and navigated underneath the harp to check for a pulse or breathing. His skin was cold to the touch, and there was no life left in him. It was impossible to ascertain from a glance if the harp delivered the final blow by crushing his chest or if the fall itself had taken his life. She turned her attention to the broken balcony. A tumble from that height could certainly be lethal, especially if you brought a harp down with you. At a glance, it appeared he must have fallen backward over the railing. Had he been pulling the harp out of the gallery and misjudged the distance of the railing? How terrifying. Bless his soul. Siobhán crossed herself, stood, and

26

gestured for everyone to back away from the body.

"Do something," Leah said. "Somebody *do something.*"

Siobhán wished she could. But that was one Christmas miracle even Santy and his sleigh couldn't deliver.

CHAPTER 2

"We have to move the harp immediately," Harry called out. "I need a few men."

"We can't." Siobhán pushed forward, glancing at the body underneath the harp once more. "He's gone," Siobhán said. "Please, back away."

"No." Leah lunged forward. Siobhán grabbed her and held her back. "I'm so sorry. You must wait outside. The guards are on their way." It was too late for an ambulance, and the scene had to be preserved. It was the only way for the guards to figure out exactly what happened. Siobhán let go of the renowned musician but stood nearby in case Leah tried to lunge forward again.

"We can't just leave him like that!" Anguish poured out of the young wife.

"I'm sorry. You want answers, right?" Leah nodded, tears running down her face, her slim body vibrating. "It's the only way. Like a car accident — we must leave everything for the guards to piece together exactly what occurred."

"What does it matter?" Leah said. "He's gone."

It was too easy to forget that not everyone thought like a guard. "I'm so sorry," Siobhán said. "The truth always matters. I know this is a terrible shock."

Harry Williams pointed to the broken rails of the balcony. His hand shook. "Isn't it quite obvious what occurred?" He took off his glasses and whipped a red handkerchief out of his pocket. It so complimented his mustard yellow coat that Siobhán was transfixed for a second. He stuck his glasses back on, then immediately glanced at the railing again as if to check whether he was seeing things.

Siobhán wasn't about to pontificate on how many things in life were more complicated than they first appeared. Perhaps it was a straightforward fall. Even more reason to preserve the scene so that it could be quickly ascertained. "Moving the harp won't help him now." No doubt the balcony rails were old. Had Enda been leaning on them? What was the time of death? Had he died on impact? Was the fall the cause of death or the crushing weight of the harp?

These were the foremost questions swimming around her mind, and the only way to answer them to satisfaction was to preserve the scene. "Who was the first to enter the mill?"

Heads swiveled as they regarded the question and one another. "I opened the door," Catherine said. "Several pushed inside at the same time."

"We were so behind," Moira said. "But I wouldn't say we shoved our way in."

"Were the lights on or off?" Siobhán asked.

"Off," Moira said. "None of us ventured in very far."

"I turned them on," Catherine said. "They're to the left of the door."

Siobhán took in the space. The lighting was coming from the sides of the mill, and there was a stark spotlight on the center of the room where the body lay.

"What does any of this matter?" Leah asked.

"It may not. But the guards will want to know every possible detail."

"For an accidental fall?" Harry Williams asked.

"If the lights were off when you entered, it only means one thing." Siobhán pointed to the gallery. "He was up there, rooting around in the pitch black. Can anyone explain why he would be attempting to move a harp in the dark?"

Everyone followed her gaze. "He didn't like wasting electricity," Moira said. "But I don't see him wandering around in the dark."

Siobhán left the rest unsaid: *And a dead man can't turn off the lights.*

At least they were focusing their panic on facts, which could help calm the nerves.

"Maybe he had his torch with him," Leah said.

If that were the case, a torch would be found in the gallery. At least it was something for the guards to work with. "Come on, let's go outside. Help is coming."

Leah resisted. "Enda," she moaned. "My Enda."

"Torch or no torch, I don't understand one thing." Moira thrust her way up-front as Harry took Leah's arm to guide her out. She pointed to her father. "Why on earth is he in his pajamas?"

Pajamas? Siobhán turned back to the body and looked once more. Sure enough, underneath his tan trench coat she spotted red material. Wellies, a coat, and pajamas. Had he come here in the middle of the night? Why? *Poor soul.* Siobhán crossed

31

herself again, a reflex as natural as breathing, a habit she couldn't break even as a guard. She finally ushered everyone out the door. Once outside she conjured the scene, trying to commit it to memory. Stone walls, a timber floor, timber ceiling, and a second-floor gallery that appeared to be used for storage. The lights to the left of the doors. Hallways to the back left and right, leading to the bathrooms. The body and the harp in the middle of the floor, staring up at the broken railing. As she was going over the scene, classical music began to play. It was faint, and it was coming from inside the mill. She couldn't ignore it. Was there someone else in the space? Up in the gallery? She opened the door and slipped inside. The music was louder and indeed coming from the second-floor gallery.

"Who's there?" Her voice echoed in the space. The music cut off. Then started again. Was it a ringtone? Was it Enda's phone? She had no backup, no jurisdiction, no trust built with anyone in this community. The guards were on their way. But if someone was in here, she couldn't just ignore it. She crept forward. Straight ahead, narrow wooden stairs led upward. Should she go up and check? Before Siobhán could make another move, a figure emerged in the hall, a blur hurrying toward her. As the person drew closer, Siobhán could make out a tall woman in her mid-to late thirties taking long strides. She didn't see Siobhán until she nearly barreled into her. Then she stopped, stared at Siobhán, and screamed. Siobhán threw her arms up. "It's okay, you're alright, luv, I'm a guard."

"Sorry, sorry," the woman said, her hands over her heart. She glanced at the body. "I can't." She covered her eyes with long, slim fingers.

"What are you doing in here?"

The woman put her hands down. "I came in with the crowd. I saw poor Enda and . . ." She clutched her stomach. "I have a weak constitution. I had to rush to the ladies' room."

"Are you okay now?"

She nodded. "I think so." She pointed. "How did he end up like that?"

"The guards will have to figure it out." Siobhán stopped to listen. She could no longer hear the music. "Were you playing music?"

"Music?" The woman frowned. "I'm a harpist."

Siobhán knew nothing about harp players, except that she loved the sound of the soothing, trilling music that made one feel as if they were floating on a cloud in the heavens, and she guessed those long fingers were helpful when it came to that particular instrument. They stopped and looked at the harp on top of the late Enda Elliot. "That's not mine," the woman said quickly.

"Any idea why he was getting it out of storage?"

She shook her head. "I didn't even know they were storing a harp here. Mine is outside in my vehicle."

"Perhaps more than one harpist was scheduled to play?"

The woman blinked. "That's not possible." She shook her head as if trying to convince herself. Her eyes filled with tears. "Can we talk about this somewhere else?"

"Of course." Siobhán took her arm as they headed for the door. "I heard classical music just a few moments ago coming from in here. Was it you? Or your phone?"

"No. I swear. It wasn't me." The woman's hands trembled at her side. "My phone has a normal ring tone, and it's in my vehicle."

"What is your name?"

"Ruth."

"Nice to meet you, Ruth. I'm Siobhán O'Sullivan. It's going to be alright." They hurried outside.

"Thank you," Ruth said before disappearing into the crowd. People had gathered in clumps. Cigarette smoke and gossip hung in the bitter air. Siobhán found Moira standing with a young man and a young woman with matching blond hair. They all had their arms around each other.

Moira nodded to Siobhán, broke away from the two, then gestured to them. "These are my other children, Paul and Orla."

Siobhán nodded. "Nice to meet you. I'm sorry for your loss."

"This is James's sister," Moira said to the pair.

"Lovely to meet you." Orla offered her hand. She was in her twenties with bright blue eyes. It was a bit odd to shake hands so formally during this moment, but Siobhán grabbed onto Orla's black leather glove and shook it. "My sister is very much in love," Orlo added. "I'm so happy for her." The declaration was accompanied by tears and a sniffling nose. "Hopefully next year my love can come. Mam said one new man was enough this year." From the look on her face, she resented that decision.

"We're happy for them as well," Siobhán said, which was only partly true.

Orla looked over Siobhán's shoulder. "Are they here? I can't wait to see them."

"They should be here soon," Siobhán

said. "I can try giving James a bell in a minute." She didn't look forward to sharing the news with him or Elise. Perhaps it should come from Moira. It would be better to deliver the news in person. Everyone was still in shock.

Orla's face looked hopeful, then soured. "I can't believe Grandfather is gone. Before his big concert. We were all so looking forward to Christmas this year."

"I hear you won't let them move the harp off my grandfather," Paul said. He was tall but stocky.

Everyone stared at Siobhán as if expecting her to apologize or at the very least explain herself. "It must seem harsh. Official procedures. I'm truly sorry."

"Of course," Paul said with a slight grimace. "I understand you're a guard and you're doing your job." He turned to his mother. "The shipment," he said, snapping his fingers.

"What, dear?" Moira asked.

"They're delivering the cases today."

"More cases?" Moira sounded horrified.

"Yes, many more." He stuck his hands into his pockets and rocked back on his heels.

"Many more?" Moira Elliot's lashes fluttered, and she seemed on the verge of fainting.

"Imagine the demand after the concert." He stopped rocking and bowed his head. "Of course, that was when this was going to be celebratory." He lifted his chin and gazed at the mill. "I was hoping to convince Grandfather that this should be the permanent home for Elliot's Irish Cream."

"Permanent." Moira closed her eyes briefly, then seemed to shake it off. "Have them take it to the house instead," she said as a pained expression overtook her face. Despite a tragic death, the unbearable facts were that life marched on.

Paul met Siobhán's gaze. "I own Elliot's Irish Cream."

He seemed to think this would mean something to her. "Do you now?"

He leaned in. "You haven't heard of Elliot's Irish Cream?"

"I have," she said.

He turned to his mam with a satisfied grin. "See?"

"Just a few seconds ago when you mentioned it," Siobhán added quickly.

"Do *you* see?" Moira said to her son. His face fell.

Guilt needled Siobhán. She hadn't meant to be cheeky. "But it sounds lovely," she added, heaping on the last-minute salve.

It did the trick. He brightened a bit. "It's only the best Irish Cream in all of Ireland." It could hardly be the best Irish Cream in all of Ireland if she'd never heard of it, but she wasn't here to argue about alcohol. He pinned his eyes on her. "Or we will be. One day."

"Congratulations," she said. To some it may have seemed like an odd thing to be speaking about, given the circumstances, but death had a way of making everyone uncomfortable, and people reacted in different, and often odd, ways.

"You must meet my cows one day soon."

"Must I?" She imagined a slew of eager cows in front of her, waiting to be introduced.

He clutched his mobile phone. "They're prize-winning cows. The land I'm leasing has perfect elevation, just above sea level, with consistent temperatures all year long, not too cold, not too hot. Due to these near-perfect conditions year-round, the pastures contain the highest concentration of vitamins, and of course the cows are grass fed. No chemicals of any kind." He leaned in as if letting her in on a secret. "Organic."

"I see."

"That makes for happy cows."

"Wonderful." She prayed they had come to the end of the discussion on vitamins, and pastures, and the general well-being of cows.

He wagged his finger. "But that's not all. I have a secret weapon. Would you like to know what it is?"

"For heaven's sakes," Moira said. "Now? Of all times?"

Paul gave a quick glance to his mam, then leaned closer to Siobhán. "*Music.* I hired young lads to sing to them. Cows love music, did you know that?"

"*Moo*sic, is it?" Orla said. Siobhán laughed, but soon wish she hadn't.

"I'm not jokin' ye," Paul said. "Cows love it no matter how you pronounce it. Did you know dat?" He was waiting for Siobhán to answer.

"I can honestly say I never gave it a thought," she said.

This seemed to cheer him up. "Indeed. It was Grandfather who gave me the idea."

"He certainly did not," Moira snapped.

Paul threw her a look of exasperation. "He did, Mam. Indirectly."

"Indirectly." She harrumphed.

"He was talking about how music changes your very soul. Uplifts you. I thought, if it works with people, why not cows?"

"Why not?" Siobhán said. He was a very good salesman, and she had to admit she was keen to try this Irish Cream.

"Yes. I took me guitar to the field one day and started to play. And don't you know, they all came running over. Running, I tell ye. They were captivated. I played 'til me fingers bled."

"Don't exaggerate," Moira said. "It's undignified."

Paul laughed at his mother with a nod of his head her way, then winked at Siobhán. "Happy cows make the best cream. They're the happiest cows you'll find anywhere on earth." For a second, Siobhán was imagining sad cows in remote corners of the earth, then switched to imagining cows on other planets, whooping it up. Paul held up his mobile phone, then lowered his head to the screen, making his chubby face look as if it had been plopped onto his torso without a neck. "I can't get a signal."

"It's better at the house," Moira said. "You should take Orla home with you."

"I'm not a child," Orla said.

"Orla is studying at Trinity College," Moira said proudly. Orla pursed her lips as if embarrassed that her mother felt the need to mention it.

Trinity College in Dublin. Where Siobhán

nearly went to college. She felt a twinge of *What Her Life Might Have Been.* "Wonderful."

"Her first year," Moira said. "Thanks to my father." She stopped as if suddenly remembering he was gone. "Now we just need to work on Elise."

"There's more to life than college, *Mam,*" Orla said. "A lot more."

Moira frowned. "Don't you start. When I was your age, no one encouraged me to go to college. You have no idea how lucky you are."

"Having us wasn't the life you wanted, is that it?" Orla said.

"Don't be cheeky," Moira said. "You should be grateful for the opportunities you've been presented."

"I'd say raising children is quite the education," Orla continued. "It's nothing to be ashamed of."

"Don't go putting words in my mouth," Moira said. "I don't know why the conversation has taken this turn. My father has just died and yet my children are going to be the death of me."

"Mam!" Orla cried. She lunged at her mother and ambushed her with a hug.

"Sorry, Mam," Paul said. "We're in shock." He leaned in. "Maybe you'd like a tip of Elliot's Irish Cream?"

"I certainly would not." Moira wrestled her way out of the hug. "You can thank me by continuing with your education, Orla. Your grandfather was very proud of you."

"I graduated from Trinity," Paul chipped in.

"Yes," Moira said, her voice sour. "You did." It was obvious that she was not on board with his Irish Cream or happy cow adventures. Siobhán somewhat found herself on Moira's side. She wished Gráinne and James would finish University and was going to do everything to encourage Eoin, and Ann, and Ciarán to go. "It's hard to suddenly stop making decisions for them," Siobhán said.

"You had to grow up fast, didn't you, dear?" Moira's gaze made Siobhán feel like a butterfly pinned to a board. Apparently, Elise had filled her mother in on the tragic passing of Naomi and Liam O'Sullivan. Killed nearly four years ago by a drunk driver in a car accident. How profoundly one's life could change in a moment. She had to drop her plans to go off to college — Trinity College in Dublin, no less — to help raise her siblings and keep their family bistro running. Although she'd never regretted the decision, there were moments when she allowed herself to wonder about what her life would have been like had they lived. She probably would have never become a garda. She couldn't imagine that. How fortunate she was to find her calling.

Speaking of guards, she was saved by the crunch of gravel under tires and looked up to see a guard car finally pulling in. The car parked, and a large man stuffed into a tiny Garda uniform climbed out. He nodded at folks as he headed for the entrance.

"Barry Cooley," Moira said to Siobhán. "Garda Cooley," she called to him in greeting.

"Moira." He tipped his hat and focused his brown eyes on her with a mixture of concern and kindness. "What's the story?"

"It's Enda," she said. "He's been crushed under a harp."

Garda Cooley's jowls bounced as his head shot up in surprise. "A harp is it now?"

"It is, so," Moira replied.

When Moira didn't offer any more, Siobhán stepped up. "He took a fall from the second-floor gallery. It appears the instrument fell on top of him."

Garda Cooley removed his hat for a moment and placed it over his head. "I am very sorry to hear that now, Moira, very sorry indeed."

"Thank you," Moira said.

"Tis a terrible shock, and what a loss, not only to the music community but certainly a loss to our little village," Cooley continued.

This was personal to them. Siobhán understood that. But she was also eager for them to start securing the scene. "I kept everyone away from the body," she said, hoping it would get his momentum going.

Garda Cooley stuck his cap back on, and his eyes narrowed. "What's a harp doing in a whiskey mill?"

"Musicians have been storing instruments in here for the Christmas Eve concert." Moira's voice sounded tight, as if she was struggling to be polite.

"Right, so," Garda Cooley said. "I should have thought of dat."

"On that topic," Siobhán said, "in the mill I ran into a woman named Ruth. She said that it wasn't her harp and she had no idea why it had been stored there or why Enda would be trying to fetch it."

Garda Cooley raked his eyes over Siobhán as if he'd just now noticed her. "And you are?"

She stuck her hand out. "Garda O'Sullivan. Visiting from Kilbane."

"Garda," he said with firm shake. He

44

turned back to Moira. "Now about this harp?"

Moira shrugged. "Perhaps my father intended on surprising Ruth with it," Moira said. "Maybe that was his big announcement."

Siobhán's ears perked up. "Big announcement?"

Moira nodded. "My father was being very dramatic about it, but he proclaimed he was going to make a big announcement at the start of the concert. I have no idea what it was."

If it was the harp, the surprise was on him. Siobhán wished she could control the thoughts that popped into her mind. She'd have to settle for being grateful that nobody else could hear them.

Garda Cooley jerked his head toward the door to the mill and then nodded at Siobhán. "You want to show me?"

"Of course." She waited until they were at the door, away from the others. "I heard music from the balcony when I was ushering out the last person. There may be someone inside."

He stopped short. "Music?"

"Classical music. From the sound of it, and the way it started and stopped, and started, and stopped again, I think it was a ringtone."

"Enda's phone?"

"It's possible. Whoever's phone it is, it sounded as if it was coming from up in the gallery." It was also possible that someone else was inside.

Cooley rubbed his chin and eyed the door. He was a thoughtful man, which boded well for the investigation.

"I was about to go up to see if I could find the source of the music when I encountered Ruth hurrying out of the ladies' room."

"Was she the source of the music?"

"She said she was not. I helped her outside. I didn't hear the music again."

Garda Cooley reached for the radio at his hip. "Let me call for backup. I need a list of everyone who is here, but I also need them gone. Can you help with dat?"

"Of course." As the guard headed back to his car to make the call, Siobhán asked Moira to handle the taking of names. "Then he needs everyone to vacate the scene."

Moira's face was a portrait of anxiety. "Are you staying?"

Siobhán nodded. "He seems willing to have me along for now."

Moira gripped Siobhán's arm. "Make sure they treat me father right."

"Of course."

"Do you need the name of the undertaker?" Moira dug in her handbag as if she was searching for the number.

Siobhán gently placed her hand on Moira's shoulder. "We won't need it just yet."

"Pardon?" Moira seemed stricken by the statement.

"If they're given the go-ahead to move the body, he'll be taken to Cork University Hospital, where the state pathologist will have to do her work before he's moved to the undertaker."

"I see."

"There's also a chance his body will have to remain in the mill until the state pathologist arrives." It was an unfortunate fact that it often took time before a body could be moved. At least he was inside away from the wind and the cold.

Moira pursed her lips but stopped digging through her handbag. "He would hate all this fuss."

He would probably hate being dead even more, but Siobhán kept this to herself. "After you collect the names, can you help get everyone home?"

"Of course."

"My siblings." Siobhán let the sentence hang.

"They'll come home with me," Moira said. "I'm sure Garda Cooley can drop you off when you're finished. We'll take you to your guest house later."

"Thank you." Siobhán hurried to their car so she could grab a notebook for Moira — Siobhán had learned to keep several small ones with her at all times — and let her brood know what was going on.

"Elise's grandfather is crushed under a harp?" Gráinne repeated. Her nostrils flared, and her black hair blew in the wind, revealing several neon blue streaks. Third in the birth order and now officially an adult, she had the air of a petulant teenager. Once again, it occurred to Siobhán that Leah Elliot and Gráinne were probably going to get on like a house on fire, and jealousy sliced through her. It wasn't always fun to be the mature one. "And you're staying?" Gráinne asked.

Siobhán pretended not to notice her sister's outrage. She promised them this would be a no-work holiday. "Just for a few minutes to talk to the guards."

"You promised," Ciarán said. "You said this holiday was about music and fun." The

48

youngest of the six, Ciarán was no longer a boy. At thirteen, he was tall and had cheekbones and lashes that girls would die for. Siobhán tried very hard not to tell him this too often. Puberty was hard enough. His voice was in the process of dropping, and his moods vacillated between child and rebel.

Her heart pitched. She took his hands. He yanked them back. "I know, petal. And I meant it. It *will be.* But a terrible accident has occurred, and I have a duty to help. I'll be back at the farmhouse soon."

"We don't even know these people," Gráinne said. "We're out in the middle of nowhere. Do they even have a telly?"

Watching telly and eating chocolates were admittedly two of their favorite holiday activities. "We're not here to watch shows," Siobhán said. "We're here to appreciate classical music, and take in this gorgeous landscape, and enjoy a different kind of Christmas."

"Look how well that's turning out," Gráinne clipped.

Siobhán pointed toward the cliffs in the distance. They couldn't see the ocean from here, but it was close and you could smell it. "Look at this view."

Gráinne pointed to the mill. "I'm sure it's

better than *that* view." She slapped her hand over her mouth. Then crossed herself. "I'm horrible," she said. "I didn't mean it at all."

"I know, luv." Siobhán put her arm around Gráinne and squeezed. "We'll make the best of it, I promise."

"It's okay," Ann said. "Elise is going to be family. You have to help." Ann was slightly younger than Gráinne but often more grounded. The peacekeeper. "I bet we can go on some amazing hikes." She was the most athletic of the six. Siobhán forced herself to run most mornings, but Ann was the one who actually enjoyed sports. She threw her arms around Gráinne. "And later you can paint my nails red and green."

Gráinne shook her head, then glanced at Ann's nails and nodded.

"Thank you," Siobhán said to Ann. Siobhán wanted to squeeze the life out of all of them. Growing up so fast. Every minute together was precious. And here she was, breaking another promise. "Get to know Elise's family a little," she encouraged. "That's why we're here."

"You'd better not take long," Gráinne said. "There's only so much classical music abuse I can take."

"I won't. Stay together."

"Why?" Ann said. "I thought this was just

an accident?"

"She worries about us, that's all," Eoin said, giving her a look. "She'll be with us before you know it."

"Of course I will."

"What about James and Elise?" Eoin asked.

"Try calling him," Siobhán said. "We shouldn't break this news to them over the phone."

"On it," Eoin said, holding up his phone. "Oh. There's no signal."

"Moira said it's better at the farmhouse."

Eoin nodded. "I'll call them as soon as we arrive."

Siobhán slipped away before she could be talked out of staying and hurried to the entrance of the mill, where Garda Cooley waited. As Moira collected names, she was diligent about sending them on their way, and slowly cars pulled out from their spots in front of the building.

"I can't believe this," Garda Cooley said. "The whole town was chuffed to bits the orchestra was on its way." He shook his head. "We should have seen this coming."

Siobhán straightened. "Oh?"

"Enda Elliot wasn't well. We've been called out to find him a couple of times."

"Find him?"

Cooley nodded. "Wandering around in the dark. Moira won't say as much, but I think he had the beginnings of dementia."

"I see." How sad. Moira had seemed surprised by it. Had that been an act put on for Siobhán's benefit?

Everyone had pulled out by the time two more guard cars showed up. Garda Cooley directed several guards to the back entrance as he and two others took the front. "Why don't you wait out here." It wasn't a question.

Wait out here? After everyone else had left? Siobhán clenched her fists. "Are you sure? I can lend a hand if you need it."

"I could use a lookout," he said, gesturing. "In case anyone tries to come in. You know yourself how people are."

"Of course." She made herself take a few deep breaths. Perhaps she or Macdara would have done the same if the roles were reversed. *Macdara.* If only he were here. She brought out her mobile phone. There was barely a signal. She sent a text:

Elise's grandfather just died.

There was no use texting the entire story. She'd fill him in when she had a signal. She stared at the screen, but no reply came in. She texted James.

We have news. Expect a call from Eoin.

She hoped he could get a signal at Moira's. She really didn't want Elise to hear the terrible news over the phone. If they talked to James first, he could break it to her. Siobhán stared at the empty field where everyone had parked their cars, which meant Enda Elliot had either been dropped off or arrived on foot. Had he been wandering again? That might explain what he was doing here in his pajamas. If he'd been suffering from dementia and his family had ignored the symptoms, they were going to blame themselves. It must be so painful to admit when a loved one isn't behaving like himself. But the consequences of ignoring it could be deadly. She wished she'd gone back to the farmhouse with the rest of them. It was one thing to be out in nature with a group of people, but Siobhán was shocked at how alone she now felt, with the bitter wind picking up and freezing her to the bone. Why ask her to stay and then not let her in?

A black car pulled into the lot and idled. Minutes later, Elise emerged, her hands filled with wrapped presents. She was petite with brunette hair and big brown eyes. Siobhán had mixed feelings about her. She was bossy with James. And mercurial. But at times she could be sweet, and it was obvious she was in love with James. "Why are the guards here?" She had a smile on her face, not expecting bad news. The car shut off and James ambled out, throwing worried glances to the guard cars.

"It's a rental," he said, pointing to the car. "What do you think?"

"Lovely," Siobhán said, heading them off. "We tried to call you, but there's no signal."

Elise nodded. "It's always that way out here. Part of the charm." She tried to move around Siobhán.

"I'm sorry to be the one to tell you. Your grandfather took a fall."

"A fall?" She glanced at the old mill. "Is it his hip?"

Siobhán cleared her throat. "He fell from the second-floor gallery in the mill. A harp fell on top of him."

Elise stopped smiling. James took the presents from her and returned them to the car. "Has he been taken to hospital?"

"I'm sorry," Siobhán said, throwing a glance at James. "There was nothing anyone could do."

"What do you mean?" Elise demanded. James put his arms around Elise, reading the scene quicker than she was. Part of that was shock.

"He's passed, luv."

Elise blinked. "Passed what?"

Elise needed to hear it in plain language. "He's dead."

Elise shook her head. "No."

"I'm so sorry."

"Stop saying that."

"Your mother and siblings have gone back the farmhouse with the others. The guards have things at hand here."

"We'll go," James said, giving Elise a squeeze.

"He's . . . still in there?" Elise asked, pointing to the mill.

"I'm afraid he has to stay in there until the state pathologist arrives or gives permission to move him to Cork University Hospital."

"The hospital? But you said he's dead."

Siobhán nodded. "To do an examination of the body."

Elise opened her mouth and then shut it. It was ghastly business, and there was often no way to soften it. "I want to see him."

"Not right now."

"Right. Now!"

James hugged her tighter. "Let's get you home."

Siobhán held up a finger. "I'm going with you. Let me just leave a note for Garda Cooley on his car."

Siobhán wasn't going to stand out here and freeze like an eejit if he didn't want her help. The business about being a lookout was nonsense. There were other guards standing along the perimeter now; they could be the lookouts. And as horrible as she felt for Enda's family, she had her family to think about. They didn't deserve to have Christmas ruined. It was a tragic event, and they would support the Elliot family the best they could *while* enjoying their holiday. Death had a way of reminding Siobhán that they did not have unlimited Christmases ahead of them. It was imperative that they do their best to enjoy every single one. Starting now.

Siobhán returned from leaving the note on Cooley's car to find Elise and James head to head in a heated discussion. Shouldn't James be comforting her? How had an argument erupted so quickly? "Please," she heard Elise say. "Don't say a word to anyone. Especially to Siobhán."

CHAPTER 3

Moira's white farmhouse was set back in a large field surrounded by rolling hills and although Siobhán couldn't see cliffs or the ocean, the smell of sea was in the air, evidence that it was nearby. It was the ideal spot for a family home, despite the weather that most likely drove a number of blow-ins away during the off-season. But Siobhán loved the forlorn atmosphere; there was something so devastatingly beautiful about the remote landscape. Nature was king in this corner of the world. A fat pine wreath with a big red bow beckoned from the door, candles flickered in the windows, and white smoke curled out of the chimney.

Siobhán parted from those heading for the house, opting to remain outdoors a little longer and explore the property. She needed to clear her head. What on earth had Elise and James been arguing about? *"Don't say a word to anyone. Especially to Siobhán."*

This was going to be her life now. James would take a wife. And this particular wife would make him keep secrets. The haunting sound of a violin filtered through the air, growing louder as Siobhán neared the closest hill. Leah Elliot stood in a small valley at the base of the hill, playing a soft melody, to a very captive donkey. Siobhán stopped. It was heartbreakingly sweet. She wanted to record it, but was aware that this was a grieving widow, and the intrusion would ruin the moment. What was it she read about Leah? It was in an article she'd come across online. *"She only speaks music."* Siobhán was suddenly furious that no one in her life had ever made her take music lessons. Maybe Ciarán would like a violin for Christmas. Who was she kidding, he'd rather have the donkey. And to be fair, it was a rather cute donkey. Siobhán could imagine him in their back garden, braying every morning to be taken for a stroll around town. Their pup, Trigger, would be furious with them. Both man and beast apparently had trouble getting used to newcomers.

Siobhán thought of the song she'd heard playing in the mill. She could hum it to Leah and see if she recognized it. But when she took a moment to try to conjure it up, she couldn't formulate a tune. It had been too faint and too quick. She should have brought one of the musicians in with her when she first heard it. Had the guards already discovered the source of the music?

Siobhán had turned away from the widow when the playing stopped.

"Hey," Leah said.

Siobhán turned back. "Hey. I'm so sorry to interrupt. You play so beautifully."

"Thank you." Bow still in hand, she wiped her nose with her sleeve.

"I'll let you be."

"No," Leah said. "Stay."

Siobhán pointed to the donkey. "He's adorable." The donkey bared his teeth and brayed. Leah laughed, but it soon turned into a cough, and then a good cry. "Would you like to come inside and I'll make you a mug of tea?" Siobhán asked. She could use one herself.

"I should have been here," Leah said. "If I'd come into town with Enda, he'd still be here."

"You can't blame yourself. No one can turn back time."

"I would have. But I wanted to spend some time with my family in Dublin, and Harry was coming later, so he offered to drive me."

"You can't change the past. Please don't torture yourself."

Leah nodded but didn't seem convinced. "I told myself it would be good for him. To have time alone with Jason."

"Jason?"

"His son. From his second wife, Faye."

"Oh."

Leah packed her violin in her case, snapped it shut, and yanked it up. "That's why I haven't gone to the house yet. I'm so angry with him. Where was he? Why wasn't he with him?"

"With him?"

Leah nodded. "Enda was in his pajamas, which meant he wandered out in the middle of the night, don't you think? Why didn't Jason watch over him?"

"Perhaps he was sleeping?"

Leah sighed. "I suppose it's not fair to take my anger out on him. That's why I'm out here, hoping to calm myself down."

"How old is Jason?"

"He just turned twenty-one. Which means the second wife is cut off."

"Pardon?"

"Enda agreed to make payments to Faye until Jason turned twenty-one."

"I see. Is Faye here?"

Leah shrugged. "I would imagine she's

coming for the concert, but I just arrived myself, so I'm in the dark."

It must be odd for Jason. Having nieces and nephews that are close to his age. They should be more like cousins or siblings. A second wife. Siobhán wondered how much drama it had caused when Enda married Leah. Apparently his first wife, Moira's mother, had passed away. But the second one was still alive, which meant divorce. It was rare for someone of Enda's age to get divorced in Ireland. Surely it had caused a stir. But Siobhán wasn't going to crack open that subject with wife number three.

"Does Jason get along with Elise, Orla, and Paul?" she asked instead.

Leah started to walk toward the farmhouse. Siobhán followed. "There's a lot of tension in the Elliot family. Enda wasn't the easiest man to deal with. Geniuses rarely are." Their wellies sunk into the mucky ground as they walked. As they neared the back of the house, they found Moira pacing by the door. She had removed her pink hat but was still wearing her fur coat. She caught Siobhán looking at it.

"It's real," she said with a sigh. "My father's gift from a previous Christmas. I wore it to please him." She stroked the fur. "And now I'll wear it to remember him."

61

Her voice cracked.

"I wouldn't dare wear mine," Leah said. "Too many eyes on me as it is."

Moira gave a sad smile. "My father never was good at buying individual gifts. All the women in his life, no matter the relation, always got the same thing."

"Every year," Leah said with a laugh. Moira joined in, and for a moment the two seemed to share a special bond.

Siobhán gestured to the house. "Is everyone here?"

Moira nodded. "People are cooking. And drinking. Your siblings are darling." This time she sounded genuine.

"Thank you," Siobhán said. "They'll do."

"Drinking," Leah said, opening the back door. "Now there's an idea." She entered and the door slammed shut behind her. Siobhán and Moira exchanged an uncomfortable glance.

"I can leave you be, if you prefer to be alone," Siobhán said.

"Actually, I was waiting for you." Moira pinned her eyes on Siobhán.

Siobhán hadn't expected this. "Me?"

Moira shifted her gaze to a thick patch of trees bordering her property to the east. "I want to go to my father's house. I was hoping you'd come with me."

"Where is his house?"

Moira pointed to the trees. "Just through there. I want to see if his lorry is still in the drive, and just have a quick look in the house. I can't understand why he was wearing his pajamas."

This was Siobhán's opportunity to address the discrepancy. "Garda Cooley said it's not the first time he was found wandering?"

Moira clamped her lips shut. "My father loved to walk. People see an old man out walking in inclement weather and they assume he's off his head. But I assure you, he was never in his pajamas." Was that the breaking point for her? Wasn't wandering in the middle of the night alarming no matter how he was dressed? Either Moira was in denial about her father's health, or she was lying. "Will you come with me?" It sounded more like a cry for help than a request.

Siobhán hesitated. Technically she'd feel better getting the approval of the guards to enter Enda's home. Then again, there was nothing to suggest this was anything other than an accident, and even if that wasn't the case, the death occurred several miles from here. She didn't see any harm in going to Enda's house.

"Has Leah already been to the house?" Even if Moira was willing to usurp the widow, Siobhán was not.

Moira shook her head. "No."

"Do you need to check with her first?"

Moira's expression soured. "It was my father's house. She rarely stayed there with him."

"Why is that?"

"They were a very independent couple. Leah is young. West Cork isn't her scene."

"Is Jason at the house?"

Moira's eyebrow shot up. "How do you know about Jason?"

Siobhán was taken aback. It was as if Moira didn't want her to know about Jason. There was definitely drama in this family. "Leah mentioned him. She wondered why he wasn't out looking for Enda."

Moira sighed. "He left a few days ago to pick up his mother in Dublin. Enda insisted. He was even going to have ramps installed at the mill for the concert."

Siobhán was having trouble following. "Ramps?"

"Oh. I guess Leah didn't tell you everything. Faye is in a wheelchair."

"I see. That was very considerate of Enda."

Moira frowned. "I agree, although it wasn't quite his style to be considerate. He was putting so much energy into this concert. It was as if it had to be perfect." Moira slapped her hand lightly on top of her head several times. "I can't believe I forgot all about Jason and Faye." Her face bore the weight of responsibility. "I don't want to give them shocking news over the phone."

"Perhaps you should simply give him a bell to let him know you need to speak with him the minute he arrives."

"I certainly will." She gestured to the left. "As soon as I've had a look around the house."

"Let's go."

The ground was hard in some spots, mucky in others. A bitter wind whipped through as they made their way toward the trees. Siobhán wished she was inside the farmhouse with a mug of tea, a thick slice of brown bread slathered with butter, and the lovely peat fire. She hoped this excursion of Moira's wouldn't take long.

"Did you play an instrument growing up?" Siobhán asked.

Moira laughed, a bitter sound that was soon swallowed up in the wind. "I tried. Heaven knows I tried. First the violin. My father said I played like a saint."

"That's nice."

"Saint Patrick. But instead of driving all the snakes out of Ireland, he said my playing had driven all the feral cats out of the village." Laughter escaped Siobhán before she could reel it in. Moira laughed along with her. "We tried piano next. I gave my father headaches. The flute was the last. He would simply walk in the room while I was practicing and shake his head. When I started having visions of knocking everyone over the head with it, I tossed it into the ocean one day and never picked up another instrument."

"It must have been difficult, growing up in his shadow."

"Shaking off the dreams of a parent is never easy. My mother wasn't musical either. But she worshipped my father."

"I read that she passed. I'm sorry."

Moira nodded. "I forgot that you can read up on my family. Sometimes I forget that we're famous."

"I must admit your father's career is very impressive. As well as Leah's."

Moira murmured in agreement. "My mother's been gone almost twenty-four years now, don't you know. How on earth is such a thing possible? I miss her like it was yesterday."

"I'm sure you do."

They stepped into the trees, and Siobhán could feel the temperature drop. Although it wasn't a full-throated woods, one could stand inside and imagine they were in one. Siobhán shivered. "You poor thing," Moira said. "We're almost there." They emerged onto an almost identical piece of property with another farmhouse. This one larger than Moira's and painted a deep blue. Enda's house was set up slightly higher than Moira's, and from a distance you could finally see a cliff jutting up. It was a gorgeous view, and if these were happier times, Siobhán would be heading for it to gaze out at the ocean. Against the dark green of the pine trees, and the soft green of the hills, it made a very impressive picture. She turned back to the house. The windows were framed in black. Siobhán had never lived anywhere but above the family bistro, and for a moment she imagined what her life would be like in a house like this. An identical pine wreath hung on the front door. "The house is gorgeous."

"Thank you. I picked out the color."

Siobhán tutted. "It makes a statement."

"Houses are my thing." Moira's eyes lit up with excitement.

"Are they now?"

Moira seemed to come alive. "I'm in charge of many of the vacation rental homes in the area. I love looking at them, renting them out to the summer blow-ins, sprucing them up." She gazed at the house. "I had the house painted as a surprise. I thought the bold color embodied his success."

"I'd say." It was certainly a house worthy of a successful man. Or woman.

Moira seemed to deflate. "He hated it."

"He did?" Siobhán was getting a picture of a man who could not be satisfied, and of a daughter who never stopped trying to please. What a wretched way to live.

"I think it's because I picked it out." Her comment solidified Siobhán's theory. How could he hate such a beautiful color? One thing was clear — this was a complicated family. She supposed all families were complicated in their own ways. Imposing their desires on one another, withholding love and disapproval if one didn't behave in a certain way. Once more she was reminded how lucky she had been. How lucky all of them had been. *Thanks, Mam and Da.* Siobhán turned back to the house. She thought the color fit in with the windswept pastures.

"It's here." Moira crossed the front of the house and pointed to a white lorry in the drive. It was similar to the one Theodore Baskins had been driving, only instead of caked with dirt, this one was clean and shining. "Why did he walk to the mill?" Moira said out loud as she began to inspect the lorry.

"Maybe he was low on petrol?" Siobhán didn't believe that, but she was trying to find a reasonable explanation. She glanced inside the cab. Keys hung from the ignition. "The keys are here."

"They are?"

Moira glanced in, and a hard look settled over her face. "Oh."

Siobhán wandered to the back of the lorry. The left tire was flat. "It's the tire."

Moira hurried over. "He must have already used his spare." Everyone who lived out here was probably taught how to change a tire. Enda had come out, tried to start his lorry, then realized he had a flat. Instead of taking the time to change the tire — perhaps Moira was right and there was no spare — he decided to walk to the mill instead. What was the hurry? He hadn't even taken the time to dress. It would help the guards to learn the time of death, so they could create a time line of when all this took place. "I'm going inside the house," Moira announced, pulling out a set of keys and heading for the back door.

"Before you enter," Siobhán said, hurrying after her, "will you take a moment to see if anything is out of place?"

Moira stopped, her eyes darting around as if she expected someone to jump out at her. "Why?"

"Just a precaution." A terrible fall. A dark mill. A flat tire. Both could be perfectly innocent. They probably were. But it was still better to be safe than sorry. Moira took her time inspecting the grounds. "Nothing is out of place."

"You're sure?" Siobhán didn't want to frighten her, but the flat tire gave her an uneasy feeling. Or maybe it was the nature of her job, causing her to see mayhem everywhere she went. He was an old man who took a terrible fall. And brought a harp down with him. Nothing unusual about that. . . .

Moira diligently followed Siobhán's suggestion. Her gaze went from the front door to the path leading out to the lorry. She took in the windows. "I can't see anything out of place."

"Do you want me to wait out here?"

"No, please come inside." Moira opened the front door, and Siobhán followed. They stepped into a large living room. The floors were made of thick pine, the walls painted a lovely eggshell white. The sparse but tasteful living room furniture faced the windows overlooking the field. There was a peekaboo view of the ocean, which sent a thrill through Siobhán. She could sit here all day with a cuppa, feet propped up, gazing out to sea. It was too bad that wasn't going to be an option. An open kitchen with an island sat at the back of the house, looking out onto a front garden. A stairwell was directly across from the back door. The decorations were simple, yet elegant and homey.

"Leah did the interior," Moira said. "It's too sparse for my liking."

"I thought Leah didn't spend much time here."

"She doesn't. But she knew my father. His head is so muddled he needed a space like this."

Head so muddled. She waited to see if Moira would say more. Had Enda Elliot taken to wandering around at night? Moira did not expound on the subject. "It's very tranquil," Siobhán said.

Moira headed for the stairs. "I need to find a suit."

For the undertaker. The business of death. "Take your time." She really wanted a cup of tea, but it would have to wait.

"There's a kettle on the counter," Moira said, reading her mind. "Make yourself a cup of tea."

71

"Would you like one?" Siobhán asked. She wasn't going to have one if it was just for her. *Please say yes.*

Moira hesitated. "That would be lovely."

"Grand." Siobhán found the kettle and turned it on. A yellow tin marked TEA sat on the counter, and cups hung above it. In the cupboard, she found biscuits. She was starving. As the kettle started its journey to boiling, Siobhán looked around. Nothing seemed out of place. If Enda had left in the middle of the night, he seemed to do so calmly.

A hook near the back door caught her eye. Patches of dirt underneath it suggested that an item used to hang there. It was the only dirty spot in the entire place. The spot was large, so her guess of an extra set of keys was eliminated. What else did people hang from hooks? An apron? That didn't explain the dirt. . . .

"Siobhán." Moira's voice rang out from upstairs. It was the tone that was jarring. She sounded frightened. Siobhán hurried up the stairs. They creaked all the way up, as if protesting the intrusion.

Moira stood at the top of the stairs. She looked old in the half light, and frankly somewhat eerie. Dark circles under her eyes suggested she hadn't been sleeping. "Are you any good at passwords?" In her hand, she held an iPad.

"What's going on?"

Moira descended with the iPad. "This was in the middle of the bed. It's open to a security feed — some kind of video — but it requires a password."

"Heavens, I couldn't begin to guess. Does it give the name of the security company?"

Moira nodded. "It's not a local company. Perhaps he found them online. Pushing security cameras." From the tone of her voice she didn't approve.

"I would say the first step would be contacting whoever this security company is."

"I'm going to ask Leah first. Maybe she knows the password."

"Come have tea while you do." *And a biscuit.*

"Alright," Moira said. "I will, so."

Finally, some order in the world.

Leah Elliot stared at the iPad as if she was afraid to touch it. Moira had fetched her from next door, and they were urging her to drink the hot tea. *Horse it into ya,* as Siobhán's da used to say. Leah remained in her coat, scarf, and hat, shivering in the kitchen as she clutched her mug. "Try *Cho-*

73

pin, Beethoven, or *Mozart.*"

Moira immersed herself in the screen, tapping away the various suggestions. Her shoulders drooped, and she looked up. "No."

Leah shrugged. "Do you think it's important?"

"Not necessarily." Moira glanced at Siobhán as if to negate the statement.

"Try *Enda Elliot,*" Leah said.

Moira laughed. "I'm sure it's not . . ." She tapped it into the screen anyway, then stopped, tilting her head and frowning. "It worked."

Leah nodded. "He always did like the sound of his own name." She said it matter-of-factly. But Siobhán couldn't help but wonder. Had there been marital discord, or was Leah's statement just a part of her personality?

"He had cameras at the mill," Moira exclaimed. Siobhán and Leah huddled over Moira's shoulder. The screen showed a barren landscape from the vantage point of a camera above a door.

"You didn't know this already?" Siobhán asked.

"He talked about placing them there," Moira said. "But I didn't know he followed through."

"He was paranoid about leaving the musical instruments unattended," Leah said.

Siobhán stared at the screen. "Isn't this a safe town?"

Leah and Moira exchanged a quick glance. "We're not without a few begrudgers," Moira replied. "But I can't imagine anyone in town stealing musical instruments."

"Theodore Baskins," Leah said.

"Because he stole Enda's award?" Siobhán prompted.

Leah nodded. "When Enda found out it was missing, he went mental. We had just had a birthday party for Enda at the house. My husband hated having people in his space. He wouldn't rest until he found the culprit."

"I'm surprised Theodore was invited," Siobhán said.

"Catherine was invited," Moira said. "She knew we didn't want Theodore, but she's a stubborn woman."

"She's paid the price, I suppose," Leah said.

Siobhán had to know more. "What makes you say that?"

"Catherine used to make a living selling her paintings to tourists in the summer."

"Because the shops in town allowed her to sell from their establishments," Moira pitched in.

"And they would hang her artwork on their walls, and give out her information if anyone inquired about them."

"She does beautiful watercolors of West Cork," Moira said.

"Yes," Siobhán said. "Didn't she say she was painting a mural for the concert?"

"Yes," Moira said. "I think it may have been a fresh start for her with the village. Mend some fences."

"How so?" Siobhán asked.

"No one promotes her art anymore," Moira explained. "Gradually everyone in the village grew so weary of Theodore that finally people insisted that until Catherine was smart enough to cut him off, they weren't going to extend their kindness anymore."

"Is Theodore really that bad?" Siobhán asked.

"He's a buffoon," Moira said. "A drunk, a cheat, a leech. I think he's burned every bridge in this village."

"I do feel bad for Catherine," Leah said. "One can't help who they love."

"They certainly can," Moira said. "Catherine is afraid to be alone, so desperate she can't see how truly vile that man is."

Siobhán had learned enough and was now

eager to steer them away from the romantic life of their neighbor. "How did Enda figure out it was Theodore who stole his award?"

"We all knew it was Theodore," Moira said. "Who else would it be?"

"Catherine finally came forward when she found the award stuffed in their laundry bin," Leah said.

"How long has he lived in West Cork?"

"Five long years," Moira said. "He's very charming. Convinced everyone in the village he was some kind of a big-shot writer. Called himself an award-winning reporter. Turns out all he has is a little blog for which he gave *himself* an award."

"Did he admit to taking it?"

"He said it was probably a joke," Leah said. "That he was only messing."

That was a new one. "*Probably* a joke?"

"He has no problem admitting that he blacks out when he drinks," Moira said. "Then has a big laugh over it. 'No harm done,' he said."

Apparently, harm was done. "Was there anyone else in town who had a problem with Enda or didn't want the orchestra to visit?" They were still staring at the screen, and Siobhán was still trying to make sense of why Enda had cameras installed. It didn't appear as if anything was going to happen.

"Enda could be aloof," Leah explained. "Some in town took offense. Once he became famous, everyone wanted to be his best friend."

"My father came here for peace of mind," Moira said. "To get *away* from crowds. There were some locals who were insulted if they couldn't get him to socialize when he was home. Typical begrudgers." The conversation was interrupted by movement on the screen. A figure emerged on the video. Moira gasped. Siobhán and Leah leaned in. At first Siobhán assumed the quality of the video was suffering. She had no other way of making sense of the dark blob moving in jerky movements toward the door. As it approached, it became clearer. Someone was wearing a hooded costume. It very much resembled the Grim Reaper.

"Is this a joke?" Leah asked.

"This is what roused Enda from bed at . . ." Moira leaned in and looked to the time stamp at the corner of the screen. "Half past midnight."

In the video the door to the mill creaked open. "Did the person use a key?" Siobhán asked.

"It's too dark to tell," Moira said. "That owner of the mill is very lax with the keys, but Enda had threatened the life out of

78

anyone who didn't lock it."

The figure slipped inside, and the door slid shut behind him or her. Even though Siobhán knew the outcome, she found herself watching while holding her breath, hoping for a different ending. For the next few minutes the screen didn't change. "Let's fast-forward," Leah said. She took control of the iPad. "There." She set it back down.

At 1:10 an older man in a trench coat and wellies approached the door to the mill. "It's my father," Moira cried out. "How did he get there so fast?"

"How long should it have taken him to walk?"

"Forty-five minutes," Leah said. "At least."

"Five minutes to pull his wellies and coat on, discover the flat tire —"

"Flat tire?" Leah asked. They filled her in. "He must have ran the entire way."

"Perhaps the adrenaline," Siobhán said. In his right hand he clutched something. All three of them leaned in.

"Enda." Leah's voice came out as a whine, a plea. "Don't go in there."

Siobhán pointed to the object in his hand. "What's that?"

Leah and Moira shook their heads. Although he obviously had some kind of object in his hand, the image was too dark and grainy to clearly make out what it was. Enda stopped to peer into the cameras. He had a scrunched face, an angry expression. He opened the door. "Who's in there?" His voice was garbled in the wind.

"Call the guards," Leah yelled at the screen. "What are you thinking?"

"He's thinking it's some young one, acting the maggot," Moira said.

They were glued to the drama as several minutes of silence ticked by. This time they did not fast-forward. They sat for five minutes, staring at the screen. "It's killing me," Leah said. She took the iPad and maneuvered the time line ahead. At 1:40, the door to the mill slid open and the Grim Reaper figure sprinted away. No matter how many times they played back the video feed, Enda, they knew, would not come out.

Siobhán played it again anyway. Leah and Moira turned away. The person waited forty minutes in that mill for Enda to arrive. Then another thirty minutes before slipping out. It suggested patience and planning.

Thirty whole minutes. Was Enda pushed right away? Or had some kind of argument taken place? What exactly happened in there? Did they argue? Did the person push

Enda off the balcony? Was it his or her intention all along? "Are there any cameras inside the mill?" Siobhán asked.

Moira shook her head. "I remember my father grumbling that the owner refused to pay for any cameras. And yes, my father had money, but he was also thrifty. He thought the cameras on the door would be enough."

A fatal mistake.

"That creature was on foot," Moira said, pointing to the screen.

"Or his or her vehicle was parked out of view of the camera," Siobhán said. "Do you know if anyone else knew the cameras had been installed?"

Leah shook her head. "He didn't mention it to me."

"I only knew he was thinking about it," Moira said. "I never followed up, and he never mentioned it again."

"Would he have used local lads to install it?"

Moira nodded. "We can ask the owner of the mill." It wouldn't have taken much for the grapevine to spread the news that cameras had been installed. There was no other reason a person would disguise themselves in a dark cloak. The person *knew* the cameras were there. That's why the person wore a costume. Because he or she was recognizable in town.

"What about Jason?" Leah asked, as if she'd just remembered him. "Where is he?"

"He left a few days ago to pick up Faye in Dublin," Moira said.

"Oh," Leah said. "We could have given her a ride."

"He rented a special van for her."

"Special van?" Siobhán asked.

"For Faye's wheelchair," Moira reminded her.

"Of course." She'd almost forgotten. It definitely wouldn't be easy to navigate this rugged landscape in a wheelchair.

Leah turned back to the iPad as a look of concentration overtook her pretty face. "What does this mean?" Leah said. "Someone witnessed Enda's fall?"

Moira shook her head. "Are you joking me?" She pointed to the screen once more. "Enda was murdered. Someone waited forty minutes for him to arrive. Then didn't emerge for another thirty minutes and was in disguise. The creature was intentionally waiting for my father. Lured him up to that gallery and pushed him to his death. That's what this means."

"Murdered?" Leah fixed her big eyes on Siobhán, as if waiting for her to refute Moira's claim.

Siobhán began to pace. "I have to agree. In addition, Enda's tire was slashed, and 999 was never called. And if I remember correctly, the lights in the mill were off when Catherine opened the doors that Saturday morning."

"Yes," Moira said. "She turned them on."

"We can't see whether there were lights in the video, but wouldn't you assume your father would have turned the lights on as soon as he stepped into the mill?"

"He certainly would have," Moira said.

"Then the person in the cloak must have turned them off when he or she was leaving," Siobhán said. "I have no doubt this was foul play. We need to get this video to the guards right away."

"I never want to see it again," Leah said, shoving the iPad at Siobhán. "You're a guard. You can have it."

Moira nodded. "I concur."

Siobhán took the iPad. "I'll get it to Garda Cooley." He'd given her his business card, so she'd place the call immediately. Siobhán thought of the music she'd heard playing. If Enda was murdered, then the murderer may have returned to the scene of the crime and was hiding up in the balcony. Perhaps the person dropped his or her mobile phone during the struggle and had returned to fetch it. Was it the ringtone of a killer Siobhán heard? Did the guards find anyone hiding in the building?

Ruth said she'd been in the bathroom. Could it have been a lie? Just because she claimed she was in the bathroom and it wasn't her ringtone didn't mean it was the truth. Siobhán would pass this along to Garda Cooley as well. She knew firsthand it wasn't going to be easy for Garda Cooley to investigate his friends and neighbors. Especially this close to Christmas. The same people he saw every day in the shops and pubs and restaurants. The people he sat next to in mass and prayed with. The people he celebrated with, and mourned with. Yet that was the job of the guards, and Siobhán could only hope he would put duty first. Justice required it. Enda Elliot deserved it.

Siobhán turned to the women. "You have to keep this news to yourselves for now."

"You mean we can't tell everyone my husband was murdered?" Leah sounded outraged.

"I'm sure it won't be long before it comes out," Siobhán said. "But we don't want to get ahead of the guards on this. All we have right now is a theory. We must let Garda Cooley follow the evidence. The state pathologist will have to decide the manner of death."

Leah chewed on her lip but did not respond. Was she going to be a wild card and go against Siobhán's wishes?

"I can't believe this," Moira said. "Who would murder my father? This close to Christmas? Who would do something so evil?"

"I don't know," Siobhán said. "But we're going to find out."

On the way out of the house, Siobhán stopped at the hook, the empty one, with the smudged dirt underneath. She pointed. "Do you know what used to hang here?"

Moira stared at the spot, then turned away with a shudder.

"Yes." Leah stared at it, her face tightening. "Enda's hatchet."

Siobhán felt prickles dance along the back of her neck. "He kept a hatchet in the kitchen?"

"He did, so," Leah said. "He'd chop firewood right outside the door."

"Why not leave it outside?"

"He didn't like it rusting," Leah said. "He liked to keep it as sharp as possible."

As sharp as possible. The images on the iPad flashed in front of Siobhán, and she mentally tried to run through a plausible scenario. First, Enda Elliot watches someone breaking into the mill on his iPad. He's incensed. His worst fear is coming true. He's in such a hurry, he pulls on his wellies and coat over his pajamas, no time to get dressed. He wants to catch the thief in the act. He runs to his lorry. The keys were still in the ignition, which means he tried to start it. Something is wrong. He gets out and discovers his slashed tire. He doesn't call 999. When he arrives at the mill, there's an object in his hand.

A *weapon.* He knew he was being messed with. Taunted. Lured out to the mill on a dark winter's night all by his lonesome. Did it mean the person lying in wait in the mill also knew that Enda's wife had yet to arrive and his son had left to pick up Faye Elliot? Doesn't it stand to reason that an enraged Enda Elliot ran back into his kitchen and picked up his sharp-as-possible hatchet? And if so, that evening, in the old, stone whiskey mill, just days before Christmas, just who had reason to be afraid of whom?

CHAPTER 4

Stepping outside, Siobhán found the cold air a welcome relief. Her nerves were on edge, and she had to place a call to Garda Cooley. Moira and Leah headed back to Moira's house as Siobhán set off for the road where Moira said she'd get the best signal for her mobile phone. Living in such a remote place had its drawbacks, especially in times of trouble. Add the holidays and the weather to the mix and it could be downright deadly. If this was a murder, then they were now stuck in this remote location near cliffs with a killer and a missing hatchet. *Happy Christmas.* A bout of self-pity sliced through her. Was it too much to ask to have one nice week where murder was the furthest thing from her mind? How could she keep her promise to have a joyful Christmas with these developments?

Enough. Think about Enda Elliot. He certainly didn't plan on this either. He spent his life making beautiful music, only to have it cut short before his big concert.

Then again, he'd walked *toward* trouble in the middle of the night with a hatchet. Even so, he still deserved justice. And the type of person who could push an old man to his death was a danger to all. The road finally came into view. Perhaps the figure who entered the mill had simply *witnessed* Enda's fall? And for some reason was afraid to call it in?

But what of his slashed tire? And that gruesome outfit? And the forty minutes spent waiting for Enda to arrive? The pieces certainly looked sinister, but the state pathologist would need hard evidence to support a finding of murder. Siobhán glanced at her phone. Moira was right, she now had a signal. She fumbled for Barry Cooley's business card and then dialed.

He answered after the first ring. "Garda Cooley."

"Hello. Garda O'Sullivan here."

"I got your note," he said. "No worries."

"My note?"

"The one you left on me vehicle." He sounded exasperated.

"Oh, yes. That's not why I'm calling."

"We've been given permission to move the body to Cork University Hospital. It looks like he took a tumble." Garda Cooley was apparently the type of man who gave information, not listened for it.

"You might want to hold off on that assessment." Before he could interject again, she filled him in on the slashed tire, the video, and the missing hatchet.

She heard the sound of wind rattling through the phone before he spoke. "I'm still at the mill," he said. "Can you get a lift here and bring that iPad?"

"Of course. I'll be right there."

She hung up. She assumed someone would give her a ride. She turned up the drive to return to Moira's house. She had only taken a few steps when she heard a vehicle approaching from behind. A familiar white lorry streaked with dirt pulled up alongside her, and Theodore Baskins leaned out.

"Are ya lost?"

"No, thank you," Siobhán said. "Just heading back to Moira's." She hesitated. "But could I get a lift to the mill?"

Theodore's smile faded. "I don't think the guards will let you anywhere near it."

"I've been summoned by Garda Cooley," Siobhán said. "I'm a guard myself."

He arched an eyebrow, then grinned. "Hop in."

She held up her mobile. "Just texting Garda Cooley that you're giving me a lift. He's expecting me." *In case you're a psychopath.*

"Not a bother. I'll get you there in one piece."

She hopped into the passenger seat. There was an odor in the lorry; it smelled a little like fish. "I knew there would be drama this year," Theodore said. "But I never imagined this."

"No one ever does." *Except for the one who planned it.*

"I'm sure you've gotten an earful about me already, have ya?" His question came with a cheery tone, but she wasn't going to get dragged into the local drama.

"No," she lied. "I think everyone is focused on the tragedy that occurred."

"Right, right," he said. "Well, you will hear things, mark my words. Don't believe your ears. This village can be chilly to outsiders, and I'm not talking about the weather."

"I see."

"Been living here five years and they still consider me a blow-in."

"What brought you here in the first place?"

"I was writing for a travel blog." He leaned toward her, and the van swerved. "I'm a freelance writer."

"Lovely." *Watch the road.*

"I fell in love this area. One of the few places left on this planet where you can lose yourself in the wilderness and feel like the only man on earth."

It was surely not one of the last places, nor was it completely remote, especially with the folks streaming in for the concert, but one could glean more information from a subject if one refrained from insulting the subject. She hadn't needed Templemore Garda College for that lesson; she'd learned it in the trenches of siblings. "Are you working on any stories at the moment?"

He frowned at the question, as if she was trying to catch him out. "A bit of blogging. Journalistic articles. Some poetry."

"Do you write for the town newspaper?"

He shook his head. "They wouldn't know talent if it bit them in the arse. I do what I can here and there. Mostly online. Not nearly enough to make a living."

"How do you make a living?"

"I fill in at the fish market," Theodore said. "Cleaning, and packing the slippery little buggers." That explained the smell in the lorry. "If it weren't for Catherine, I probably wouldn't have stayed. It's not easy to be the black sheep of the village. Unless, of course, there's a party. Then everybody loves me." He threw his head back and laughed, swerving slightly.

Siobhán gripped the door handle. "I see." He was a talker. It was best to keep her words to a minimum and let him spill. "It must be exciting to have all these famous musicians in town."

He glanced at her. "Why is that?"

"Seems like the concert would make a good article."

"I would have been more than willing. But would anyone in town publish it, or read it if they saw my name on the byline?" He shook his head. "Not a chance."

"Why do you stay?"

"I told you. I love it here. I'm not going to let other people run me off." Siobhán noted he said that he loved it here. He did not say he loved Catherine. Did it mean anything? If she hadn't just insisted she'd heard no gossip about him, she'd be tempted to ask him about stealing Enda's award. Perhaps she could get him to spill some gossip of his own.

"What did folks in town think about the age difference between Enda and Leah?"

Theodore laughed. "The Beauty and the Beast?"

"Is that what they say?"

92

He shrugged. "It's what I say. Can you imagine being married . . ." He stopped. "I suppose there's no use speaking ill of the dead."

At least he had limits. "You're right. I was just curious."

"I'm sure there was plenty of talk. You know yourself. But I've heard more tongues wagging over Catherine and I."

"How did you two meet?"

"I rented her guest house at the back of her property. Moira is in charge of the rentals. If she wants to blame someone for me and Catherine, she should look no further than herself."

"She mentioned she handles the rentals in the village," Siobhán said.

"It's not luxury accommodations by any means," Theodore said. "I think that's where you'll be staying."

"I see." Was he purposefully trying to upset her? "We don't need luxury. A clean bed and a roof over our heads will do." They were approaching a small wooden bridge, and the lorry bounced over it. Below them, a small creek gurgled.

"Wait until you see Catherine's watercolors," Theodore said as they settled back on the road. His voice swelled with pride. "That's how I first fell for her. Art over age."

He gripped the steering wheel. "Enda of all people should have respected that. No one blinks at his third marriage to a woman young enough to be his daughter, but everyone's a critic when an older woman is with a much younger man." He flexed his hands on the steering wheel. Dirt was caked underneath his fingernails.

She was dying to ask him if he was out late last night, but she didn't want to tip him off to a possible murder inquiry. If he was a real writer, he'd be all over the story and he had no idea what was about to hit. It had been a mistake, she realized, as they drew closer to the mill, to ride with him. If he wasn't liked in town, that may even extend to Garda Cooley, and she needed the guards to trust her. Guilt by association. Unfair, yes, but she didn't write the rules of the world. She hadn't been thinking straight. At least the iPad was tucked well into her handbag. But later, Theodore Baskins would wonder why she was returning to the crime scene, or he wasn't much of a writer. How could she have been so foolish?

She recognized the turn they had just taken. The mill was within walking distance. "Stop," she said. "I'll get out here."

"What?" She'd startled him, and he

swerved. "The mill is just ahead," he said.

"I'd rather walk the rest of the way." She tried to keep her voice light and airy.

"I see." He jerked the car to the right and screeched the brakes. She'd insulted him.

"Thank you so much for the ride."

"You're welcome." He stared straight ahead. She tried to think of a reason for wanting to walk the rest of the way. She came up empty. She hopped out of the lorry and waved. He nodded his head and screeched off.

Siobhán's heart was still thudding as she approached the mill. She had to side with Moira, there was something off-putting about Theodore Baskins, and it wasn't just his bravado. There was an angry edge to him, like a kettle ready to boil over. Three guard cars remained in the lot. Barry Cooley ambled over from a huddle with other guards, half an unlit cigar in his large hand.

"Dirty habit," he said, lifting the cigar. "But whatever gets you through, am I right?" He stuck the stub in his gob.

"I won't argue that," Siobhán said.

They watched the iPad video in Garda Cooley's vehicle with the heat on. Barry Cooley played it three times without saying a word, then leaned back and shoved the chewed-on cigar back in his pocket. "Did

Moira have any idea who the figure could be?"

"No." Siobhán wasn't going to mentioned Theodore Baskins. Moira had no proof, only a strong bias.

"Theodore Baskins," Cooley said. *So much for trying to keep this fair.*

"What about him?" Siobhán said. Thank goodness she'd had the sense to ask Theodore to drop her off before the mill, even if she had insulted him.

"He threw an All Hallows' Eve party a few months back. If anyone was sneaking around in costumes in the middle of the night up to no good, it would be him."

"I wouldn't call that hard evidence," Siobhán couldn't help but say. "It could have been anyone in that costume." It was always dangerous to jump to conclusions. It was equally dangerous to confront a local guard about jumping to conclusions. Life was a constant lesson in picking your battles.

Cooley rubbed his chin and stared out the window. "This complicates things."

"Yes. It certainly does."

He patted his pocket as if to make sure his cigar was still there. "This does clear up a question I had."

"Oh?"

"I can see Enda pawing through items in

96

the balcony, organizing things. But it made no sense that he would lean on the railings of the balcony."

"You're thinking he was pushed?" Siobhán did too, but she didn't want Cooley to think she was putting ideas in his head. Best let him sort it out for himself.

"I'm going to have my investigators check the scene to figure it out, but it fits what I've seen so far." Garda Cooley leaned his head back for a second and sighed. "Happy Christmas," he muttered. He picked up a travel mug and drank, then put it down and looked at it forlornly. "Sorry I can't offer you any."

"I just had tea, I'm grand." She stared out the window at the mill, wishing the old stones could tell her a story. "Did you find a mobile phone or a hatchet anywhere in the mill?"

"We did not."

Siobhán chewed on this. If it was an accident, not reporting it was one thing. Taking the dead man's mobile phone and hatchet before sneaking off was another. It was becoming very clear. Enda Elliot was murdered. "We definitely need to find out who else was in there."

"We?" He arched an eyebrow.

"Sorry. Habit."

He gazed out the window. Laughter erupted from a clump of guards in the distance. "I'm sure you're a very capable guard, but we can't have any outside interference."

"Of course."

"Just so we're clear."

He left the rest unsaid. Not that she needed it vocalized, she knew what he was trying to say. *Stay out of my case. You must have large hands and a fat cigar to work here.* "Very clear."

Cooley picked up the iPad. "Thank you for this. I'll be questioning everyone. Don't let any of the guests leave."

It took everything she had not to snap back that she thought she wasn't allowed to interfere. How was she supposed to keep guests from leaving? Anger coursed through her, and an uneasiness she couldn't quite place. It was just the stress. And a deep itching from within. She wanted to be involved. It was in her nature. But this was a good thing. She would stay out of it. This way she could keep her promise to the rest of her siblings, and they could simply focus on being together while the local guards solved the murder. If Macdara was here, he'd have a sarcastic retort to the notion of Siobhán staying out of a case. He'd also be itching to be involved himself. They were two peas in a pod. Enda and Leah were bonded by music, Catherine and Theodore by writing and painting . . . were Siob hán and Mac-dara bonded by criminals? It was a slightly depressing thought. Still, there was no one she'd rather fight crime with.

"Hopefully the state pathologist will be able to determine if he fell or was pushed," Siobhán said. She wondered if Jeanie Brady had the holidays off? She was an excellent state pathologist. It would be nice to see her again. Siobhán was going to have to buy some pistachios just in case. Nothing could light Jeanie Brady up like a bag of pistachios.

"I'll have the forensic team examine the harp tracks," Cooley said with a laugh and a shake of his head. "Never thought I'd say that." This was indeed a fascinating case. "I'll drop you off at Moira's." He started the car and headed off. During the short ride home he chatted about West Cork and how much they'd been looking forward to the orchestra. He drove her through a main street in the village so she could see the Christmas lights in the shop windows and street lamps wrapped in garland and bows. Christmas music played through the streets, piped into speakers at the top of a pole.

"It's lovely."

"The turning on of the Christmas lights is always my favorite part. And the Christmas markets." Siobhán hadn't pegged him for one to celebrate the holidays; it was a sweet discovery. "It won't stay that way for long. Not if this was a murder," he said, his voice thickening.

"It's during the worst times that we need the Christmas spirit most of all," Siobhán said. She truly believed that. Christmas wasn't just a day, or an event, it was a spirit. Markets and lighting ceremonies, and shopping, and cooking, and attending pantos before Christmas. Midnight mass on Christmas Eve, and time with the family. A big feed on Christmas Day. Then off to the pubs on Saint Stephen's Day. *Nollaig na mBan* on January 6, otherwise known as Women's Little Christmas. Siobhán had never really celebrated it, but it seemed to be making a comeback in Ireland, or perhaps it was wishful thinking. She was all for it. A day when the men stayed home to tend to chores while the women got together for their own celebration. And here, they all seemed eager for the Polar Bear Swim on Christmas morning. She couldn't imagine jumping into those frigid waters, bless the souls who braved it.

"You're right, you're right," Cooley said,

returning to her comment about the spirit of Christmas. He put on the radio and soon "Christmas in Killarney" by Bing Crosby filled the vehicle.

"Forget Killarney," Cooley said with a grin. "It's Christmas in West Cork." *With all of the suspects at home. . . .*

When he arrived at Moira's farmhouse, she asked to be let out near the road. "Trying to get a mobile signal?"

"Yes," she said.

"Here should do it."

They exchanged pleasantries, and he drove off. She stayed by the road holding up the phone until she reached a spot with the strongest reception, crossed her fingers, and dialed. Detective Sergeant Macdara Flannery picked up right away. "Hey, boss."

His deep voice warmed her. "Hey, Dara."

"How's the jolly?"

She shut her eyes, wondering how to play it. It didn't sound as if her text had gone through. She had to tell him that Enda was dead, but did she need to worry him about a murder? He'd leave his mam and come straight here. She wanted nothing else. But she couldn't do that to him. Force him to choose. He'd be here the day after Christmas, and that would have to be soon enough. "There's been some sad news," she

101

said. "But we're all hanging in there."

"What's the story?" Her supposition had been spot-on, concern immediately filling his voice.

"Enda Elliot is dead."

"Ah, stop."

"There's more." She had wandered slightly up the drive, and from a distance she could see the space between Moira and Enda's houses. Was someone sneaking up on Enda's house? She fixed her gaze. Whoever it was, the person's movements were erratic, flashes of color popping up and down as if the person was ducking for cover and then peeking up. "Sorry, I'll call you back."

Siobhán clicked off and headed for the woods. The figure — she couldn't tell if it was a man or a woman — crouched on her approach, and then when she was closer, whoever it was sprung up and took off toward the cliff. A small white ball, like on the end of an elf cap, bounced as the figure ran. Was the person dressed as an elf? Siobhán propelled herself forward, giving chase. "Hey!" she shouted. "Wait!" But whoever it was, he or she had no intention of waiting. Siobhán ran until she could no longer catch her breath, the cold air squeezing her lungs. She was feet from the cliff when she came to an abrupt stop. *That was stupid.* The person was fast, she'd give credit where credit was due. She edged forward and peeked down. There was no one there. To her left was another patch of trees. They were thick, and Siobhán was in no mood to venture farther. She was a runner, and most likely so was the so-called elf. The mysterious person was not only fast but knew this terrain well enough to hide from the likes of Siobhán.

She headed back for Moira's house, scouring the ground where she estimated she'd first seen the figure. From here, one could easily see the back of both Enda and Moira's house. A voyeur? A skulking reporter? The killer?

Cooley said that Theodore Baskins was one for costumes. Maybe everyone was right about him. If he was trying to get a story, he had probably realized he wouldn't get it by being forthright.

She crouched, as if re-creating the person's movements might offer some insight. Something sparkled on the ground. Tiny sparks of something green. She looked closer. It was glitter. She ran her gloved hand over it. Did it come from the runaway elf? She looked at her black glove, which now sparkled with the shiny emerald bits.

She tried to see if the elf had dropped more, perhaps leaving a trail in his or her wake, like festive breadcrumbs, but alas no luck.

Before she could formulate any more theories, Moira's back door flew open and Elise, Paul, and Orla stepped outside. They huddled for a minute, then broke apart. Elise was doing the talking, gesticulating dramatically. It appeared as if she was lecturing her siblings. Paul suddenly looked up and peered intently into the trees. Did he see her? He locked eyes with her and frowned, then lifted his hand in a somewhat puzzled greeting. Now *she* looked like the stalker, voyeur, killer. Siobhán stood up, then waved and headed for them with a grin, as if crouching in the woods was a totally normal thing for her to be doing.

"What's the story?" Elise asked, staring at Siobhán's head.

Siobhán touched the top of head where stray bits of pine clung to the strands. She pulled them out. "There was a man. Or woman. Dressed in red and green. Crouching in the woods. I tried to approach, and whoever it was took off. I chased them for a while." She turned her gloved hand toward them. "I think the elf left behind some glitter."

"Are you joking me?" Paul asked. He

sounded amused. "Why would an elf be hiding in the woods, like?"

"Trying to see if we're naughty or nice," Orla sang.

"Definitely naughty," Elise said while looking directly Siobhán.

They sounded so cheerful. Siobhán suddenly realized why. Very few people knew that Enda's death had taken an even more sinister turn. But she wasn't going to be one to whisper the word *murder*. With the wind in this town, it would travel through soon enough. "I was worried it was a reporter." *Or voyeur. Or killer.* "Watching the houses."

Paul stepped forward. "Why do you say that?"

"I stood where the person stood. The two things in the sight line are Enda's house and this house."

"Theodore Baskins," Paul said. "Spying as usual." He strode toward the cars in the drive.

"Hey," Siobhán said, hurrying after him. "Wait."

Paul stopped. "I won't have him messing with us in our moment of grief."

"You don't know that it was him."

"Who else would it be?"

"I have no idea."

"That's right, you don't. But I do. It was

105

Theodore Baskins, and I'm not letting him get away with this."

"I understand you're upset. But we have to let the guards handle it."

"We?" Elise spoke for the first time. "Since when do you involve yourself in my family's drama?"

Since I learned that your grandfather may have been murdered. "I just think we've had enough trauma for the morning. Your mother wouldn't want her children running off to confront people — especially based on nothing but speculation."

"She's right," Orla said. "We need to be here for Mam." Her voice had started out timid but then gathered strength.

Paul turned back, kicking dirt with the toe of his runners as if it had personally offended him. "He's lower than low."

"You should get your guitar," Orla said. "Join the others."

"Others?" Siobhán asked. Just then she heard music coming from inside the farmhouse. The musicians were warming up, doing what they do. "You're a musician too?" Siobhán asked Paul, hoping to distract him.

"I told you I played my guitar for my cows."

"Right. Sorry. I forgot."

He looked away. "Grandpa Elliot wasn't

impressed."

Orla linked her arms with her brother's. "You're a fabulous guitar player, and Grandpa only had an ear for classical music."

"Paul sings too," Elise said. "In a local café."

"For me supper," Paul added with a laugh.

Siobhán was touched to see the sisters try to cheer him up, and it seemed to be working. "That's wonderful," Siobhán said. "I'd love to hear you play."

A lorry pulled into the drive. It was green with a painting of a cow and an enormous bottle of Irish cream on the side. The cow appeared to be laughing. The name ELLIOT'S was sprawled across the top. Elise's mouth dropped open. "You bought a lorry?"

Paul swallowed. "I just paid for the advertising."

"With what money?" Elise asked.

"Did Grandpa know?" Orla chimed in. The sisterly cheer was gone.

"Gotta check on me shipment," Paul said. He jogged off toward the lorry.

"Mam seemed upset when she came back from Grandpa's house," Orla said, giving Siobhán the once-over. "Did something happen over there?"

"It's been a very upsetting day," Siobhán

said, hoping that would be enough to satisfy her.

Elise tensed. "That's not an answer."

What Siobhán really wanted to do was some grilling of her own. *"Don't say a word to anyone. Especially to Siobhán."* What didn't Elise want Siobhán to know?

"Where's James?" Siobhán asked instead.

"He's inside," Elise said. "With the others."

"If you're hungry, there's enough of a feed for all of Ireland," Orla said.

Hungry. She'd forgotten that people get hungry. The only thing she'd eaten so far today was the biscuit in Enda's kitchen. Her mind flashed to the missing hatchet. She hadn't noticed it in the video when the mysterious person *exited* the mill, but if he or she had confiscated Enda's hatchet it could have been hidden under the dark cloak. But what if it wasn't? Where was the hatchet now?

CHAPTER 5

In the distance, Paul Elliot unloaded crates of Irish Cream from the lorry, his arms flexing with each haul. Siobhán followed Elise and Orla into Moira's house, stepping into a large kitchen. Elise hadn't been exaggerating — every surface was covered with offerings from the neighbors, the cooker was in use, and simmering pots gurgled on the stovetop. Unlike Enda's sparse living areas, Moira's house was homey and cluttered. Siobhán preferred it that way. She merged into the living room, where there was a peat fire roaring, and stopped to take in the familiar and comforting scent. *Home.*

The orchestra members and fellow musicians sat in a relaxed circle in the room, entertaining children at their feet. It took a few beats to recognize they were playing a sophisticated version of "Jingle Bells." Her brood, apart from James, looked on enthralled, fat mugs of cocoa in their hands and a plate of biscuits in front of them. Relief settled over Siobhán's shoulders. James and Elise immediately snuggled in a corner. Elise's eyes were red from crying. Harry Williams stood by the fire, gazing into it. He caught Siobhán's eyes and nodded. She nodded back, then knelt next to her siblings. "Hey," she said, gesturing to the musicians. "They're something, aren't they?"

"Deadly," Eoin said. He threw a look over his shoulder. "The cooks booted me from the kitchen."

"They don't know what they're missing." Siobhán patted him on the shoulder. She meant it. Eoin was a talented chef. He was also growing into his looks. Gone was the acne that used to cover his face, gone was the backward baseball cap, and in its place she found a handsome young man. His growing talent as a graphic novelist was impressive too. Gráinne glanced over, placing her hand at the side of her mouth as if to spill a secret. Her long nails were painted neon blue to match the streaks in her hair. "When are we checking into our place?"

"Checking in?" Siobhán said. If Gráinne was expecting a fancy hotel, she was going to be sorely disappointed.

"I almost forgot," Moira said, coming in

from the kitchen. She handed Elise a set of keys. "Would you take them over to the guest house?"

"Of course," Elise said.

"House?" Ciarán said. "We get a whole house?"

Moira smiled. "It's nothing spectacular, but yes, there's quite a few of you, isn't there? So it's all yours."

"Yes!" Ciarán said. Ann tussled his hair.

Moira caught Siobhán's eye, then moved into a hall off the living room. Siobhán quickly followed. "Did you speak with Garda Cooley?" Moira asked.

"Yes. He has the iPad, and I've given him all the information. I assume someone will be in touch to have a look at Enda's lorry."

"Did they identify the person in the video or find Enda's hatchet in the mill?"

Siobhán shook her head. "I don't know. I'm being kept out of the investigation." Of course, Cooley had told her a few things, but she wasn't about to share anything. Everyone who had been in town when Enda was pushed was a suspect. Especially someone like a daughter. Siobhán grasped Moira's hand. "We have to keep this to ourselves for now."

"You don't think he fell, do you? You think he was pushed." Moira seemed intent on getting Siobhán to answer her.

"It's too early to say. That's why the guards need *all* the information. They'll sort it out." Siobhán kept her gaze steady. She was proud of herself for not blurting out what she was really thinking. *Yes. He was pushed. And someone in this house might be a killer.*

Moira nodded. "I hope the guards figure it out quick."

"Me too." Siobhán glanced into the living room, then back at Moira. "In the meantime . . . have you mentioned the video, the flat tire, or the hatchet to anyone?"

"No," Moira answered quickly. "Have you?"

"Only Garda Cooley. Let's see what they make of it. It's best not to get everyone worked up."

Moira's gaze shifted to the living room, where the musicians were putting down their instruments for a break. "Because one of us could be a killer."

"I hope not." She patted Moira's arm, although she knew that was little consolation. "I saw someone running through the trees just a few minutes ago," Siobhán said. "Dressed as an elf?"

Moira stared as if waiting for a punch line. "Are you joking me?"

"No. I take it you have no idea who it could be?"

Moira frowned. "Theodore Baskins."

"That's what Paul said." The Elliot family had a definite bias against Theodore Baskins. Then again, they were the ones who had been neighbors with him for years, so perhaps their ire was well deserved.

"He's always lurking," Moira said.

"He lives next door?"

Moira shook her head. "Catherine lives next door. He mooches."

"I see."

"It's our three houses, the guest house, Catherine's painting cottage, and then no one for miles." Was it likely, then, that their killer was one of the people in this little cluster of houses? "I hope you like your lodgings," Moira said, with a tone that suggested their conversation had come to an end. They merged into the living room.

"I'm sure we'll love it."

"If you want to join us, we'll be going into town soon to meet Jason."

"We'd love to join you," Siobhán said. Besides wanting to meet Jason and his mother, she was ready to do a bit of Christmas shopping with her siblings. They could all use a little bit of cheer.

"Your guest lodgings are the back of the

field, between my home and Catherine's main house. Elise will take you there. Meet back here in two hours and we'll all head into town."

"This is it?" Gráinne croaked, hands on hips as they stood outside the guest house.

Unlike Moira's cozy farmhouse or Enda's dramatic home, the structure before them resembled a series of interconnected shacks that looked vulnerable to being felled with one sharp wind.

"Catherine Healy and Theodore live in the main house," Elise said, pointing to a yellow house in the distance.

"Is this a barn?" Ciarán asked. From the tone of his voice, he was hoping the answer was yes.

"It is," Siobhán said while ruffling his ginger head. "There was no room at the inn."

Elise frowned. "You're lucky to get rooms at all. Everyone wanted to be here for the concert."

"We're very grateful," Siobhán said. "We just like to mess around."

Elise stuck the key in the door and turned dramatically. "Ready?"

"Yes!" Ciarán said. "I'll go first in case anything jumps out at us."

Elise opened the door and they stepped into a small, dark kitchen. Elise pawed the wall. "Wait, wait, there's light."

At the end of this tunnel. The light flicked on, illuminating new counters, a sink, and a cooker. Everything else was old wood. The floors, the walls, the ceiling. With each step the old boards let out a squeak of protest. At least it was clean. Behind the kitchen was a small living room with a fireplace. Another door led to two rooms with four sets of bunk beds. "There's wood right outside," Elise said. "It should warm things up in no time." It could probably burn it all down in no time, too, but Siobhán quickly shoved the thought away. It was nearly Christmas; they were in a beautiful, rugged setting; and despite a murder, there was still going to be a Christmas concert with re-nowned musicians. There was still going to be *Christmas.* Siobhán was determined to think positive starting right now.

"Eoin and I will start the fire," James said.

"What about me?" Ciarán asserted.

"Forget Eoin," James said. "Ciarán and I will see to the fire."

Eoin put on a mock-angry face, then ruffled Ciarán's hair. Siobhán felt guilty for having done the same minutes earlier. Ciarán swiped Eoin's hand away.

"How many bedrooms?" Gráinne asked despite staring at the two rooms.

"Two," Elise said. "But they each have two sets of bunk beds."

"I like the farmhouse better," Ann said, keeping her hands folded as if she was afraid to touch anything. "Could I stay there?"

"Right with you," Gráinne said.

"All this place needs is a good peat fire, and Christmas decorations," Siobhán said.

"A tree?" Ann said.

"Why not," Siobhán said. "A tree, and lights, and prezzies." Presents. She couldn't wait to start shopping.

"Just not the tree from behind the mill," Eoin chimed in.

"Too soon," Siobhán said, and Eoin roared with laughter.

"We didn't bring our ornaments," Ciarán said. "Or our train set." At Naomi's Bistro back home, they set up a train most years. It had been a tradition their father, Liam, started. Every time the train chugged around, black smoke curling out of its stack, sounding its horn, Siobhán felt the spirit of her parents filling the bistro with love. Once the kitchen filled with scents of cookies and pies, and the peat fire crackled in the living room, there was no doubt they were home. An added bonus was that the locals loved watching the train go around as well. Young ones eyes lit up, and they'd let out squeals. Truly, there was no place like home for Christmas. Siobhán felt a pang of homesickness. They would have to do whatever they could to hang on to their Christmas cheer.

"I'm sure folks around here would be happy to lend you a few ornaments," Elise said. Her expression said otherwise.

Ciarán fixed his eyes on her as if he was taking names. "How many is a few?"

"We could also get creative," Siobhán said.

"Creative how?" Ann asked.

"Decorate our tree from nature or found objects. Ribbons, berries, wildflowers, shells, driftwood, rocks. Maybe a starfish for the top of the tree." Her brood stared at her openmouthed. "We'll add some white lights from the hardware shop. It will be grand."

Everyone gave it a beat. "That's not the worst idea I've ever heard," Gráinne said.

Siobhán put her hand on her heart. "Be still."

"Rocks?" Ciarán asked, caught between outraged and all-in.

"Is there anything else you need at the moment?" Elise asked. "There's tea and biscuits in the cupboards and milk in the refrigerator. Later you can collect whatever you'd like to eat from Mam's kitchen, and you can get anything else you need in town."

"Sounds like we're sorted," James said. "Thank you."

Elise gave him a puzzled look. He did sound overly polite.

"Do you get along with Jason?" Siobhán couldn't help but ask Elise.

"I suppose. Not that we see each other very often." Elise rifled through her handbag. "I have no doubt he will regret his last conversation with my grandfather."

"Oh?"

Elise slung her handbag over her shoulder and nodded. "They got in a terrible row."

Siobhán's interest was piqued. "What about?"

"I don't know. Jason and Grandfather were both at his house. We could hear them screaming at each other all the way over here." She shook her head. "The lungs on him."

"What were they saying?"

"We couldn't really make out the words. My guess, it was over Jason's mam. He never got over his father leaving Faye after her accident." *Accident.*

"What happened?"

Elise waved the question away. "It was a long time ago."

She did not want to say anything more

118

about it, and Siobhán knew not to push. "This argument took place just before Jason left for Dublin?"

Elise nodded. "Immediately after, Jason screeched off in his car. That's the last we saw him." *Interesting.* Everyone's alibi would need to be carefully vetted. *By the guards.* Siobhán had to remind herself that this was not her case. Elise put her hands on her hips. "Not everyone can be as cozy as the O'Sullivan Six." Elise's voice was cheerful, but there was a judgmental edge to the comment that Siobhán didn't like.

"I'm looking forward to meeting Jason and Faye," Siobhán said lightly, hoping to shift the mood.

"Why would you be looking forward to meeting my uncle?" Elise didn't sound snippy, just genuinely curious.

"The more the merrier," Siobhán said when she couldn't think of anything else. Elise stared at Siobhán. It was an unsettling habit of hers, how she openly watched people without speaking. Siobhán could only imagine what that look was going to do to her brother over the years. She turned back to her brood. "Let's make a list of the things we'll need from the shops."

"Don't buy any food," Elise said. "You'll only be here to sleep, and we have loads at the house."

"Except chocolates and crisps," Gráinne said. "They don't count as food."

"If we get a tree, how will we get it back here?" Ciarán asked.

"It should strap to the top of the car," Siobhán said.

"If you're willing to pay extra, someone in town will be willing to deliver," Elise said. "But don't buy any Christmas gifts, we're going to pick names later."

"Ah," Siobhán said. "The Secret Santa."

"Secret Santa?" Gráinne, Ann, and Ciarán asked in stereo.

"Yes," Elise said. "It's a family tradition. Instead of everyone buying for everyone, we all pick a name out of a Santa cap. That's the only gift you'll have to buy. And this year it has to be music related." Elise either did not notice the slack-jawed, horrified faces staring back at her or was pretending not to notice. "Be back at Mam's house in a couple hours and we'll go into town."

James and Ciarán loaded wood and kindling into the fireplace. "We'll be leaving soon," Siobhán said. "We should hold off on lighting it."

"I was thinking I'd stay here," James said. "I can get the fire going so that it will be warm by the time we have to go to sleep."

It was true that Siobhán didn't want any of them to be frozen. But her brother had been acting strange since he'd arrived. Were he and Elise arguing? It had always been on and off with them, which is why their upcoming nuptials worried her slightly. It was probably good they hadn't set a date yet. *Just a venue.* The abbey in Kilbane, where Siobhán had always intended to marry. She'd yet to have that argument and probably never would. "There will be plenty of time to get the fire warm," Siobhán said. "I'd rather you come with us."

He sighed. "I'm tired. Was thinking of having a lie-down." He was definitely chewing on something.

"We're still buying each other gifts, aren't we?" Ciarán asked.

"Yes," Siobhán said.

"No," James said. "We're picking a name from a Santa cap."

"That's for her side of the family," Siobhán said. "We can all pick a name for their tradition, but we're certainly all exchanging Christmas gifts amongst ourselves."

James didn't respond but looked terrified of the prospect of going against Elise's wishes.

"Music related," Ann said. "I don't even know what that means."

"They're all musicians, dummy," Ciarán said.

"How do I know what to buy a professional musician?" Ann said.

Excellent point. "No name-calling," Siobhán said. She didn't like the music-related part either. Wouldn't musicians have everything music-related already? Restricting their choices also took all the fun out of Christmas shopping. Draw a name from a Santa cap. But Elise was going to be family, and they had to go along to get along, didn't they? At least a little bit. Especially when they were all already grieving Enda. They had to keep the peace and try to enjoy whatever moments they could given the circumstances. "I bet we'll find ornaments of musical instruments and that sort of thing in town," Siobhán continued. "We'll just consider it a fun challenge. Like decorating our tree with items from nature."

"How are we supposed to shop for one another in front of one another?" Gráinne complained.

"You'll have to be a little sneaky, I suppose," Siobhán said. "And we'll have to agree to respect one another. If you see something you want to buy, you can ask the rest of us to leave the shop for a minute."

James sighed. "Elise won't like it."

"She doesn't have to know," Gráinne said.

"Are you asking me to lie to my future wife?"

"It's not a lie, you're just not telling her." Gráinne shot Siobhán a look as if she couldn't believe James wasn't getting it.

Siobhán turned to Eoin. "Would you mind taking everyone outside to look for Christmas ornaments in nature? I want to speak to James for a minute."

"Why can't you speak to him in front of us?" Gráinne again. She was in a prickly mood.

"She's going to set him straight about Christmas," Ciarán said.

"Nobody is setting anybody straight. Outside with ye, now." They were all going to turn on one another if they didn't cheer this little shack up.

"Maybe it's a surprise," Ann said, looping her arm in Gráinne's. "It is the season for surprises."

"Exactly," Siobhán said. Even though the surprise was that she wanted to find out why her older brother was acting so peculiar.

"Come on, you's," Eoin said. "Last one to find a pine cone is a rotten egg."

■ ■ ■ ■

"What's the story?" Siobhán asked the minute they were alone. James had the fire roaring, and he was staring into it as if contemplating diving headfirst. "What is it? You're scaring me." *Did you drink?* Were there any AA meetings in this remote location? The answer was surely a yes, and Siobhán was prepared to drag him there if necessary.

"It's not a big thing," James said. The tone of his voice belied the comment.

"What's not a big thing?"

He crossed his arms. "Elise told a little white lie."

"Okay." *Definitely didn't sound okay.* Siobhán perched on the edge of the sofa.

He leaned back and folded his arms across his chest. "We didn't just arrive."

"What do you mean?"

"We've been in West Cork for days." He paused. "We stayed downtown at an inn."

She didn't know what she was expecting, but this was not it. "Why not just tell us that?"

"That's the thing. I don't know."

"You asked her. Right?" James shook his head. "Why not?"

"I just assumed she wanted her privacy. Before all the family and holiday madness began."

"And now?"

"What do you mean?"

"It's obviously bothering you."

James unfolded his arms and perched on the sofa. "I need to talk this through, but you have to promise me you won't over-react."

Siobhán crossed her fingers at her side. "I promise."

"I ran into Moira. She told me about Enda's flat tire. And the video." *Great.* Moira had just lied straight to her face about not telling anyone. What else was she lying about? James turned to her, worry etched on his face. "Is this turning into a murder probe?"

"Between us, okay?" Siobhán said. James nodded. "Yes. I believe it is." He swore under his breath. James was still holding on to part of this story, and that worried her more than ever. She patted his shoulder. "As long as you don't lie to the guards, you're fine."

He pulled away. "I can't go through this again. I can't." Siobhán knew what he was talking about. James had been accused of a murder once before. Years ago. Next to their parents' death, it was the most traumatic event of their lives. It was also why Siobhán was a garda today. She stared at her brother by the warm light of the fire, and for a second she was startled to see her father's face looking back at her. James was too young to look so old.

"The guards will be asking everyone their alibis. Lying to family is one thing. Elise cannot lie when the guards ask for your alibis. Understood?"

James nodded. "I'm going to have to speak with her."

"Are you expecting an argument?" He chewed on his lip. Siobhán stood, hands on hip. This was getting painful. "What aren't you telling me?"

"If I tell you . . . it cannot leave this room."

"I can't promise you that."

"Then I won't tell you."

"James. This is serious. You cannot lie to the guards."

"Maybe I won't have to."

"Was Elise with you all night?" James looked away. *She wasn't.* That's what was bothering him. "How long was she gone? Where did she say she went?" James put his head in his hands. "I promise I'll do everything I can. You have to tell me."

"We were at the inn last night when she

got a call around half eleven. It was Paul. She said there was an emergency family meeting."

The family that lies together. . . . Siobhán didn't want James to see her reaction. He should be worried. That wasn't a little secret — getting together suddenly in the middle of the night for an "emergency meeting" was a big one. "Did she say who in the family attended this meeting?" *Where did they meet? Was it in the mill? Did they all witness Enda's fall? Did one of them push him and they were all covering up?*

James put his head in his hands again. "I got the feeling it was just the siblings."

Paul, Orla, and Elise. Siobhán couldn't help but pace; it often helped her think. "What time did she return?"

"I don't know. I fell asleep. You know me. I'm dead to the world."

It was true. James was the heaviest sleeper she'd ever known. Always had been. "When did you wake up?"

"Thirty minutes before we showed up at the mill."

"And Elise was back in your room?"

"Of course."

"Did you ask her what time she got home?"

"She said she was only out an hour."

127

She said. James wasn't sure he believed her. "What was the name of the inn?"

"Why?" Now that he'd confessed, his defenses were setting in.

"Because there are probably cameras. Or night staff. Someone who could either collaborate her alibi or . . ."

"Or catch her in a lie."

"Yes," Siobhán said truthfully. "Or catch her in a lie. Which is why — no matter what — you must make her understand. Elise cannot lie to the guards."

CHAPTER 6

The O'Sullivans stood on a footpath in town, with Christmas cocooning all around them. Candles flickered from windows, and pubs and shops had their front windows decked out in holiday cheer. Christmas lights ran the length of the street, giving the overcast day a bit of sparkle. Blown-up Santas and snowmen beckoned from outside the hardware shop. A young man exited an inn, pushing an older woman in a wheelchair — presumedly Jason and his mother, Faye Elliot. He had dark hair slicked back and wore an old-fashioned suit, making him look as if he'd just stepped out of a 1930s movie. Enda's son was young and handsome. Jason stopped in front of Elise, Orla, and Paul as an awkward silence hung in the air. Finally, stiff hugs were exchanged. Elise turned to the O'Sullivans.

"This is my half uncle Jason and his mother, Faye."

Siobhán noted that she could have just introduced him as her uncle. Was it intentional? Was she placing him just outside the family? If he was offended, he didn't let it show. He smiled and nodded throughout additional handshakes and exchanges of "Sorry for your loss."

"It's quite the shock," Jason said, putting his hand on Faye's shoulder.

Faye Elliot wore a fur coat, similar to the one Moira had been wearing this morning at the mill. She must have noticed Siobhán looking. "This was Enda's Christmas present from the past," she said, stroking the fur. "Moira, Leah, and I decided to wear ours to honor Enda. It's quite out of fashion, politically speaking, but Enda meant well."

"It looks very warm," Siobhán said. *It was real.* And as Moira had pointed out, Enda had bought it for multiple recipients. *The women in his life.* Out of fashion was putting the controversy of wearing fur mildly. Had he not realized that real fur was offensive to many these days? She had enough personality quirks, she was not going to start lecturing dead men. Even if she wanted to. Just a little.

"He could be a generous man at times," Faye said. "Until he wasn't."

130

Jason squeezed his mam's shoulder, then let go. "May he rest in peace." Everyone crossed themselves.

"Have they arranged mass or the funeral yet?" Faye asked.

"Mam is working on that," Elise said. "She's discussing it with Leah."

"Leah." Faye said the name as if it were a bad taste in her mouth. "How is the poor dear?"

"I haven't seen much of her," Elise said. "She's always with that British man."

"Harry Williams," Siobhán said. "He's a renowned conductor."

"That's the one," Elise said.

"She's terribly sad," Orla said. "I saw her crying and playing her violin to a donkey."

"A donkey?" Ciarán said. "I want to see a donkey."

"Are you joking me?" Ann said. "I've seen at least six of them since we got here."

"I haven't see a single donkey," Ciarán said.

"That's because you've always got your head buried in a screen," Siobhán said. "Put it down for a while and you'll be amazed what you see."

"If I see one, I'm taking a picture, so my head will still be in the screen," Ciarán pointed out.

"Are we going to pop into the shops?" Gráinne asked.

"Don't buy anything yet," Elise said. "We still have to draw names."

"We're still buying for one another," Gráinne said. Beside her, James winced.

"No," Elise said. "We're picking names out of a cap."

"We just love exploring new shops," Siobhán said. "We're just here to have fun." Elise gave her a look that conveyed her suspicion that the O'Sullivans might be going rogue with the Christmas gift exchange.

"We should get to the house," Jason said as a van pulled up alongside them. "That's our ride."

Did he mean Enda's house? Siobhán supposed it wasn't a crime scene, so they were free to go to his house. But the guards might think otherwise, especially if they wanted to check on the slashed tire. She glanced at the inn behind them. Was it the same one Elise and James stayed in? She never did get a straight answer out of James.

"I take it you weren't here last night?" Siobhán couldn't help but ask.

Jason shook his head. "I left to pick up Mam two nights ago." He sighed. "I don't know why he went to the mill in the middle of the night. Other than he was paranoid about the instruments being stolen. Maybe if I had been home, I could have stopped him. Do we know yet why he was trying to get a harp out of storage at that hour?"

"We do know that your father's lorry had a flat tire," Siobhán said. "Were you aware of that?" If Moira was spilling the beans, there was no reason Siobhán couldn't scatter a few more around and see if anything sprouted.

Jason shook his head. "No. But my father didn't use his lorry much anymore. For all I know it's been that way for ages." If that was the case, it made his death less suspicious. Yet one could not ignore the sinister images on that video. In a town like this, wouldn't it be easy to know if anyone had a Grim Reaper costume?

"What vehicle do you use when you're here?"

"I don't," Jason said. "I prefer to walk."

Faye had been wheeled into the van and strapped in. "I'm afraid that's partly due to me," Faye said. "I was in a vehicular accident. That's why I'm in a chair."

"I'm very sorry," Siobhán said.

Faye waved it away. "It's in the past."

Jason got in the vehicle. Siobhán continued speaking with him. "Just in case the lorry hasn't been that way for ages, you might want to stay clear of it until the guards arrive."

Jason frowned. "Why?" He got out of the car and fixed his blue eyes on Siobhán. "My father's death was an accident, wasn't it?"

"Yes," Elise said. "A terrible fall."

"Enda was always prone to accidents," Faye said.

The comment seemed to tie Enda Elliot to the vehicular accident Faye mentioned. Siobhán waited to see if Faye would fill in a few more blanks. Instead she turned her head and looked out the window. There was definitely more to *that* story. Siobhán would have to try to suss it out later. "It was a pleasure to meet you," Siobhán said.

"Was it?" Faye asked. "I'm just wife number two. *Not* the charm." She smiled as if she were just joking, but it didn't reach her eyes. She pushed a button and the window slid up. The doors closed and the van pulled away. Siobhán turned to James.

"We're going to hit the shops," Siobhán said. "And maybe get some chocolates."

The younger ones cheered.

"Sweets are your answer for everything, aren't they?" James asked in a playful tone.

"Never underestimate the power of chocolates and crisps," Siobhán said. "That's the only love advice I'm ever going to give you."

The main street had a bookshop, a souvenir shop, a charity shop, a hardware shop, a sweetshop, and general gift shop. They hit all of them, and little by little Siobhán's mood lifted. She bought a book for each of her siblings, trying to find something that matched each of their wide interests, loving the new book smell, conjuring memories of books given to her by her mam and da, sitting by a peat fire with a mug of hot chocolate, entering a fictional world. *Bliss.* There were multiple purchases at the sweetshop, as they booted one another out on the footpath in order to buy in secret. It looked like all of the O'Sullivans appreciated the power of sweets, especially during the holidays, where calories certainly didn't count. Siobhán was thrilled to note that the gift shop was large and varied enough for everyone to shop in separate corners, thus avoiding prying eyes. Lights twinkled from the ceiling, and Christmas music played overhead. Siobhán kept her eyes peeled for something musical, given the upcoming gift exchange.

There was a single shopkeeper behind the counter, a middle-aged woman with dark hair pulled back with a red ribbon, and a welcoming smile. Siobhán approached. "Do you have any gifts that have a musical theme?"

"My, I don't recall any. What type of gift are you looking for?"

"I don't know, to be honest. I think we're all directed to find something with a musical theme."

She placed her hand on her heart. "Is it in honor of poor Enda?"

"It's probably in honor of the orchestra and their guests," Siobhán said.

"Are you with the orchestra?"

"No. We're friends of the family."

The woman leaned in. "Is it true? Did he fall from a balcony?"

"It's a difficult time for the family," Siobhán said, not giving away any details.

"Is it true he died in the middle of the night?"

"I really don't have any details."

The woman bit her lip. "There was talk of a harp." Beat by beat she had the story. The West Cork grapevine was alive and well. "I'm sorry, I don't feel it's my place to talk about this."

"Of course. I just wonder . . ." She shook her head, then turned back to her cash register. "Never mind."

Siobhán nudged forward. "What do you wonder?"

She looked around, then made eye contact with Siobhán. "I might have seen him that evening."

She had Siobhán's full attention. "You mean Enda?"

The woman nodded. "I certainly saw *someone.*"

She was drawing it out, wanting attention. Siobhán leaned in. "Whatever do you mean?"

"I'm never out that late, mind you. But I was invited to a Christmas party with friends, and I stayed out way too late. It was dark when I was driving home. I saw someone out hitchhiking. Near the wooden bridge, don't you know."

An image of the bridge over a creek popped in Siobhán's mind. She'd crossed over it with Theodore Baskins on their ride to the mill. "What time was this?"

"It was around half past one in the morning." Enda Elliot was dead in the mill at half past one. But was this the killer? The woman placed her hand over her mouth as if she'd just confessed something naughty. "I'd had a glass of wine at dinner, and I waited hours just to make sure I was okay to drive."

"What was the person wearing? Was it a man? Woman?"

The woman frowned. "Honestly, it was dark, and I wasn't expecting anyone out at that hour. I only saw a figure, regular height, dark clothing, thumb stuck out alongside the road."

Dark clothing. "Can you describe anything about the clothing?" Siobhán didn't want to put the word *cloak* in the woman's mind.

She shook her head. "A dark coat, I think. Something long. Maybe a trench coat?"

Maybe a cloak? But if the killer was trying to hide his or her identity, why on earth would he or she hitchhike? "Did you stop?"

"Heavens, no. Not at that hour. It's not safe."

"Of course. Have you told the guards?"

She reached back and played with the ribbon in her hair. "Do you think it's important?"

"Probably not. But better safe than sorry." Siobhán had to calm down. The village didn't know it was a murder probe yet, and she didn't want to be the first to light that wick.

"Enda fell, didn't he?" *Perhaps it was too late.*

Siobhán shrugged and waved it away as if it didn't matter. "As I said, I don't have any

138

details."

The woman nodded. "Enda was a difficult man. But a musical genius. I don't envy the road ahead of them."

"What's your name?" Siobhán said it as if she just wanted to be friends, but she intended on calling Garda Cooley so he could question her about the person she saw near the bridge.

"Alison."

"Lovely to meet you. I'm Siobhán."

Alison leaned across the counter. "I hear both wives are together for the holidays."

"I'm sure that's common these days."

"Faye Elliot is a woman of class." From the sounds of it she wasn't so sure about Leah. Siobhán felt strangely defensive of wife number three.

"I just met her, she seems lovely," Siobhán said. "As does Leah Elliot."

"Faye would have to be lovely, wouldn't she? To forgive him? After what Enda did?"

"What he did?"

"She's in a wheelchair."

"I'm aware."

"Enda put her there."

It appeared Siobhán would be getting this story sooner than she thought. "What happened?"

Alison looked around. Besides her brood,

139

there was no one else in the shop. "He was driving. It was a winter night, just like the ones we're having now. Rained for days. He took a curve too fast and the vehicle rolled upside down."

An accident. "I see." *Had he been drinking?* She didn't ask.

"I suppose it was so long ago now that it has all been forgiven."

Had Faye forgiven Enda? What if she hadn't? What if she'd been planning something like this for years? He'd not only left her after the accident but eventually traded her in for a much younger, able-bodied wife. That had to sting. Then again, Faye was certainly not the figure in the Grim Reaper costume, and she couldn't have navigated the stairs up to the second-floor gallery in the mill. If Faye Elliot was behind Enda's murder, then she would have needed help. Her son, Jason? Siobhán realized Alison was staring at her with rapt interest. "It's good when family can forgive and come together," Siobhán said.

Alison nodded, then suddenly looked up as if remembering something. "The hardware shop."

"Pardon?"

"They have plastic snowmen."

"Okay."

"They play 'Frosty the Snowman.' "
Siobhán frowned, wondering why Alison
thought she looked as if she was in the
market for a plastic snowman. "You said
you needed something musical?"

"Oh. Wonderful. Thank you." That wasn't
quite what she had in mind for a musical
gift, but it was nice that Alison had been
listening. Siobhán bought some festive
cookie cutters and a pine-scented candle
for their guest house, then eyed a few other
bits for a future visit.

"Can we break for tea and chocolate
now?" Gráinne asked, approaching, hand
on hip, as if she expected an argument.

"Yes, pet," Siobhán said. "That's exactly
what we should do."

After tea and heavenly chocolates, they
finished at the hardware shop. Christmas
trees lined the footpath, making Siobhán
swell with cheer as memories of Christmas
trees past marched through her head. That
is, until she saw who was selling the trees —
the old man who had dragged Eoin by his
ear. He recognized them too. Siobhán had a
sinking feeling that the price of trees had
just gone up. All of the O'Sullivan Six got
involved in the pick — touching trees,
shouting, "What about this one?" with

everyone standing back to decide. Ciarán finally found the one. It was tall and full, with several bits sticking out at odd angles; if it were a person, you might say the tree was a bit of a dolt. "He's cute," Ann said. They all agreed. He was cute, and silly, and imperfectly perfect.

"That's a beauty," the old man said, rubbing his chin and casting a glare Eoin's way. "That one's going to cost you."

"We'll pay up as long as you can deliver," Siobhán said.

"He's like Ciarán with his hair sticking out," Eoin added with a gentle punch to Ciarán's shoulder.

"We can make him pretty," Gráinne said, eyeing him like a potential beauty customer. "With the right grooming and decorations." They also picked up a tree stand and, after much debate, decided a string of white lights would look beautiful in their cottage (shack) and on a tree adorned with items from nature. Siobhán found herself excited by what they might find. This was the spirit of Christmas, getting creative, working together. When they reached the counter and Siobhán hoisted her handbag, Eoin pushed her away. "It's on me."

"On you?" Siobhán said.

"We both know the price went up because

of me." He nodded and removed his wallet. Tears filled her eyes. "Don't you dare," he said as he handed the money over. "Dry your eyes."

She had to turn to a wall of stockings and cry to them. Eoin worked hard in the bistro during the day and poured whatever energy he had left into his graphic novels. They'd actually been getting some traction. Ironically, his main character was a superhero version of her. Flying through fields and lifting sheep over her head, of all things. But she couldn't be prouder — of all her siblings, and the quicker they grew, the more she wanted to freeze them in time. The old man grinned. "I'll deliver this beauty this evening." On the way out, Siobhán checked out the singing plastic snowman. Instead of jolly, he looked as if he'd remove his plastic carrot nose and stab you in your sleep. She wouldn't buy this snowman for her worst enemy. Siobhán kept her distance.

CHAPTER 7

After shopping and tea, the O'Sullivans returned to Moira's house, which was nearly the same as they left it. The kitchen was still in full use, and Elise had been spot-on. Not only was there enough food, but at this rate they could feed the entire village. The living room held only a few folks, so many more were outside, standing in clumps, getting some air despite the chill and a growing wind. It was late afternoon. What a day it had been. Siobhán finished her tea and stepped outside. Within minutes a garda car pulled up. Garda Cooley stuck his head out of his vehicle, caught Siobhán's eye, and jerked his head indicating he wanted her to join him. She did.

"Take me to Enda's house, and lead me through what the two of you found."

"Of course." Her eyes flicked to the kitchen window where Moira stood with her head bent, speaking with Faye. Jason, Orla, and Paul huddled outside. The sound of a violin wafted out from the living room. *Leah.* Enda's house should be empty.

Garda Cooley exited his vehicle with a wave at the others before following Siobhán through the small patch of woods to Enda's house. Once there she took him through everything, starting with the flat tire, moving on to the iPad, and ending at the wall where a hatchet once hung. "He took it with him," Cooley said, staring at the dark spot on the wall. "And now it's gone."

"It's not clear from the video that he's carrying a hatchet," Siobhán said lightly. "But it's a good working theory."

"If it walks like a duck and talks like a duck, it's a duck," Barry Cooley said as if that was the end of the matter.

"That outfit the person was wearing," Siobhán prodded.

"Big enough to hide a hatchet underneath," Cooley finished.

"Any thoughts on where someone would have acquired such a costume?"

"Plenty of women in the village sew," Cooley said. "Catherine Healy is known for it. But she sews mainly for one person, and that person likes his costumes."

Theodore Baskins. Was he going to keep an open mind and follow the evidence, or

145

was he going to skew the evidence to point at his preferred suspect?

They returned to the backyard. Siobhán pointed out the spot in the woods where she'd seen the person in red and green sneaking through, dropping glitter, and then running away.

"What I tell ya? Another costume." He stared out at a spot in the distance and sighed. "I don't like opening a murder inquiry right before Christmas."

"You'll want to speak to the shopkeeper at the gift shop in town. Alison?"

He nodded. "Why is that?"

"She said she saw someone hitchhiking on the road around half one in the morning. Near the old bridge."

Cooley removed a notebook from his pocket and jotted it down. Then he stuck the unlit cigar in his mouth. "I'll be bringing yer man in for questioning."

"Theodore Baskins?"

"You do catch on quick."

"It's hard not to notice he isn't well liked."

"He's caused a lot of trouble. Wild parties. Bragging. Snooping. Stealing. Besides Catherine, I cannot name a soul in town who would give the lad the time of day."

"Is it because he's English?" The past was never entirely forgotten. And here, in this part of West Cork, anyone who hadn't lived in this village their entire life was considered a blow-in.

"No, it's because he's a bollocks. Pardon my language."

"No worries." She was just happy he was confiding in her. "Did he have a beef with Enda?" Motive was often key to solving a murder, and sadly, it was often family members who had the biggest reasons to kill.

"Theodore once stole a trophy of Enda's. And I'm not talking about one of his wives." He stuck his cigar back in his pocket.

"And?" Siobhán asked, wondering if Garda Cooley had anything to add to the story.

He frowned. "And what?"

"What happened?"

"Catherine found the trophy in her laundry basket, and she returned it to Enda."

At least the story was the same. "And you think that's a motive for murder?"

"What if Theodore was nosing around in the mill, stealing instruments? Enda catches him red-handed. Theodore doesn't want to get in trouble, so he pushes him to his death."

"Were there any instruments missing?"

"Do you think he'd actually steal an

instrument after that?"

She took that as a no. As far as they'd been able to ascertain so far, nothing was missing from the mill, and the figure on video had not been carrying any instruments when he or she exited. It was too bad the video quality was so poor. It was impossible to make out even the height and weight of the person. That was the problem with murder inquiries — absolutely anybody could be the killer.

"Finally," Elise said, hoisting up a Santa cap. "We're all here." Here was Moira's living room, where all the musicians and family members had crammed in, including Catherine Healy and Theodore Baskins. Before they began, Moira sidled over to Siobhán, her intense gaze never leaving Theodore.

"I don't want him in my home," she said in a harsh whisper. "I intend to ask him to leave." She took a step toward Theodore. Siobhán put her arm gently on Moira's shoulder.

"Wait." Moira stopped, her jaw clenched. "I need to get to know all of the suspects. You don't want to set off any alarm bells."

"I can't stand the sight of him."

"It's better to have him where we can keep

an eye on him. Try to get your mind on something else." Moira shook her head but took a step back and folded her arms. "There's no use starting a war with your neighbors at this moment."

"Because it's Christmas?" Moira seemed surprised.

"Because you have no hard evidence that Theodore did anything at all to your father."

Elise began passing around biros and torn sheets of paper. It was late into the evening, and Siobhán was dying to snuggle into bed.

"Don't tell me we're playing a game." Orla sounded bored already as she twirled a strand of her long blond hair around a slender finger.

"Elise loves games," Paul said with a wink. "Don't you, sis?"

"Are we writing down our alibis?" Gráinne said with a laugh. Siobhán knew her sister was joking, but she was so close to the mark it made her cringe.

"Why would we need alibis?" This came from Jason, who, Siobhán had noted, had already been paying extra close attention to Gráinne. She was a black-haired beauty who so far showed no signs of attaching herself to any man. Gráinne shrugged and examined her nails, which was her tell when she was nervous. She was so used to being flippant, she'd most likely forgotten she was no longer in her safety web of just family. Or she was sweet on Jason Elliot.

"I'm sorry," Gráinne said, treating Jason to a shy smile. "I was only messin', but there's a time and place for everything, and this was neither."

"Not a bother," Jason said quickly as the two held their gaze.

Siobhán nearly choked. She had never heard her sister apologize in her life. It made her give Jason a second look. She supposed he was somewhat attractive, in a stuffy way. Not the kind of man she'd ever pictured Gráinne dating. But she'd learned that it was impossible to pick out partners for other people.

The thought led her to glance at Catherine and Theodore, who stood stiffly by the door as if they were prepared to flee. Catherine was still in a flannel shirt, Theodore Baskins in a leather coat and wearing sunglasses of all things. Leah and Harry Williams sat next to each other as well. Very close. Leah stared into the fire.

"Everyone write your name on the sheet of paper, then stick it in the Santa cap," Elise said, dropping her name in and passing the hat to her left.

"If you must know," Moira announced in

a loud voice, before Siobhán could even think to stop her, "I think my father was pushed off that railing."

A gasp sounded as Siobhán inwardly groaned. The gasp came from Orla. She flew out of her chair.

"Mam?"

"What on earth do you mean?" Jason stood, chest pushed out. "Pushed?"

"I knew it," Faye said. "I knew he wouldn't lean against a railing. I can't even see him rummaging up there for a harp!"

"Especially when I already have a perfectly good harp," Ruth said. "That old thing up there couldn't be tuned in time for the concert."

Siohban knew nothing about harps and had only glanced at it, but it certainly didn't seem like some old thing. It looked very dear. If Ruth was putting on an act and pretending otherwise, the gnawing question was, Why?

"Siobhán and I found a video on my father's iPad," Moira said. "It showed someone else entering the mill before Da. And they were dressed in a costume."

Heads swiveled, then landed finally on Siobhán. She stood unblinking. This was a growing disaster, and she had yet to learn how to harness the power of time travel.

"What kind of costume?" Catherine Healy asked.

"Wait," Siobhán said before Moira could answer. She glared at Moira to drive the point home. *Shut your piehole.* "I assure you, the guards are investigating. It's important that we all remain calm, and please do not jump to any early conclusions."

Leah turned to face everyone. "I saw the video too. Enda woke in the middle of the night because he had an alarm system on the doors to the mill. The video showed this strange person — in a Grim Reaper costume entering at a little past one in the morning."

Siobhán hung her head. What was wrong with these people? They should stick to playing music and let the detectives do the detecting. Giving away details only the killer would know would set this investigation back. What's done was done. Siobhán prayed that Garda Cooley wouldn't blame her for their discretions. She turned and stared at Theodore Baskins. With his sunglasses on it was impossible to tell if he was having any reaction at all. Catherine moved closer and linked her arm in Theodore's.

"How odd," Catherine said.

"A Grim Reaper?" Harry Williams said. "Odd is putting it mildly. It sounds horrifying." Siobhán got the distinct impression he was putting on an act, pretending to be hearing this for the first time. Just how close were Leah and Harry Williams?

"Why didn't you tell us any of this?" Jason asked. "Especially me. As his only son I think I had a right to know."

"We were asked to keep this quiet," Siobhán said. "I'm afraid I'm going to have to tell Garda Cooley that everyone knows. It would have been better for the investigation if you didn't."

"Is that why you were asking me all those questions?" Jason asked, turning to Siobhán. "Were you trying to see if I had an alibi?"

"No," Siobhán said. "I'm not on this case."

"Neither of us were even in town," Faye said. "We'll make sure Garda Cooley knows that."

"Let me guess," Catherine Healy said. "The guards are going to go after Theodore."

"Of course they are," Theodore said. "But I was at home all night." He put his arm around Catherine. "Wasn't I, darling? Or should I start calling you Darling Alibi?"

"This is hardly the time for humor," Moira said.

"My apologies," Theodore said. "But my story still stands." He turned to Catherine.

"Yes," she said, dropping Theodore's arm and stepping slightly away from him. "We were in all night."

Moira crept closer to Catherine. "All night, you say? Why I swore I heard Theodore peel out in his lorry around half nine."

She did? Siobhán clenched her fists. Why hadn't she mentioned this earlier? Was she making it up? If so, they were all playing a very dangerous game.

"You must have been mistaken," Catherine said.

"I know the sound of that lorry, and I heard it clear as day," Moira said.

"Even though it was in the evening," Gráinne added unhelpfully.

"Whatever you heard, it wasn't me," Theodore said. "Unless you think you can pick the sound of my lorry out from all the others on the road, I wouldn't repeat that to anyone."

If Moira was intimidated by Theodore's comment, she didn't let it show. Instead, she continued to glare at Catherine. "Are you still taking sleeping pills?"

Catherine blinked rapidly, then frowned. "What are you suggesting?"

"I'm suggesting you were sound asleep when Theodore snuck out in the middle of the night."

"Half nine is hardly the middle of the night," Theodore said. Catherine gave him a look. He held up his hands. "It wasn't me, I'm just saying . . . if it was, that's hardly the middle of the night."

"I have to agree," Gráinne said. "As a fellow night owl." This time Jason was treated to a full-on smile as Gráinne wound a streak of blue around her finger. He had the decency to blush.

"Why are you harping on Theodore?" Catherine asked.

"Who else would break into a mill in the middle of the night?" Moira said. She turned to Gráinne. "Is half twelve the middle of the night, luv?"

"I suppose that's getting closer," Gráinne said. "I guess it's relative to what time one goes to bed and gets up."

Siobhán was slightly proud of her logic there, although the interruptions were getting them nowhere.

"Who else would break into the mill in the middle of the night?" Catherine echoed. "Besides your father, you mean?"

Moira whirled on her. "He had a concert to plan."

"That's not what I'm on about."

"Out with it then." Moira straightened.

"He's been doing a lot of that lately, hasn't

155

he? Wandering around in the middle of the night?"

Faye rolled her wheelchair forward, forcing Moira and Catherine to part. "We cannot start bickering amongst ourselves," Faye said. "Besides, at that hour we were all sleeping."

Not a creature was stirring . . . But of course that was a lie. Way too many creatures had been stirring. First there was the matter of the emergency family meeting. Those creatures were stirring. Faye's comment suddenly snuck up on her. *We were sleeping.* She turned to her. "I thought you two weren't in town last night."

Faye opened her mouth and then shut it. "We arrived late last night. After ten."

"That means you were in town," Moira said. "Why did you lie?"

"We weren't roaming around," Faye said. "I certainly didn't roll myself to the mill."

Jason cleared his throat. "I didn't leave the inn until morning when I went to fetch us some breakfast. I suppose the guards will hear that from the innkeeper."

Siobhán turned to James. "Were you and Elise staying at the same inn?"

"It's the only one in town," Moira said.

"Staying at the inn?" Elise said. "James and I didn't arrive until this morning." Her face did not give any hint that she was lying. "Not that anyone would think I'd hurt my own grandfather."

Paul and Orla exchanged a look. Paul started to cough, Orla pounded him on the back, and Siobhán stared at James. He refused to meet her eyes. *The three unwise men. Very unwise.* Siobhán was going to have to have a heart-to-heart with her soon-to-be sister-in-law. Her lies could not continue. Too much was at stake.

"The guards will do a thorough investigation of everyone," Siobhán said. "Every detail of your alibis will be checked out, and all possibilities are on the table."

"Thorough investigation," Theodore said with a laugh. "You obviously don't understand this village." He crossed his arms as if daring someone to contradict him. No one did.

"In the meantime, we have to find a new venue for the concert," Harry Williams said.

"Concert?" Paul said. "I assumed it was canceled." They continued to write their names on slips and drop them in the Santa cap as they conversed.

"No," Moira said. "We talked it over. The musicians want to continue with the Christmas Eve concert in honor of Enda."

"I've agreed to step in as conductor,"

Harry Williams said, standing and giving a slight bow. *The rival conductor steps up.* Siobhán had a feeling Enda Elliot would be less than pleased with that development. Exactly how ambitious was the handsome Harry Williams? Or did he have designs on more than just Enda's position? She could certainly see how easy it would be to fall in love with Leah.

"Enda would be honored." Moira touched Harry's arm, then dropped it abruptly as if afraid she was being forward. Harry Williams bowed again and his gaze shifted to Leah, where it remained for several seconds before he turned away.

"I don't mean to be rude, but is there a nip of whiskey in the house?" Harry asked.

"Of course," Moira said.

"No need, Mam," Paul said. "We have Irish cream."

Harry Williams studied Paul with a patient smile. "I'm more of a whiskey man myself."

Paul straightened up as if the very notion offended him. "We won an award."

"I heard. Congratulations." He turned to Moira. "Whiskey, if you please."

"Whiskey it is." Moira hurried out of the room as Paul sulked in the corner.

The Santa cap made it back to Elise. She held it up and swung it left and right, as if performing a magic trick. "Next we'll draw names. Whoever's name you draw, you will be that person's Secret Santa. You can buy them a series of small gifts or one big gift. Our theme this year is something musical."

Someone coughed, and Siobhán wondered if it was an attempt to cover a groan.

"Secret Santa," Ciarán said. "Cool."

"And because we don't all know one another, everyone should spend time speaking with everyone else about their likes and dislikes, get to know each other. Gifts should be thirty euro or less. If you draw your own name, return it to the hat and pick another. Use your imagination and creativity. If you're musical, you could even play someone a song."

This time there was a definite groan, and it came from Gráinne. She held up her hand as if she were in school waiting to be called on.

Elise's jaw tensed. "Yes, Gráinne?"

"Please. If you pick my name, do not cheap out by playing me a song."

There was stunned silence, and then Leah broke the tension with laughter. Genuine from-the-belly laughter. At first, Gráinne looked startled, then she started to laugh. Moments later, everyone was laughing with her. Leah's laughter subsided and a second later, she was sobbing.

Harry was the first to rush to her side. He put his arm around her. "There, there." It only made her cry harder.

Ruth navigated to another corner, and seconds later harp music wafted into the air. Soon it was joined by a violin. And then a bass. Leah wiped her eyes, her breathing going from jagged to steady as she began to sway with the music. Even Gráinne could be seen brushing a tear from her eye when the song finished.

"Fine," Gráinne said. "My Secret Santa can play me a song." Laughter reined again as Elise passed the cap.

When it reached Siobhán, she pulled a name out and glanced at it. *Theodore Baskins.* She cringed a little as she passed the hat on. The rest in this group would be certainly happy that she picked his name. Perhaps all he required was a bottle of award-winning Irish cream. Then again, it was supposed to be musical. Was Theodore Baskins even into music? *Whoever changed their ringtone to classical music certainly was. . . .* Had the guards figured out the source yet? She forced herself to focus on the here and now. She was eager to find out which names her siblings had drawn. When all the names were picked, Elise encouraged them to mingle as musicians gathered to play Christmas songs. Paul brought out his Irish cream and Siobhán said yes, she'd love some poured over ice. He was more than happy to oblige, and it became obvious as he stood staring at her that he intended to watch her drink it. She smiled and took a sip. The sour notes hit the sides of her tongue immediately.

"Well?" he said.

"It's something," she said. It took forever for him to go away. She immediately poured the rest down the kitchen sink and reached for some water. Exactly how much money had he poured into this business? Perhaps his cows weren't as happy as he claimed.

"Enda was right," Moira said, startling her from behind. "It's horrid, isn't it?"

"Unfortunately," Siobhán said.

"He wasted so much money. He'll never get rid of that inventory."

"Tis a pity." Just how upset was Enda about his grandson's failing business? Siobhán filtered back into the living room. She put her arm around Ciarán. "Show me who you picked." Ciarán was reaching into his pocket for the slip of paper when Elise's voice cut across the room.

"No! Siobhán! You cannot ask whose names they drew. That's cheating." Heads swiveled to Siobhán as heat crept up her neck.

"Busted," Gráinne said.

Siobhán put her hands up as Ciarán shoved the name back in his pocket. "I hear you. Not a bother." *It so was a bother.* James threw her a look she couldn't interpret. She understood the gist of it. *Don't make my life any more difficult than it already is.* She thought of Macdara and realized the last time she spoke to him she cut off the call to chase an elf through the woods. She'd better try him again and apologize. She found her coat, then slipped outside and hurried down to the road, hoping he wouldn't be too browned off with her.

CHAPTER 8

"Hung up on me?" Macdara said when Siobhán reached him. "I just assumed you lost the signal."

Darn. I should have stuck with that. "Good. I was worried you were browned off."

"I wasn't browned off then, but now that I know you hung up on me, I might be."

From his tone of voice, he was messing with her. "Will it take you long to get over it?" she asked.

"Give me a sec." He whistled a tune, then stopped. "Over it. So, what's the story?" She filled him in on their Christmas shopping and the Secret Santa name draw, and she vented for a bit about Elise. Then she asked after him and his mam, and he in turn filled her in on the past few days. Kilbane, he said, was rather quiet for the holidays, especially with Naomi's closed. She silently vowed that next year they would be home for Christmas. She missed Kilbane and

O'Rourke's, and Maria, and Bridie, and Annmarie. And of course she missed Macdara Flannery most of all, but he would be here soon.

"I do have some news, but you have to promise you won't change your plans." Siobhán had to tell him what was going on. Enda Elliot was a famous man, and the news was going to spread quickly.

"What is it?" He was on guard, she could hear it in his voice.

"It's possible that Enda Elliot was pushed from the gallery."

Silence. After a few seconds she was wondering if he had cut her off. "Are you coming straight home?" he asked.

"Everyone is staying. Supporting the family. Even the orchestra is still going to play. Only now the concert will be a tribute to Enda."

"You're not getting involved in the case, are you?"

"They have their own guards here, as you know, and Garda Cooley has made it clear I'm not to involve myself in his investigation."

Macdara mumbled something under his breath. "Why did you hang up on me again?"

"I thought I saw someone in the woods."

"What do you mean by someone?"

"Just one of Santa's little helpers." She tried to make light of it. "Turns out it was just an elf sprinkling glitter."

"Mam and I are coming." She hadn't fooled him for a second. That was the downside of having a fiancé who was an excellent detective sergeant.

"Macdara. You'll be here soon enough. Stick with your original plans, or your mam will kill me."

"She loves the orchestra."

"We both know she wants to spend Christmas with her son. I don't even know where you'd stay. The single inn in town has been booked for ages because of the concert. We're sleeping in a very rustic cottage — I might call it a shack — with bunk beds."

"Promise you won't go running off into the woods alone."

"It's not really a woods. Just a patch of trees."

"I don't care. Just stay safe."

"I will. I promise. And Dara?"

"Yes, boss?"

"I want this to be the last Christmas we ever spend alone."

"It will be."

Tears came to her eyes, but she didn't want him to hear them in her voice, so she said her goodbyes, hung up properly this time, and tried to think of something to get her mind off missing the blue-eyed, messy-haired man with the lopsided grin. In the new year they were going to have a wedding to plan. They should at least think about setting a date. She would speak to him about it when he arrived. And until then, she had plenty to keep her busy. She had to find a Secret Santa gift for Theodore Baskins, for one. For some reason the plastic snowman came to mind. Maybe she'd been wrong about it. Maybe a party animal like him would love a plastic singing snowman.

When Siobhán returned from her phone call, she was surprised to see a group outside waiting for her, all huddled around her siblings.

"They all want to help find items for our tree," Ciarán said.

"We didn't get to decorate the mill, so this will be perfect," Leah said.

"Sounds lovely," Siobhán said. "But I don't even know if the tree has been delivered."

"We can get a head start," Ciarán said.

Siobhán shook her head. "It will be dark soon and we're all exhausted." It had been one of the longest days of her life, and she was eager for it to end.

"First thing in the morning," Elise said. "We'll meet you outside the guest house, and we'll all find items for your tree." Everyone heartily agreed. Siobhán thanked them and smiled. She couldn't have asked for a nicer group of people. Minus one. The killer. If only she knew which one it was.

The wind howled all night long. It took Siobhán ages to fall asleep, her feet hung over the edge of the bed when fully stretched out, making for uncomfortable contortions, keeping her awake. At some point she finally drifted off, but when she woke up, her back was sore and her poor little toes were ice cold. She wrapped a shawl around her and put on the kettle for tea. Soon the rest of the six were awake, with Ciarán peeking out the window, waiting for the others. The tree had arrived sometime in the night, and the lads had it set up in seconds. True to their word, Elise and the others landed bright and early ready to scavenge for ornaments.

Orla gravitated to Gráinne and Ann. "Can I join the two of you?"

"Not a bother," Ann said. "But we're going to power walk it."

"I'm in," Orla said, pumping her arms.

"What are we looking for again?" Paul asked.

"Items from nature," Siobhán said. "Anything we can hang on the tree. As long as it isn't too dirty or crawling with bugs."

"I don't mind bugs," Ciarán said.

"No bugs," Siobhán repeated.

"What about a ladybug?" Ciarán demanded. "They bring good luck."

"Or a glowworm?" Ann chimed in.

Siobhán sighed. "No bugs of any kind, even if they sparkle and bring good luck. Everything else is a go."

Leah and William gravitated toward each other, and Catherine Healy stood by Jason and Faye. "I'll have to watch from here," Faye said. "Why don't you all agree to meet back here in an hour with your finds?"

"I'll help you inside the house first," Jason said to his mother. "Would you prefer to be at Moira's or Father's house?"

"Moira's, dear," Faye said. "I can bake my Christmas treats." It would be impossible to navigate these mucky fields in a wheelchair, so even though they had lied about their alibi, Faye was not high on Siobhán's list. That didn't mean Jason was in the clear, even if he was handsome and good to his mam. After all, why lie about when they got into town? Paul lifted Faye out of her wheelchair as Jason folded it and brought it into the house. "Such a strong young man," Faye said as Paul carried her inside, his full cheeks flushing at the compliment.

"It's from carrying cases of Elliot's Irish Cream," he said as they disappeared inside.

Theodore Baskins stood off to the side smoking a cigarette, and if his scowl was any indication, he was not in a festive mood. Ruth and Moira headed off without a word to anyone else. Jason and Paul exited the kitchen, waved at Faye through the window, and headed off. Leah and Harry scooped up Siobhán's brood, and the hunt for Christmas ornaments made in nature began. It was a perfect activity, something to get them hiking and focusing on a bit of cheer. In the distance, Siobhán could hear Leah and Gráinne chatting away. She'd been right about the two of them hitting it off. Siobhán looked about to see who was left to go scavenging and found Theodore Baskins the sole person still standing around. Given she had to buy his Christmas present, she decided she might as well give it a go.

"Shall we?" she asked.

He blew smoke into the cold winter air. "What do you need me for?"

"I thought you might tell me stories about living here while I scavenge."

"Stories?"

She shrugged. "I just assumed a writer like you would have some good tales. But if not, no worries."

"Are you trying to appeal to my massive ego?"

"That depends. Is it working?"

He laughed, then flicked ashes off his cigarette into the wind. "If you don't mind horror stories."

Siobhán started to walk, heading for the road. "I'd prefer something on the lighter side."

"Gossip?" he said, as if he had something good to offer up.

"If you must."

"Leah and Harry Williams look awfully cozy, don't they?"

"Not that kind of gossip." He was right though. And if she had noticed it and Theodore had noticed, then others did too. What about Enda? Was he jealous of Harry Williams? Had he noticed?

"I thought they all hated me because I'm English. But they act like Harry Williams walks on water." He shuffled behind Siobhán. "Enda would be furious. His wife and his nemesis romantically entwined."

170

"Nemesis?" Siobhán sincerely wanted to admonish Theodore, as there was no proof that Leah and Harry were having an affair, but she had to follow the tongue-and-time rule — bite and bide. She'd learned she could squeeze more information out of a suspect if she didn't needle them first.

"Now he has a better chance of luring Leah to London," Theodore said, waving his arm in a flourish. "Not to mention coveting the wife. After Moira's bombshell about this Grim Reaper character, I'm starting to think Enda's death wasn't an accident."

Siobhán got the feeling he was turning the tables, scavenging not for Christmas ornaments but information. She wasn't going to bite. "Faye seems like a lovely woman." Theodore must know something of her accident. Would he volunteer anything?

"She might be lovely, but I wouldn't say the same about her son."

"What are you insinuating about Jason?"

They had been walking along the road toward the small bridge where the shopkeeper had seen someone hitchhiking around the time the figure had entered the mill. Siobhán stopped to look down at the gurgling creek. Theodore bent and retrieved something from the ground. He held up a

171

large gold button. "Is this the kind of thing you're looking for?"

"Looking for?"

He cocked his head and gave her an amused smile. "To decorate your tree."

"Right, so." It was beautiful. Ornate, and much larger than a normal coat button. "Yes," she said, delighted. "It will make a beautiful ornament." Theodore offered a shy smile and handed it to her. "I'd love to get a little closer to the ocean, see if there's any driftwood or shells."

"Follow me," Theodore said with confidence.

They crossed the road and then cut through a pasture, and there it was — a steep cliff and, below it, the ocean. As they drew closer, she feared Theodore was going to do something ridiculous like scale down or, worse, jump. "If you want to get down by the water, we'll have to go back to the house and fetch my lorry."

She hesitated. Did she really want to get in a vehicle with him? She'd be furious if any of her siblings took a ride from him without letting anyone know. He'd given her a ride once already, and seemed harmless. Maybe he was right. Maybe they didn't like him because he was young, and English, and living with an older Irish woman.

Maybe he was a bit cocky and off-putting, and eccentric. It didn't mean he was dangerous. "Let's head back toward your house and see what we find," she said. "If we strike out, we can head to the ocean."

"Not a bother." They turned to begin walking in the other direction.

"Do you know much about Faye's car accident?"

"Such as?"

"Was Faye driving?" She wanted to see if his stories would match the others.

Theodore shook his head. "From what I've heard, Enda was driving."

"What happened?" Siobhán normally avoided the topic of car accidents, but she had a feeling this story could be important.

Theodore shrugged. "I don't know all the details. Everyone around here has a slightly different version of what happened. It was around this time of year, I believe. A holiday party. Dark ice on the road. No doubt drink involved. And a third version is that they were arguing. Enda took a curve too fast, and the car rolled over twice before landing in a ditch. Faye ended up in a wheelchair, unable to bear children." He stopped there, which was annoying given there was obviously something left unsaid.

"Are you saying Jason is adopted?"

173

Siobhán asked.

"No. Catherine said they used a surrogate to carry Jason." Faye must certainly have mixed emotions about Enda. "Jason and I have something in common," Theodore continued.

Now this she had to hear. "Were you conceived by a surrogate?"

Theodore laughed. "No. I wasn't left in a manger either." He took a moment to reflect on what he was about to say. "I only meant that the pair of us are outsiders. Even if he was Enda's son, he was always an outsider. Enda treated his three grandchildren more like children."

Orla, Paul, and Elise. The same three that called an emergency family meeting the night of Enda's murder and had yet to confess it to anyone other than James. Before she knew it, they were back at Moira's house. The others were nowhere in sight. She hoped they were having better luck scavenging than she was.

"What do you say?" Theodore said. "Quick ride to the ocean?"

"Why not." Maybe she would find some nice shells. They headed over to Catherine's and hopped in the lorry. They fell into a comfortable silence, and Theodore put on a radio station playing Christmas songs.

174

Theodore was a fast driver, and the roads were filled with dangerous curves. The music stopped and an announcer came on.

"West Cork is mourning the tragic death of orchestra conductor Enda Elliot. The guards are looking for anyone who saw a strange man hitchhiking near the creek bridge."

No, no, no. What have they done? Ted swerved to the right, and the lorry bounced as it straddled the road and a dirt path. "Sorry." He swerved again to get them back on the road. Siobhán's heart hammered in her chest. "Why do you think they're asking about a hitchhiker?"

Because they're too stupid to keep their gobs shut. "I haven't the faintest idea."

"They're shutting you out, are they?"

"Who?"

"The local boys. You're not good enough to be on the case, is that it?"

"It's not my jurisdiction, nor do I wish it was."

Theodore nodded. "I suppose Enda's will might shed some light on the situation," he said as the lorry descended a hill leading toward the ocean.

"Oh?"

"Does he leave the bulk of it to Leah or his second wife? His only son or his only

175

daughter? Split evenly?"

"I hope he will be fair to all."

"Moira was at our house the other day, and I'm not trying to point fingers . . ." He let the thought hang in the air as if waiting for Siobhán to encourage him to point fingers.

"Yes?"

"I heard her asking Catherine about declaring someone mentally unfit." He waited for her to process it.

"I see." She mulled it over.

"I think Moira was rattled by Enda's decline. I think he had a serious undiagnosed issue. We all saw it."

"What exactly did you see?"

"Enda behaving irrationally. The night walks. The arguments."

"Arguments?"

"Screaming at Moira at the top of his lungs. Paul even had to step in one day."

This was news. "What happened?"

"They were all standing at the back of the house. Enda was wielding a hatchet." He pulled over into a small parking lot. "We can walk from here."

"What do you mean, wielding a hatchet? Was he threatening them with it?"

"I didn't say that. But I also didn't see him chopping any wood. I did hear him

176

grumble about Jason several times, and then Paul literally wrestled the hatchet out of his hands."

Siobhán had been right. Theodore was holding on to stories. And what a story it was. Moira didn't mention this incident. She downplayed any mention of her father having a mental decline. And when Siobhán pointed out the missing space on the wall, Moira didn't chime in to tell her what had hung there. It was Leah who mentioned the hatchet. If Theodore was telling the truth, and days before the murder Enda was threatening them with a hatchet, why didn't Moira mention it? Was she trying to cover for an ailing father? Was she trying to have him declared unfit? That seemed worth following up on. She'd pass it along to Garda Cooley the next time she saw him. She hoped he wouldn't broadcast over the radio every tip she gave him.

They exited the vehicle and made their way to the edge of the ocean where frothy waves lapped a rocky beach and the wind blew hard. Despite the chill, it was gorgeous. She could see herself retiring here. Walking along the ocean every day hand in hand with Dara. She found several shells and pieces of driftwood, and finally some sea glass. She was looking forward to this

177

Christmas tree adorned by nature.

"If you hear anything about the will, would you let me know?" Theodore asked as he stood staring out at the waves.

"Me?"

He laughed. "Don't play dumb. As a guard, you have way more access than I do, even if the boys are keeping you at arm's length."

"Why do you care about his will?" *Did he have a personal interest?* He didn't think Enda was going to leave him anything, did he?

Ted skipped a pebble across the surface of the water. "I'm hoping Catherine is in it."

"Why would Catherine would be in it?"

"She's been a neighbor and friend for over thirty years. She's due."

She's due. Good neighbors and friends didn't act out of greed. They simply did what was required of them. The payback should be having a good friend and neighbor in return. Was this just Theodore hoping to cash in, or was Catherine also itching to receive? Siobhán got the feeling this was all Theodore Baskins. Maybe the rumors about him were true. He was only after money. She very much doubted that Catherine Healy would be in Enda's will. And if she was, Siobhán hoped the woman would boot

Theodore Baskins out the door before collecting a single euro from Enda's estate.

They were the last to return to Moira's house. Everyone brought their treasures over to the guest house and piled their findings into a large wooden bucket by the door. There were shells, and driftwood, and pine cones, and sea glass, the gold button, and a coin or two. Siobhán held up the gold button, marveling at its size and shine.

Ciarán plucked a silver coin out and held it up next to the button. "Silver and gold!" he said.

"Silver and gold," Siobhán repeated, clinking her button with his silver coin.

"Should we start decorating?"

"We waited long enough, we most certainly should decorate now," Gráinne said.

"We'll also need to give these a good washing," Siobhán said, gesturing to the bucket. "Any volunteers?" Ann and Ciarán eagerly volunteered. Siobhán cheered. "The job is yours."

"Can I see that button?" Siobhán had forgotten she was still holding it when Ruth edged forward and snatched it out of her hand. "That's strange."

"What?"

"I think it's off a cloak donated to the costume department."

"Cloak? Costume department?" The image of the figure draped in a black cloak entering the mill rose in Siobhán's mind.

"The village has a local theatre," Ruth said. "They planned on dressing certain characters for the concert. The three wise men, elves, Santa."

Elves . . .

"I should take this button to the costume department and see," Ruth said. Then she gasped.

"For heaven's sake, Ruth," Catherine said. "Why are you being so dramatic?"

"I just remembered, the costumes had been moved to the mill. Do you know if we're allowed in yet?"

Siobhán was grateful that Ruth didn't mention the Grim Reaper costume, although it wouldn't be long before someone else made the connection. "May I see?" Siobhán took the button from Ruth before she knew what was happening. If the button was from the cloak of the person sneaking into the mill, it was evidence. Where had she found it again? *By the bridge.* Where the shopkeeper had seen someone hitchhiking at around half one in the morning. With the gold button tucked safely in her coat pocket, Siobhán headed for the road to call to Garda Cooley.

CHAPTER 9

Garda Cooley stood in front of everyone gathered at the guest house, still examining the gold button resting in his plastic evidence bag. He turned to Siobhán. "Ruth, we will arrange to meet at the mill to see if the cloak in question is missing."

"Of course, Garda," Ruth said.

"Was there more than one cloak?" he continued.

"No," Ruth said, her voice timid. "There was only one. Catherine Healy donated it." All heads turned to Catherine.

"It was Theodore's costume," she said. "From last year's All Hallows' Eve extravaganza."

"That's right," Theodore exclaimed. "That was a brilliant party." His grin faded when he noticed everyone staring at him.

"Is that the one where you slept in the bathtub?" Paul said.

"I did," Theodore said, laughing and slapping his leg. "Woke up cuddling a bottle of shampoo." He looked around, hoping for laughs, but found none.

"Why didn't you remember this when I mentioned the Grim Reaper outfit?" Moira asked.

"It didn't cross my mind," Theodore said.

"How convenient," Moira quipped.

"Theodore was home with me that evening," Catherine said. "And it's already been established we donated the cloak to the theatre. You can't point fingers at us just because I once made the costume."

"Let's all calm down," Garda Cooley said. "Now that everyone knows this is officially a murder probe, we'll be calling everyone into the station for questioning," he announced. "No one is to leave town until we've interviewed them."

"No one would dare leave town," Leah said. "We're still having our Christmas Eve concert." No one spoke up to dispute this fact, but uneasy looks were exchanged amongst some of the musicians. No doubt there were those who wished they could slip away in the night.

"You're calling everyone into the station?" Theodore said. "Why don't you save yourself some time and just interview us here and now?"

"Because we're going to do this by the book and record every session," Cooley said. "First thing tomorrow you'll all be given schedules to come in for your interrogation."

"We arrived the morning of the murder," Siobhán said.

"I still want to hear your accounts of everything that happened the morning you found Enda. You never know what could crack open." Siobhán couldn't argue with that.

"We arrived that morning as well," Elise piped up. Siobhán shot James a look. She was now lying to a guard. What was she trying to hide? James cleared his throat.

"When exactly did you arrive?" Cooley asked, poised to jot it down.

"I believe it was an hour after Siobhán," Elise said.

Siobhán seared her gaze into her brother until he started to fidget. "That was when we arrived at the mill," James said. He put his arm around Elise. She stiffened. "But we were in town, petal." He looked Cooley in the eye. "We arrived the afternoon before and stayed at the inn."

Elise's face blazed red. Siobhán could practically see flames in her eyes. Did Elise really expect James to lie for her? In front of his garda sister? She'd been good about keeping her gob shut up until now and minding her own business, but Elise had just crossed a line and it would not stand. Siobhán was going to have to have a talk with her.

"You'll be coming in for questioning, then," Cooley said. He gave Elise a look that conveyed he knew what she had just tried to pull. And instead of getting the heat off of them, Siobhán knew that Elise had just turned it up full blast. All Siobhán could do now was to keep it from becoming an inferno.

With the weight of Garda Cooley's announcement on their shoulders, everyone wanted to retire to their own living spaces. Elise and James remained in the pasture, no doubt arguing. Siobhán was looking forward to decorating their tree. Eoin played Christmas music through his mobile phone, reminding Siobhán of the song she heard when she first entered the old mill. Maybe she would take some time to listen to classical music to see if she would hear it again. Was it a longshot, expecting her to recognize a ring tone from sampling random classical songs? Maybe. But she was confident she'd know it if she heard it again. Maybe Garda

Cooley should call all the musician's mobile phones to hear the ringtones. Should she call him to suggest it, or would he resent the intrusion? Maybe she'd mentioned it when he brought her in for her interview.

"Wait," Gráinne said just as Ciarán was about to hang an orange leaf on the tree. "Don't lights go on first?"

"Right," Siobhán said.

"Got them." Eoin held up the box of white lights. Together they unraveled them and wound them around the tree. They turned them on and stood back to look. The soft shine complemented the rustic cottage perfectly.

"Gorgeous," Siobhán said.

"It is pretty," Ann said. "Although I prefer the multicolored lights at home."

"It's like sparkly snowflakes on the tree," Ciarán exclaimed.

"You're right, pet," Siobhán said, glancing out the small window. "It will look even prettier when we get actual snow."

"Did Mam and Da have lights with color or white lights?" Ciarán asked. Stress was planted on his face. He remembered their parents less and less every year. Siobhán put her arm around him, and was grateful he didn't knock it off.

"Multicolored lights most years. Mam

185

preferred white ones, but Da wanted the splash of color, so she kept that a secret."

"A secret?" Ann asked, edging forward.

"She wanted Da to be happy. She knew these were his favorites."

"I didn't know that," Gráinne said. "I remember we had colorful lights, but I didn't know Mam wanted white ones."

"She used to hang white ones in the kitchen."

"That's right!" Eoin said. For a few moments the three eldest were lost in time, entering their mam's kitchen in the mornings, smelling the brown bread baking, seeing the white lights twinkling while their father built a fire in the main room.

"It's not fair," Ciarán said. "I remember next to nothing." He pointed at Siobhán. "And you remember everything."

Siobhán swallowed the lump in her throat. "You're right, luv. It's not fair. But every story I tell about them becomes your story too. Because you were there. All of us were. And Mam and Da are right here." She laid her hand over her heart. "And we had wonderful Christmases."

And they did. Because there was so much love. And warmth. And laughter. There were lean times too. Stressful times. Times when they couldn't afford to make much of a fuss.

Times when Siobhán would notice her parents' bent heads and hushed voices going over the bills at night. There was the time her mam wasn't invited to a Christmas gathering of women in her knitting circle. She cried as her father put his arms around her, making fun of the women and imitating them one by one until her mother laughed. Siobhán had eavesdropped from the stairwell until James gently tugged her away. He never tattled on her either. They had not been a perfect family — such a thing did not exist — but there was laughter and love. So much love.

"Don't you dare start the waterworks," James said. They all turned. Siobhán had no idea he was in the room. She was relieved to see Elise with him. Maybe they were going to be alright. A stern chat with her was coming, but now was not the time.

"Let's get the ornaments on this tree," Siobhán said.

Elise held up a canister. "I have hot cocoa."

A cheer sounded. Elise grinned. For the next hour they didn't argue, or cry, or stress. They played music, and drank hot cocoa, and hung ornaments. They just did Christmas.

■ ■ ■ ■

Siobhán was outside trying to get ahold of Macdara when she saw Theodore in the field. Macdara wasn't answering his phone. She hoped that he and his mam were enjoying their time together. She shoved her phone in her pocket and returned her gaze to next door. Theodore was heading for his lorry. Siobhán acted on impulse and hurried over.

"Wondered if we could talk?" She wanted to ask him a bit more about the button. Why hadn't he recognized it when they found it near the bridge?

He shook his head. "I've just been called into the fishery. They're short a man."

"When you get back then." Siobhán started to head off.

"Why don't you come with me?"

She stopped. "Me?"

"You like poking your nose into things. The fishery is something to see."

He was messing with her. She didn't want him to have the upper hand. "Why not." She hopped into the lorry. "Just texting everyone and letting them know where I am," she said.

"In case I murder you?" He peeled out of

the drive with a screech, rocks and dust kicking up behind him.

"Exactly. Now they'll know to look for me at the fishery." She grinned.

"Yes, it was my costume," he said. "But that should leave me in the clear."

"How do you figure?"

"Why would I be so stupid as to wear my own costume?"

"Because you didn't expect to get caught."

"If that's the case, why would I wear a costume at all?"

"Maybe you wanted to scare Enda. Maybe you knew about the cameras."

Theodore shook his head again. "I could never think of something that complicated." Siobhán was tempted to believe him. "You have to help me. Everyone in this village hates me. I'm innocent."

"Did you know that Catherine donated the costume to the local theatre?"

"Didn't know, nor would I have cared. I never wear a costume more than once. I pride myself on originality."

"It didn't bother you that she gave it away?"

"Why would it?"

He sounded sincere. But she wasn't done yet. "When you found that button, why didn't you recognize it?"

"You must be pulling my leg. I don't notice things like buttons." She didn't believe him. This wasn't just any button. It was large, and gold, and ornate. You couldn't *not* notice this button. He was lying. If her job was to catch and punish liars, there wouldn't be many humans left walking around. But lies meant she was getting close to a secret. If he wasn't the killer, what was his secret? "Once Catherine tells the guards what she saw that night, I should be in the clear."

Siobhán was paying attention now. "What did she see?" He chewed on his lip and tapped his fingers on the steering wheel. "If you want my help — and I must agree that the guards are looking mostly at you — I need to know."

Theodore's fingers stopped tapping. "She saw Orla, Elise, and Paul huddling in their field. It was after midnight."

The emergency family meeting. Moira must not have been involved, otherwise why huddle out in the cold?

"In and of itself that's not a crime."

"They must have seen Enda come out of the house."

"The timing is close, but it's possible they missed him."

"Then why didn't they mention this to

Garda Cooley?"

Now, that was an excellent question. "Maybe they prefer to do it in private." Even Siobhán didn't believe her own answer.

"Elise tried to say she wasn't even in town."

"We straightened that out."

"Looks suspicious to me. Yet all fingers will continue to point at me, mark my words."

The fishery was housed in a large wooden building by the ocean. The waves were choppy, slashing against the rocks in angry bursts. Siobhán hopped out of the lorry, wondering how she was going to get home. She texted James.

At the fishery with Baskins. Can you pick me up?

"Calling the cavalry?" Theodore said.

"Just figuring out my ride home."

"I'll give you the tour."

It was a large open space with ten men in overalls and plastic aprons rushing about, crates of fish in their hands. "You're late," an older man barked. "If we don't get these processed we'll lose a week's worth."

"On it." Baskins turned to her. "If you really want to help, I'll let you pitch in." He held a pair of rubber gloves in front of her.

191

"Pitch in?"

"We're short several men."

"I'm sure your boss wouldn't let a newbie touch a thing around here."

"It's not like you can kill anything," Theodore said. "The fish are already dead,"

Siobhán should have known there was something fishy about his offer to bring her here. "I'd be willing, of course, but I'm sure your boss wouldn't like it."

"Boss," Theodore yelled out. "Mind if my friend helps?"

"The more the merrier," he called back.

"Do I get paid?" she yelled.

"We'll pay you in fish, how's dat?" the boss called back.

A nice chowder on Christmas Eve didn't sound bad. "Half fish, half cash?"

"Let's see how good a job you do."

Theodore Baskins couldn't take the grin off his face. That settled it. He was getting the plastic snowman as his Secret Santa gift.

Siobhán took the gloves and the apron, wondering how many slimy hands in days of yore had worn them. She slid them on, shuddering at the clammy feel on her skin. What on earth did she think she was doing? *Investigating.* Her stubborn personality had gotten her into this. Despite trying to convince herself that this was not her case, she couldn't stay out of it. And unless she proved that Theodore wasn't the killer, she had a feeling Cooley wasn't going to give anyone else a serious look. But cleaning fish? She'd taken it too far. Theodore pointed to stacks of crates in the corner. "Carry those to the assembly line."

Was that it? Relief washed over her, and she nearly laughed. She could do that. "On it." She turned to leave. "Then empty the crates of fish into the washing bin . . ."

The rest of the words evaporated when her eyes landed on the sharp knife in his hands. The glint remained in his eye, and with the light coming in from behind, for a second he looked truly menacing. Maybe this village was right to suspect him. Maybe it was this simple. Most unliked lad in in town was the killer. Case closed. "I can't thank you enough," he said. "You've renewed my Christmas spirit."

She sighed, took the knife, and headed to the crates. Minutes later, she was numb. Slime. More slime. Slippery skin. Fish odor. Things she didn't want to talk about or ever remember again. After an hour in, she found an unexpected rhythm. The hum of the conveyor belt, the slice of the knife through fish skin. Mostly it made her job feel like a parade. She was shocked when she reached the last crate, and nearly cried with joy.

"Someone is here to see you."

She turned to see a man entering the mill, and it took three seconds to recognize the tall build, the messy hair, the sky-blue eyes, and lopsided grin.

"Dara?" She ran up to him. She didn't realize she was holding the knife until she saw his gaze fall to it. Then it raked over her. Great. She smelled like dead fish and was holding a deadly weapon. *Lovely.*

He shook his head. "I knew it," he said. "I knew I'd find ya up to your gills in this thing."

CHAPTER 10

Siobhán was still in shock over seeing Macdara when the second jolt hit. Dara stepped
to the side to reveal his mam. Nancy Flannery scrunched her nose and turned her
face away from Siobhán.

"I'm so sorry," Siobhán said. "I had no
idea you were coming."

"I see your job as a garda must not be paying enough," Nancy said. Macdara roared
with laughter. Siobhán did not.

"How did you know I was here?"

"James gave me the heads-up," Macdara
said. "He said you asked for a ride." He
bowed. "Joe Maxi at your service."

"But why are you here? I thought you
weren't coming until New Year's Eve?" She
was thrilled to see him, but she didn't want
Nancy Flannery to think that she had tried
to pull the Golden Boy away from her at
Christmas.

"We decided we didn't want to spend

Christmas away from you." By we, he meant him, but Nancy Flannery was polite enough not to contradict him. "And turns out Mam is a big fan of classical music."

"A concert on Christmas Eve in honor of Enda Elliot sounds lovely," she admitted. Her hand moved to her nose, where it remained, as if she were afraid to breathe in.

"Wonderful," Siobhán said. "Where are you staying?"

Macdara shook his head. "We tried the village inn. They're fully booked."

This time Siobhán roared with laughter. Dara cocked his head and looked a question. "You're literally saying — it's Christmas time and there's no room at the inn," Siobhán said.

"Good one," Dara said. Nancy Flannery did not seem amused. Siobhán was saved by her mobile phone buzzing in her pocket. It was a message from James:
Emergency Family Meeting
Now what?

"What is it?" Dara said. He knew just by the look on her face. At least she wasn't going to have to face it alone.

"If I weren't covered in fish slime I would hug you so hard right now."

"Let's just imagine it," Macdara said,

holding his hand out like a barrier.

"One more thing. Are you going to let me ride in your car?"

Siobhán had never been so happy to shower and change clothes, even if the water was freezing. She was now back in the small main room of their guest house. Nancy Flannery was in Moira's house, hopefully enjoying a cup of tea. Siobhán and Macdara stood in front of the sofa where Elise, Orla, and Paul sat like convicted criminals. James paced outside. They had learned they were going to be the first three to be called into the guards for questioning in the morning, and apparently they were freaking out.

"Elise." Siobhán waited until Elise pinned her big brown eyes on hers. "Do you want to tell us why you snuck out of the inn in the middle of the night on Friday to meet your siblings?" *The same night your grandfather was murdered?*

Elise shrugged. "I didn't sneak. James was asleep. I walked out the door like a normal person."

Siobhán gritted her teeth. "And why did you do that?"

"We were just getting together for a wee drink," Paul said.

"You were spotted in the back pasture."

"By whom?" Elise demanded.

If Siobhán admitted she'd heard it from Theodore, they would probably dismiss it as a lie. "That doesn't matter. The person intends to tell the guards."

Elise hung her head. "This is why I said I wasn't in town. See what happens?"

"It's precisely because you tried to cover it up that you're being called in first," Siobhán said. "The cover-up is often worse than the crime."

"What crime?" Elise cried.

"Lying to a guard," Siobhán said. "You're lucky he's not charging you for interfering with an investigation."

"I don't feel lucky at all," Elise said.

"I make Irish cream," Paul said to Macdara. "It's the best in West Cork."

"Is it now?" Macdara said.

"We won an award. Happy cows. Dat's the secret."

"Enough about your Irish cream," Elise said. "Are you joking me right now?"

Paul crossed his arms. "I'm a businessman. I will not apologize for doing what I need to do."

"What you need to do right now is help us figure out who killed our grandfather," Elise said.

"It's not a crime to want to see your

siblings," Orla said.

"If one of you doesn't start talking, I can't help you." Siobhán kept her voice firm. The village guards were going to eat them alive if they didn't straighten up.

"We were having a family meeting," Elise said. "It's really none of your business."

Siobhán took deep breaths while counting elves jumping over reindeer. "I'm on your side. James said you wanted guidance for tomorrow's interrogation."

"Interrogation?" Orla said, leaning forward. Her blond hair hung over her left eye. "I don't like that word. Why does everyone keep using that word?"

"Because it's a murder inquiry," Siobhán said gently. They understood that, right? "Listen." Siobhán knelt. Her height could intimate people. Especially tiny people like Elise. "I'm not accusing any of you of pushing your grandfather off that balcony. But that doesn't mean the guards won't. You're family. You probably all stand to inherit. This is very serious. But I repeat, I cannot help you unless I know why you were all meeting outside, in the cold, at midnight." *And why you tried to cover it up.*

The siblings exchanged glances. "We were worried about our grandfather," Paul said. "Mam said he was acting strangely."

199

"Go on," Siobhán prompted.

"The night before, Mam saw Grandfather wandering around the field with a hatchet," Orla said. "Paul had to wrestle it out of his hands."

"Orla!" Elise cried out.

"Well, he did!"

"He was sleepwalking," Paul said. "No harm was done."

"Was he saying anything?" Siobhán asked. She wanted to see if he would support Theodore's claim that he was raging about Jason.

"He seemed to be upset with Jason. I think they'd been arguing," Paul admitted.

"Or maybe Grandfather didn't want Jason in the house any longer," Orla said. "Because Jason shared Mam's concerns that Grandfather needed to see a doctor."

Once again, heads swiveled. "Someone told me Jason and Enda had argued before Jason left to pick up his mother," Siobhán said.

"Jason insisted that the minute he returned with Faye he was taking Grandfather to the hospital," Elise said. "You can imagine this made Grandfather mental. Especially with the concert coming up." She swallowed. "Grandfather said he was going to cut Jason out of the will."

"Now you've done it," Orla cried. All heads turned to her. "We weren't going to start accusing each other. We promised."

"The truth will come out," Siobhán said. "I understand that you mean well. But the truth will come out."

"Why wasn't Jason at this emergency family meeting?" Macdara asked.

"He had already left to pick up his mam," Orla said.

"Were you afraid Enda was going to cut all of you out of his will?" Siobhán asked because Moira also wanted Enda to be seen by a doctor. So why single out Jason?

"He kept saying Jason was just like his mother," Paul said. "I don't think they're anything alike."

"What does that have to do with the price of tea in China?" Elise asked.

"Nothing," Paul said. "But we're not talking about the price of tea in China."

This was getting unruly. Siobhán wished she had a sheepdog to keep them corralled. "Why that night?" she pressed. "Why did you have to meet right then?"

"It's my fault," Elise said. "I had just arrived when Paul told me about Grandfather's alarming behaviors as of late. Since he'd been seen wandering around only at night, we were waiting to see . . ."

"If he was going to do it again," Siobhán finished.

"Yes," Elise said. "We were waiting to see if he was going to do it again."

Siobhán stood up and stretched. It was rather painful to be tall and kneel for too long.

"Meeting at that hour is not as secretive and odd as it sounds," Paul said. "We were always night owls, the three of us. Especially when we're all back here. We'd escape to the field to have a chat, or a nip of whiskey, or a smoke."

"Then why all the lying?"

"Mam didn't want people to know that he wasn't right in the head," Orla confessed. "Especially before the concert."

"And you did see your grandfather that night?" Siobhán asked. "Did he come out of his house with a hatchet?"

"No," Paul said. "We waited until half twelve. When he didn't appear, we gave Elise a ride back to the inn."

Siobhán turned to Paul. "But I thought you wrestled the hatchet out of his hands?" she said.

"Yes. But that was Wednesday, right after Jason left. Not Friday." He paused. "Does the iPad show what time Grandfather left his house that evening?"

The video showed the figure entering the mill at half twelve. Siobhán guessed he left the house shortly after. If the Elliot grandchildren were telling the truth, then they'd just missed him. "I can't give you an exact time," Siobhán said. There were already too many facts about the case floating around.

"We probably just missed him then," Orla said. "But he couldn't have had the hatchet with him."

Siobhán straightened up. "And why is that?"

Orla swallowed. "Because we buried it," she said.

CHAPTER 11

Siobhán and Macdara stood outside the guest house, shielding themselves from the wind by huddling under the overhang of the door. "You realize how it's going to sound," Macdara said, "when we tell the guards that the Elliot children buried the hatchet."

"I do," Siobhán said. Orla had told them they buried it Wednesday night. This was after Jason had left. Enda Elliot had been worked up and that night took to wandering with a hatchet. No wonder everyone in that family was on edge. He had obviously needed serious psychiatric help and yet because of his stature and demeanor, he hadn't been willing to accept it.

Macdara shook his head. "You can't make this stuff up."

"I need to see that video again. Enda had something in his hand. If it wasn't the hatchet, what was it?"

"Do you think it makes a difference?"

"One of our working theories was that when Enda arrived into the mill with the hatchet, whomever was in there got the fright of his or her life and that maybe Enda's death was a result of self-defense."

"But if he wasn't carrying a weapon, then it's something more sinister."

"Exactly." Siobhán thought on it. "Maybe it was a torch. After all, it was dark."

"Doesn't the mill have lights?"

"Yes. But he walked there in the dark, and when the mill was opened that Saturday morning the lights were off."

"He walked because he discovered his tire was flat."

"Your point?"

"Did he have time to go back into his house and get a torch?"

"No. But maybe he had one in his lorry."

"Let's say he did turn the lights on in the mill — you're saying the killer may have turned the lights off."

"Yes."

"You're saying a killer is conscientious about the electric bills?"

"No. But perhaps they wanted to buy time before anyone discovered Enda's body. As it was, everyone was expected the next morning."

"Buy time for what? Do you think our killer left town?"

"If the killer did, this case is going to be very hard to solve," Siobhán said. "But if the killer didn't leave town, then they either turned off the lights out of habit or were looking forward to a dramatic reveal."

Macdara slid next to Siobhán and put his arm around her. "I'm glad this isn't our case," he said softly. "So we can celebrate Christmas in peace."

"You're a very wise man, Dara. Too bad there aren't three of ya."

"Let's figure out where Mam and I are going to stay before they relegate us to a barn."

"Don't worry," Siobhán said. "If they do, I'll bring gold. You're on your own with the frankincense and myrrh."

Macdara cocked his head and grinned. "That's only because you don't have the faintest idea what those are."

"I don't," Siobhán agreed. "I really don't."

"My," Moira Elliot said, wringing her hands near her sink. The kitchen looked larger tidied up and absent all the cooks. "I'll get my list of houses, but don't get your hopes up too high. Everyone is in town for Enda's concert. *Was* in town for Enda's concert."

"We understand," Macdara said. "Whatever you can do for us would be much appreciated." Moira nodded and disappeared into another room. "Do you think she knows about her children burying the hatchet?" Macdara asked.

Siobhán rolled her eyes. "You're going to use every opportunity you can to say that, aren't you?"

"I am," Dara said. "I really am."

Moira returned with a folder. She opened it to reveal sheets with pictures of homes on them and data below. Siobhán glanced and could see that the number of bedrooms and rental amounts were among the data. "You must have every house in West Cork listed in there," Siobhán said.

Moira let out a low laugh. "I probably do. If anyone went away for even a weekend and wanted some extra income, I listed it for them."

"How did you get into that?" Macdara asked.

"Catherine Healy is the reason I started it," Moira said. "Twenty-plus years ago. She decided to go on a trip, lucky her. She was going to be gone for nearly a year and was worried about the upkeep of her place. Worried about teenagers in the village up to no good, breaking in and what have you. I told her I'd find someone to rent it. After that, I was known as the woman who could get it rented." She paused on a sheet and put her finger up to her lips. "Speaking of Catherine . . ."

"Yes?"

"I just realized that she has a spare room. And a sofa."

Macdara rubbed his hands together. "Do you think she'd rent it to us?"

"I'm sure she would," Moira said. "But we all know Theodore is the one who pushed my father from the gallery. Do you really want your mam to stay in the same house with him?"

"Theodore Baskins, is it?" Macdara said.

"That's the one," Moira said. "Dreadful, dreadful, man."

"There's no proof that it was Theodore," Siobhán said. "At this moment, everyone is equally a suspect." *Including you.* Unfortunately, now was not the time to grill her about the rumor that she actively worried about her father's declining mental health. It was generally bad form to interrogate a person while she was in the middle of doing you a huge favor.

After they left the fishery, Siobhán had filled Macdara in on the story, including the fact that the entire village was against Theo-

208

dore. She found him eclectic and peculiar but somewhat likable. She kept that to herself — no use stirring up trouble.

"I can protect my mam," Macdara said. "Although I'd appreciate it if you not tell her we're going to be staying with a possible killer. She's picky enough about the sheets."

"Let me give her a bell," Moira said, picking up her phone. Moments later, she clicked off. "That's settled. Catherine said you're more than welcome."

"Grand," Macdara said. "Thank you."

"I'm sure Catherine will be thrilled someone is willing to stay there," Moira said.

They fetched Nancy, who was in the living room spending time with the rest of Siobhán's brood, and headed next door. Siobhán was keen to have a look around Catherine and Theodore's home. One could tell a lot about a person from the way they lived. Their back door led into a mudroom, then the kitchen, and next a living room. Catherine Healy's home was messy and loud. Chaotic. Large furniture shoved in small spaces. Piles of books against the wall. Magazines falling off the coffee table. It wasn't a hoarder's home, but given a little time it could get there. Theodore was on the sofa with his feet propped up on the coffee table, a bottle of beer in his hand and rugby on the telly. It cast a spell on Macdara for a moment, and before Siobhán knew what was happening, he was on the sofa next to Theodore with another bottle and Siobhán was stuck with his mam and Catherine Healy, getting the tour of the rest of the house. They climbed the stairs to the second floor.

"Here we are," Catherine said, stopping at a large room. "This will be your room."

Nancy placed her hand over her heart. "This looks like the master bedroom."

"Don't you worry," Catherine said. "Theodore and I like to snuggle in the guest bed at times." Siobhán cringed as she knew Nancy Flannery was probably not comfortable with the comment. "I hope your son won't mind the sofa." They headed back to the living room, where the lads were still glued to the telly.

"Detective Sergeant Flannery will be grand," Siobhán said loud enough that Theodore heard her. He gave Macdara the side-eye.

"Detective Sergeant?" Theodore said, surprise ringing from his voice. "Are you here about Enda?"

"Off duty," he said. "Unless of course anyone needs me."

Catherine's phone rang from inside her pocket to the tune of "Jingle Bells." She glanced at the screen. "I have to go out," Catherine said. "Make yourselves at home. Will we see you in town this evening?"

"This evening?" Siobhán asked.

"Although the lighting of the tree happened last week, there will be carolers, and the town decorations, and of course Santy will be there for the kids. Folks are pitching in to make the best of it."

"We'll be there," Siobhán said. "With bells on."

It couldn't have been better timing, a celebration to get everyone out of their houses and away from the mill, and with a little luck, in the mood for Christmas. The village was as festive as it could be. Multicolored lights were strung down the middle of the street, a fat Santy hustled through the crowds ho-ho-ho-ing and posing for pictures with tiny tots, and the orchestra played Christmas tunes as a group of carolers in old-fashioned dress sang along. The giant tree in the town square shone bright. The O'Sullivans had come early to do a bit of shopping, and besides bits and pieces for her siblings, there was now a plastic Santa in the boot of Siobhán's car destined for

211

Theodore Baskins.

"Multicolored lights," Ann said, popping up by her side and slipping her hand into Siobhán's as they took in the tree. "Da would love it."

"Mam would too." Siobhán loved it as well, but even more so she loved the grins on the faces of her siblings. When Ann dropped her hand, Macdara took it and gave it a squeeze. He was part of their family now. The carolers launched into "O Christmas Tree," and soon the crowd joined in. Siobhán was not ashamed to admit that the entire scene turned her into a holiday-loving puddle of goo. They needed this more than ever.

"Ready for the pub?" Elise said as the carolers finished up. And of course everyone was more than ready for the pub.

It was the coziest of pubs with a lively crowd and a crackling peat fire. Trad musicians played from the corner, and Paul Elliot joined them with his guitar. He sang "Dirty Old Town," "Galway Girl," "The Girl With the Black Velvet Band," "The Irish Rover," and more of Siobhán's favorites. Once he had the crowd warmed up, he went on to a few original songs filled with descriptions of living in West Cork and his love for Ireland,

and he finished with a song about happy cows. His voice was deep and melodic, and the passion shone from his eyes when he was onstage. It gave Siobhán a twinge of sadness that such a talented musician had not been appreciated by his grandfather. *The ties that bind.* What weight family member's expectations could place on one's shoulder. Disappointment was so easy for one family member to toss out but so difficult for the recipient to take. Siobhán had once run home in tears from school when her marks were low. She stood in front of her mam and da, wondering if they would punish her.

"Don't cry, pet," her mam said. "Did you do your best?"

Siobhán nodded, a big goose egg in her throat. She had done her best. But her best hadn't been good enough. Now what?

"Your best is all we ever ask of you," her father said. "That's all a person can be expected to do."

"Best doesn't mean perfect," her mother added as tears fell down Siobhán's face. "And your best will change from day to day like the weather. Dry your eyes and set the table for supper." She had been very lucky to have such parents. She knew that now. But some folks thrived in spite of their parents and grandparents, and when it came to music, Paul Elliot was one of those folks. Siobhán was lost in thought when she felt a nudge. She turned to see that Ruth Halliday had squeezed in beside Siobhán. "Hello."

"Hello."

"You seem to like this music."

"I do. Don't you?"

Ruth gave her a tight smile. "It's lovely."

Siobhán had a feeling Ruth would rather listen to the strum of a harp. "Do you listen to this music at home?" Tension was stamped across Ruth's face. "I must confess I don't know what kind of music most people like. Or how they even play it these days. I just play instruments. But popular songs . . . I'm not quite in the loop. Something to do with streams, is that right?"

"Streaming," Siobhán said. "Yes, we do a bit of that." Gráinne, who was better versed in those things, often controlled the music at home. They also held on to an old record player of their parents, but they were using it less and less. As Ruth awkwardly chatted up Siobhán, it dawned on her that Ruth was her Secret Santa and she was trying to suss out what to buy her.

"But I can still play CDs, and it looks like Paul is selling his music CD for ten euro."

"Maybe you shouldn't buy it just yet," Ruth said, looking more nervous than ever.

"True," Siobhán said. "You never know what Santa will bring."

"Quite right." Ruth's face finally relaxed. What was the point of all this Secret Santa business if all it did was stress everyone out?

"Speaking of music," Siobhán said, "are you quite sure you don't know anything about the harp that was stored at the mill?" She left out the obvious — where the harp ended up. For all Ruth knew, Siobhán had drawn *her* name, so this was the perfect opportunity to grill her without it seeming as if she was accusing Ruth of murder.

"Such as?" Ruth asked.

"I was wondering if you knew anything about it. It looked quite dear to me."

Ruth shifted away from Siobhán. "I did take a look when I had to accompany Garda Cooley to look for the cloak."

Siobhán had almost forgotten about that. "Did you find the cloak?"

"I suppose since you're a guard it's alright if I speak with you." Siobhán nodded. Ruth shook her head. Technically that wasn't speaking with her, but the meaning was conveyed nevertheless. The person who entered the mill had at some point taken the cloak *from* the mill.

"Remind me again why the cloak was at the mill?"

"Everyone in the village seemed to use the building for storage purposes. Our local theatre rented it out last summer for a production, and the costume rack remains there."

"Who owns the building?"

"Rick Jasper. He was the old man selling Christmas trees out back."

Yikes. Siobhán would definitely never get any information out of him. Even after buying another tree and paying dearly for it. "About the harp . . ." Siobhán reminded her.

Ruth nodded. "You're right. It's something special. Although it may be in need of tuning. Even before . . ." She let the sentence hang, finishing wasn't necessary.

"What is special about it?"

Ruth lifted her chin. "I would need to have another look." Siobhán didn't believe her. She was obviously in love with harps. Obsessed, even. Siobhán had a feeling that Ruth knew the exact make, model, and worth of the one that ended up on poor Enda. But was it valuable enough that she would murder someone to acquire it? And what would Enda want with a harp anyway? "It's wonderful to see Faye looking so happy," Ruth said suddenly.

The comment did the trick, distracted Siobhán from her questioning. She glanced over at Faye, who was sitting with Jason. Her face was a portrait of pure delight.

"She looks so happy to be with her son," Siobhán agreed.

"Indeed. It's funny how time changes one's opinion."

"What do you mean?" Given that Ruth was only in her thirties, Siobhán assumed Ruth wasn't speaking about herself.

"I shouldn't gossip."

Please. Gossip. That's all I want for Christmas. "I think it's just chatting."

"I heard that Faye and Enda used a surrogate to carry their baby. It was quite a scandal back then." Ruth smoothed her skirt and crossed her legs. "I was only ten years of age, but I can remember the women gossiping after mass."

"I can imagine," Siobhán said. It shouldn't have been, but given this small village she wasn't surprised. Enda would have been one of the few who even had the money to pay for that option. Ruth's eyes flicked over Jason.

"He's handsome, isn't he?"

"He is." Was that what was happening here? Did Ruth have a crush on Jason Elliot? Just then, Gráinne appeared at Jason and Faye's table. She plopped down next to Jason and the flirting began. Ruth's face flushed, and she hurried up to the bar for another drink. She was a single woman in this remote village. Siobhán wondered why she didn't move to a bigger city where she might have a better chance of meeting someone. Some people were wanderers, while others never wanted to leave home. Siobhán was a little bit of both. She finished her drink, then headed to the ladies' room. After she was finished, she was on her way back to the bar when she saw an open hall door revealing a storeroom. Inside a pair of lads were placing liquor bottles on shelves. "It's lucky for him the old man died when he did," one said. "Imagine Mr. Elliot finding out Paul had gone against his wishes."

"Award-winning me arse," the other replied. "We'll be lucky if we go through one bottle next year." They stopped when they saw her standing there.

"Can we help you?" they asked in stereo. It never hurt to be a pretty girl, and Siobhán ambushed them with a smile. *Imagine Mr. Elliot finding out Paul had gone against his wishes.* What wishes?

"I love Irish cream," she said. "But you're saying it *isn't* the best in town?"

"It's abominable," one said in a loud whisper. "You'd do better with known brands."

"It must have cost a lot to produce."

"Not hard to do if you're rich," the other said. "Doesn't mean it was smart."

Indeed. "Did I hear you say something about Enda Elliot not being pleased with his grandson and the business?"

"Not pleased," the one closest to the door said as he made a face. "That's putting it mildly."

The other nudged his pal, indicating he should shut his gob. "A gorgeous girl like you shouldn't ask too many questions about a dead man," he said.

Siobhán stepped farther into the room. "Oh? Why is that?"

The lad put his hand over his heart. "I couldn't live with meself if we put nightmares in that pretty head of yours."

"Not to mention the rest of you," the other said, letting his eyes finish the statement by trailing all over her.

"It actually gives me a bit of a thrill," she said, touching her index finger to her lip. "Is that bad?"

"You'll be on Santa's naughty list," the first one said. "Nothing wrong with dat."

"My big ears couldn't help but overhear.

You said Enda would be furious about something?"

"Heard him say it myself, he wasn't going to loan his grandson the money to keep this business going. Makes you wonder how he got it."

The other joined in. "We all know the old man was losing it. He probably got him to sign a check in a weak moment. Because the Enda Elliot of old would have gone mental if his grandson wasted his money on this happy cow rubbish."

"I hope you lads don't mind if I get your names and digits," Siobhán said pulling out a pad of paper.

"Both of us?" the first one asked. "I promise if you pick me you'll never need another."

"Don't listen to him," the other said. "I'm your man."

"I'm afraid I'm much more methodical in my decision-making, fellas. I'm going to take down both your names and numbers."

She didn't need to tell them twice. "Thank you." She turned to go.

"We didn't catch your name," one said.

"Are you sure your pretty heads won't have nightmares when I tell ye?"

They frowned in unison. "I'm Garda O'Sullivan, and I'll be passing your information on to Garda Cooley. But don't you lads get your pretty little heads jealous. There's no doubt in my mind he'll be giving both of you a call."

CHAPTER 12

That night, instead of visions of sugarplums, depressed cows and a failing Irish cream business danced through Siobhán's head. Once she reported the story to the guards, Paul was going to have to produce all the financial records related to his company. Siobhán wasn't going to be endearing herself to her new family. Had Paul forged Enda's signature on a check or a loan document, or were those lads from the pub just making wild guesses? And if Paul did steal the money somehow, did Enda find out? Did he overreact?

Siobhán needed more information in regards to Enda's health. Correction. The guards needed to investigate Enda Elliot's medical condition. Siobhán was here on holiday. Enjoying Christmas with her loved ones. So if she didn't sleep a wink that night, the howling wind outside and wondering how Macdara was doing on Catherine's sofa were probably to blame.

When morning came, she was exhausted but relieved. She missed her cappuccino maker back at the bistro, but a cup of tea was the next best thing. An early phone call jolted her out of her morning trance. Leah was requesting that everyone gather at Enda's after breakfast for a meeting. Eoin made them all eggs, toast, and rashers, and soon after they headed over.

Leah gathered them in Enda's kitchen. Siobhán tried not to stare at the spot on the wall where the hatchet once hung. She'd yet to tell the guards about the Elliot grandchildren burying it on their property. She was waiting for her official interview. The list of things to tell them about was growing. "The guards are finished in the mill," Leah said. "We need to organize the concert. I say we start with blessing and decorating the space."

Finished in the mill. That meant Enda's body had been moved to Cork University Hospital. Pity, Siobhán was looking forward to seeing Jeanie Brady, and she'd already purchased a bag of pistachios in town. Moira stepped forward wringing a handkerchief. "Are you sure we shouldn't find a new location?" Siobhán had been wondering the exact same thing. The last time these folks had entered the mill, they'd received quite the fright.

Leah shook her head. "Enda was very excited about using the whiskey mill. He loved the acoustics. Our instruments stay more in tune with the temperatures in the mill. He would have cared more about that than anything else. We'll keep it in the mill in honor of my husband."

If anyone else objected they dare not say so in front of the widow. "When do we start?" Harry Williams asked.

"Right now," Leah said. "Let's organize rides to the mill. We can rehearse while others decorate."

Rehearse. That would be exciting. Siobhán edged closer to Macdara. "We're going to walk."

"We are?" Ann asked.

"Anyone who wants to stretch their legs can join us," Siobhán said. No one did, including her brood. "See you there," Siobhán sang as they bundled into their coats.

"What are we really doing?" Macdara asked the minute they were outside.

Siobhán stood in Enda's driveway. "We're re-creating Enda's walk." She headed over to the space the lorry used to occupy. The guards had taken it in as possible evidence.

"Let's assume he didn't know about the tire. He would have come out here first." She looked down the drive. "Then, the shortest distance is this way." She started to follow the drive down to the road. Macdara followed her, letting her do her thing. They took a left at the road, heading for the small bridge. Once there, Siobhán stopped. "This is where the woman saw the hitchhiker."

Macdara hadn't seen the video on the iPad, but Siobhán had described it to him. "And the woman from the shop said the person was wearing a cloak?"

"No. She never used that word. She said a dark coat, like a trench coat."

"In the dark perhaps she just couldn't make out that it was a cloak?"

"It's possible. Or she saw someone else entirely."

"Either way, it's smart she didn't stop."

"She got very lucky." Once they crossed over the bridge, there was only a large pasture between them and the whiskey mill. It wasn't too long of a walk. Siobhán still wouldn't want to do it on a cold winter night, and for Enda to reach the mill from his bedroom in twenty minutes, Enda had to have been running. At least most of it. If he'd had a heart attack and fallen over the rails, the autopsy would bear that out.

225

Siobhán stopped.

"What is it?" Macdara asked.

"I wonder which direction the shopkeeper was headed, and where on the bridge she saw the hitchhiker."

"The guards will probably figure that out."

"I hope so."

"You don't sound convinced."

"Perhaps I simply don't like when I'm not in control."

"You?" Macdara asked with a feigned tone of shock. "Never."

She laughed, then gave him a gentle shove. "Maybe we should help Garda Cooley out. Given that we're here and we have the morning light."

"What were you thinking?"

"Let's take some pictures of the bridge so we can ask her."

"Yes, boss," Macdara said. "Want me to play the hitchhiker?"

"Give it a go," Siobhán said. "But I'm not the type of girl that stops for strangers."

"That's too bad, lassie. I'd pick you up in heartbeat."

Macdara stood on every end of the bridge and Siobhán snapped four photos with her mobile phone. "There. That should do it."

They headed off again, and this time Siobhan filled Macdara in on her conversation with the lads in the pub.

Macdara whistled. "If Paul Elliot stole money from his grandfather, that's going to cause a stir."

She sighed. "I know. Even if he got permission it might cause a stir, given the growing evidence that Enda's mental health was failing. But by exposing this, I won't exactly be endearing myself to the Elliot family."

"I hope the guards can handle it without dropping your name."

"I have a feeling it's not easy to keep secrets in this town."

"We'll have to work that to our advantage," Macdara said.

"You mean hypothetically?"

He gave her a look. "Yes. Nothing wrong with conducting a hypothetical investigation, is there?"

"I don't see a thing wrong with it. Hypothetically."

Soon the mill came into view. Siobhán pointed. "Here we are."

Macdara whistled. "It's a good-looking building."

"Tis. I don't blame Leah for wanting to keep the concert here."

"Leah," he repeated. "You like her."

"I do. She's a musical prodigy. And beautiful. And sweet. I saw her play the violin for a donkey."

"I have a few things I could say about that, but I won't."

"Excellent decision." She hesitated near the door to the mill. From within they could hear the musicians warming up. "What is your take so far on our musicians?"

Macdara locked eyes with her. "I think Harry Williams is in love with Leah."

"Me too," Siobhán admitted. "And I think it might be mutual." Macdara reached for the door.

"Wait," Siobhán said. "I want to get a look at the back of the building."

He followed her along the side. "Any reason why?"

"Eoin ran into an old man that morning back here. Rick Jaspers. He has a Christmas tree farm in the back, and Ruth said he owns this building."

"It's not just the musicians who are among the suspects," Macdara stated as the headed on.

"You mean Jaspers?"

Macdara nodded. "What if he saw Enda go in and thought he was an intruder?"

"From what others have said, the old man doesn't really care what goes on in the mill as long as he gets a few bob out of it."

"What are your thoughts on Theodore

Baskins?" Macdara asked her.

"You tell me. You're the one whose watched rugby with him."

Macdara laughed. "Doesn't mean it was a bromance."

"What do your detective instincts say?"

"He makes himself an easy target."

"Because he's a bit outlandish?"

"Yes."

"What else?" Macdara was an excellent Detective Sergeant. She was thrilled to have him share in this case with her.

"I would keep my eye on the son," Macdara said. "If this were my case."

"Indeed." Jason. The odd son out. Siobhán stopped. They had reached the back of the mill. Christmas trees were laid out in neat rows as far as the eye could see. The sales were probably slowing down given how close it was getting to Christmas. She didn't see a sign of Jaspers.

"Are we going tree to tree to look for him?" Macdara teased.

Siobhán shook her head. "Let's mention him to Cooley though."

Macdara tilted his head. "Did he do anything suspicious?"

"He yanked Eoin by the ear. Although it wasn't without merit." She filled him in on the story. Macdara covered his mouth, trying and failing to hide his laugh. "You were saying something about keeping an eye on Jason?" They headed back to the front of the mill. "Any particular reason?"

"Have you ever noticed how intensely he watches everyone?" Macdara asked.

"I have. Especially Gráinne. I'm thinking that one might be mutual."

"It's as if he's terrified to miss a beat."

"A controlling killer."

"He was living in the house with Enda, correct?"

"Staying in the house. Yes."

"Access to the hatchet. And the lorry."

"He also lied about his alibi. The same lie Elise tried to pull off."

"They claimed to be traveling, yet they were at the inn?"

"Exactly." She sighed. "And it's not like we can just ask Faye if her son snuck out in the middle of the night. Of course she would cover for him."

"I'm assuming they had separate rooms as well," Macdara said. "Faye would have needed one on the first floor."

"I didn't think of that."

"We could make inquires at the inn."

"We could and we should." She wasn't the only one itching to get involved in this case. Macdara couldn't help himself either.

They'd arrived at the front door to the mill, neither in a hurry to go inside.

"We could also have a chat with Faye. See if she accidentally let's something slip," Macdara said.

"I think you'd have better luck with that than me," Siobhán admitted.

"And why is that?"

"You are a bit more charming to the female population."

"Just a bit?"

"Don't push it."

He threw his head back and laughed. "Using me good looks and charm, are ya?"

"Why wouldn't I?" She stopped, then physically turned him around to face the direction from whence they came. "Unfortunately, it means you have to turn around and go back to Moira's house."

"Why is that?"

"Because Faye said she wasn't coming to the mill. She'll be at Moira's house baking cookies."

Macdara put his arms around Siobhán's waist and pulled her in. "What excuse will I use for being a lazy sod and not coming in to help?"

"I'll let you use your superior intelligence to figure that one out."

He laughed again and leaned in for a kiss.

"Happy Christmas, boss."

"Happy Christmas."

Above them, snow began to fall. Siobhán squealed, and the two of them looked up, then out on the fields. It was going to be stunning covered in a blanket of white. "Great," Macdara said. "I'll be trudging back in a snowstorm. I hope I get back to the houses before we're buried."

"Best of luck to ya," Siobhán said. Then she kissed him again, laughing as wet flakes fell on their faces. Siobhán waved goodbye, then disappeared into the mill.

With lights blazing, Christmas music playing, and snow falling outside, the mill was transformed from the tragic space Siobhán first encountered to the festive hall that Enda had envisioned. The helpers were in full swing, and Siobhán was delighted to see her siblings had taken on decorating the Christmas tree. All but Gráinne. Siobhán had no idea where she'd gone off to. She snuck up on Ann, who was so startled she dropped a bulb. It smashed on the floor, sending bits of shiny gold glass scattering.

"I'm so sorry," Siobhán said. "I wasn't thinking."

"No harm done," Paul said, scooting into the mix with a broom.

"Where's Gráinne?"

"She's snooping around the costumes," Ann said, pointing to the far-right side of the venue. As Siobhán's gaze traveled over, she noticed that the steps leading to the gallery were blocked off. A sign read NO ENTRANCE. They had yet to fix the broken railing. Was it a mistake not to change the venue? Siobhán supposed there weren't many buildings in town that could hold as many people as they were expecting. And Leah was right, the acoustics were fabulous. The music washed over her in waves, vibrating through her bones, making her feel as if she were a part of the song.

"Snow?" Ciarán suddenly cried out. "Is it snowing?" There were not many windows in the mill, and that's when Siobhán realized he was starting at the wetness in her hair and on her coat. She grinned. "It is, luv. It's snowing."

"It's snowing!" Ciarán cried, barreling to the door. The crowd laughed, and a group of musicians who had been warming up played an instant few bars of "Let It Snow." More laughter rang out and then people rushed to the door after Ciarán.

"Snow fight!" James yelled, zipping past Elise.

"Don't you dare," she said, screeching

with laughter and chasing after him. Siobhán spotted Ruth standing by a rack of clothing in the corner. Sure enough Gráinne was going through them as if they were at Penny's Department Store instead of an old mill.

"What's the story?" Siobhán said, startling the second of her sisters in mere minutes.

"I'm saving them from themselves," Gráinne said. "They aren't even organized according to size."

"I don't think we need this done for the concert," Ruth said tentatively. She seemed slightly afraid of Gráinne, and Siobhán could hardly blame her.

"Shoes!" Gráinne exclaimed, discovering boxes underneath the rack of clothing.

"Don't get into those now," Ruth said as Gráinne brandished a pair of red heels. One by one the shoes in the box were revealed.

"Where are the stilt shoes?" Ruth asked. It was a rhetorical question that sent her diving into the box.

"Stilt shoes?"

"Platform, stilt, they're not real shoes of course. We had to use them when one of our little gals insisted she needed more height to get into character. I'm supposed to return them. I forgot all about them." She stared at an empty box. "They're gone.

Someone stole them."

"How much height do they give a person?"

"Up to six inches."

"Was the missing cloak hanging here as well?"

Ruth shot up and stared at Siobhán. "It was," she said. She chewed on her lip. "Do you think it's important?"

Up until now the guards had probably estimated a height for the figure in the video, despite the figure being hunched over. Even Siobhán had been thinking it had to have been a man or a tall woman. But could someone really have navigated the rocky muck in the pastures wearing costume shoes? Could it explain the clunky movements of the person in the video? She wished she could see the clip again. Did the person move differently coming out of the mill than going in? The biggest challenge was that the footage was grainy and difficult to see in the dark. But this opened up possibilities, allowing for suspects both short and tall. Even someone as little as Elise. It would be some suspect lineup, calling their mobile phones to hear the ringtone and making each one strut across the floor in platform shoes. Then again, surely the ringtone had been changed and a person could fake his or her walk. Regardless, it was amusing to imagine it, like a Killer Cinderella.

Siobhán turned to Ruth. "Is there any system for people coming in and out of the mill or borrowing costumes?"

"Does it look like there's a system," Gráinne said, still flinging through fabric. If there had been any suspicious fingerprints on anything, they were ruined now, with Gráinne's paws all over them. She suspected the killer had been wearing gloves anyway.

"Where is everyone?" Gráinne asked as she took in the near-empty mill.

"It's snowing," Siobhán said. As soon as the words came out of her mouth, Ruth and Gráinne took off for the door. Siobhán dropped a hanger and followed. She stepped outside to a winter wonderland. The flakes were fat and coming down fast. The next hour passed with attempts at gathering enough of a ball to have snowball fights, making snow angels, and sticking one's tongue out at the sky. Siobhán rarely saw snow like this, and even though she suspected it would cause a lot of treachery on those curvy roads, not to mention the work it would take to shovel it, she was loving it for now.

Leah and Harry pummeled each other, as

did Gráinne and Jason. "Look out!" she heard a voice yell, just in time to see a large ball whizzing past. It hit Theodore Baskins on the forehead.

"Ow!" His hand flew first to where it hit, then to the ground, where he bent to retrieve the object that just hit him. "A rock!" he said. "Who did that?" Siobhán turned to see a lump of people standing together, staring. Nobody apologized or took credit.

"That's not funny," Siobhán said. "Whoever threw that, I urge you to confess and apologize."

No one did. Was it a prank or something darker? Was someone gunning for Theodore?

"Why does everyone in this village have to treat Theodore like this?" Catherine yelled. "Haven't you put us through enough?"

"Never mind," Theodore said, taking her hand. "Let's go home."

"You should be ashamed of yourselves," Catherine continued. "After all I've done for everyone here. I've always been good. To everyone. And this is how you treat us? At Christmastime no less."

It was a very Grinch-like thing to do, and the jovial mood was ruined. Siobhán would have felt much better had the guilty party simply stepped up and apologized. Then again, throwing a rock at someone's head could be considered battery.

"We'd better head home. The roads will be frozen before we know it," Moira called out.

"Come on," Catherine said, taking Theodore's arm. "Let's get some ice on it."

The group returned to the mill to pack up. The lights flickered. The keyboard player laughed and played a few bars of a melancholy song. Siobhán had been headed to the door. She stopped and faced the keyboard player. "Keep playing that," she said. "Please."

"A Mozart fan?" he asked with a grin as he began to play again.

Siobhán's spine tingled. "That's it," she said. "That's the song I heard playing in the mill. And now that I hear you play it, I'm quite sure the one I heard was someone's ringtone."

Harry Williams hurried over to her. "Are you sure?" he asked.

"Positive," Siobhán said.

"That's not good," Leah said.

"No," Harry Williams said. "Not good at all."

CHAPTER 13

"Mozart's *Requiem,*" Harry explained. He had just finished playing a fuller version of the song for Siobhán on his mobile. There was no doubt now — that was the song Siobhán heard playing in the mill the morning they'd discovered Enda's body.

"Why does everyone look so somber?" They were gathered in Enda's living room as the snow continued to fall.

"Mozart died before he could finish it," Leah said. "It was a Requiem mass."

"It's one of us who killed him," Harry said, hanging his head. "An orchestra member."

"Why do you say that?" Siobhán asked. "Couldn't anyone download that ringtone to a mobile?"

"It's the symbolism of the song," Harry said. "Mozart's health was failing when he was commissioned to write it. He was convinced he was about to die and it would be his swan song."

Siobhán considered this. Enda was in failing health. But he certainly didn't play Mozart's *Requiem* from the other side. Someone else decided this was his swan song. Someone lured him to the mill. "Why do you think someone is suggesting that this concert was Enda's swan song?" Leah and Harry exchanged a long look. "What is it?"

"Enda told all of us he planned on making a big announcement at the concert," Leah said.

"What announcement?"

"We have no idea. Enda liked building suspense." Leah gave a sad smile.

"But we had a theory," Harry said. "We think he was going to announce his retirement."

"Why do you think that?" Harry threw a look to Leah, and she nodded.

"My husband knew he was starting to forget things. Enda was a proud man. He was still respected as a conductor. I think he wanted to retire while he was still at the top of his game."

Siobhán didn't know what to do with this information. It's not like someone would have killed him to *prevent* him from retiring. "This announcement — it could have been something else entirely?"

Leah shrugged. "I suppose. But I have no idea what else it could have been."

"Enda was putting all his energy into this concert," Harry said. "It looked to me like he was preparing his exit."

"Do you know who his replacement will be?"

"That's decided by people above our pay grade," Harry Williams said.

"I see." Was Harry Williams going to apply for the position? Transfer to Ireland?

"Have any of you heard any musicians using Mozart's *Requiem* for a ringtone?" Macdara asked. One by one, everyone shook their heads.

Leah stood. "We should confiscate everyone's phones right now."

"If it was the killer's ringtone, I'm sure they've changed it by now," Siobhán said. "I think the question to answer is, Why did they program the song into the phone in the first place? Was it to draw Enda up to the gallery? Would that have done the job?"

"Yes," Harry Williams said. "Enda would have recognized the tune immediately and understood the message."

"The message," Siobhán said slowly. "They were hinting that this concert would be Enda's swan song?"

"Even more sinister," Harry said. "They

were suggesting that Enda would never get to perform his last concert. Just as a student of Mozart's had to complete the *Requiem.*"

It wasn't proof, but it did point to a sinister killer. One very knowledgeable about classical music.

"Should we stop the concert?" Leah asked.

"And play into the killer's hand?" Harry asked. "I say the show must go on."

Siobhán was only half-listening. Did smartphones log ringtones? Wouldn't there be evidence somewhere of a person downloading it? It most likely depended on the carrier, the type of phone, and the user's savvy. But what was it she always heard? Nothing is ever erased?

Despite the snow, she now wanted to be the first to be interviewed by Garda Cooley. There were so many things he needed to know about, and Siobhán had to keep repeating them in her head until she got a chance to write them down. The buried hatchet. Paul's failing Irish Cream business and how Enda claimed he'd never finance it. Jason's alibi. Enda's will. The missing platform shoes Ruth had discovered. And now this. Mozart's swan song. It was beginning to look like the village guards were going to have a very busy few days leading up to Christmas.

The garda station was tiny, and the room they stuffed Siobhán in was barely bigger than a closet. At least Barry Cooley had honored her request to see him first, and he diligently took notes as she unloaded all her questions and observations. He informed her it would impossible to investigate the ringtone. Just the process of getting telephone companies to hand over records would have been a lengthy court battle. Nor did he think phones stored a user's past choices of ringtones when it was so easy to change ringtones with the push of a button.

"But this wouldn't have been a standard ringtone. The person would have needed to download the song first."

"If we narrow down a suspect, I can think about trying that avenue. But it's not a quick process and I'd need to convince a judge that we have reasonable suspicion for doing that kind of digging."

He was right. Doing things by the book was a necessary but often frustrating part of the job. They were in the middle of pondering this when a guard popped his head in the door.

"He's here."

243

Cooley packed up his notes. "Thank you, Garda O'Sullivan."

"That's it?"

He smiled. "I think we're about to wrap this case up and put a violin bow on it."

"Oh?" She frowned. "Is that a reference to Leah Elliot?"

"No. Just a joke." He held up his hand. "We heard a rumor about Theodore Baskins. A witness has just come forward, and I believe he is about to wipe Theodore Baskin's alibi clean. Would you like to sit in?"

She was surprised by the offer, but from the grin on his face, he wanted her to have a front-row seat to his triumph. Theodore Baskins. All roads led to Theodore Baskins with this guard. Either way, she wasn't about to refuse his invitation. "Sure."

She followed him into the next interrogation room, where a thin man sat at the table, seemingly trying to shrink into his chair. At first Siobhán thought it was an older man, but as she looked closer, his wrinkles had been caused by his squishing his face down. He was probably in his early thirties. His hands were stuffed in the pockets of his puffy jacket.

"I'm listening," Cooley said.

The witnessed sighed. "The night Enda

244

was killed, Theodore Baskins wasn't home. He was at my party."

Siobhán jotted a note on her pad. *Where does he live?* Cooley glanced over at it. "A mile from the mill," Cooley answered. The man lifted an eyebrow, looked at Siobhán, then nodded. "What time did he leave?"

"I saw him stumbling out around midnight."

Cooley looked over at Siobhán. "Giving him plenty of time to arrive at the mill at half past twelve." He tapped his notebook. "Just when the video shows him entering."

"May I?" Siobhán asked glancing at the witness.

Garda Cooley gestured to the man. "Go ahead."

Siobhán made eye contact with the man and nodded. "Was he wearing a cloak?"

The man frowned. "A what?"

"What was Theodore wearing?"

He shrugged. "Denims. A shirt." He shook his head. "I don't pay attention to things like dat."

"When he left. It was cold outside. I assumed he had some kind of coat?"

"Yeah, of course. A coat."

She gave Cooley a look. He leaned in. "He must have picked the cloak up at the mill," Cooley said.

"How? The person was wearing it in the video." It wasn't easy, whispering in front of the witness, and she was worried he was actually listening to every word, but there was little she could do about it.

"Maybe he stashed it near the mill. In advance."

"He just said Theodore *stumbled* out of the house. Does that sound like someone calculating a murder?"

Cooley turned to the witness. "Could it have been a cloak?"

"What?"

"His coat. What did it look like?"

"I dunno. Like. A jacket."

"Dark? Long?" Cooley prodded.

Siobhán shook her head. The witness clearly did not see Theodore in a cloak. "Could have been," the man finally said.

"Did Theodore drive to your party?"

The man nodded. "He did. But he didn't drive home. I took the keys. Catherine and Theodore took a taxi to me house the next morning to pick it up. Woke me up. I was feeling a little rough."

"He was on foot when he left," Cooley said. "Close to the mill. After he pushes Enda, he has to walk home. Over the bridge."

Where Alison the shopkeeper saw a man

246

hitchhiking . . .

Siobhán leaned in and whispered again. "What about Enda's tire? He didn't have time to slash it."

Cooley wasn't fazed. "Then the tire must have been slashed previously."

"Why would Theodore Baskins kill Enda?"

The man looked startled. "Are ye asking me? I have no idea. I'm only letting you know he was at my party."

"She wasn't asking you," Garda Cooley said before turning back to Siobhán. "Theodore Baskins is unhinged. Who knows why?" Garda Cooley shoved a form across the table to the witness. "Write down your statement and sign it."

"Yes, sir."

Garda Cooley leaned back and folded his arms. "There you have it. We'll be arresting Theodore Baskins for the murder of Enda Elliot."

Was he serious? "Based on a lie?"

"It's reason enough to get him in here," Cooley said. "I'll get a confession out of him if it's the last thing I do."

Siobhán let him vent. This wasn't good. "Theodore isn't the only suspect who lied about his alibi," she said in a calm voice. "Jason and Faye lied about theirs. Paul, Orla, and Elise tried to lie. So, yes. Now we've discovered that Theodore lied about his as well. You need to question him, of course. And Catherine. But I don't see why you're jumping to an arrest."

"You don't know why? Because you don't live here. You don't know this village, or these people."

"I know. But —"

"We're done. You can go." Cooley stood. The witness scrambled to his feet and was out the door in seconds. It slammed behind him. Siobhán stood but didn't make a move to the door.

"Has the state pathologist finished examining the body?" She had refrained thus far from trying to glean information from Garda Cooley, but this was her last chance. He was jumping to conclusions too soon.

"Yes. His death was ruled a homicide. The body is on the way to the funeral home, and don't you worry. I'm going to get that confession. Theodore Baskins is our killer."

"Would he even recognize Mozart's *Requiem* if he heard it?"

"He's been a neighbor of Enda's for six years. It's quite possible."

"But . . . don't you want to know why?"

"I intend on asking him just that."

"Arresting? Just based on one witness?"

Cooley held up two fingers. "Two wit-

248

nesses. Remember Alison, the shopkeeper you met?

"Yes."

"She identified Theodore Baskins as the man she saw hitchhiking on the bridge."

"When I spoke with her, she said she couldn't identify the man."

"She was terrified."

"She didn't seem terrified."

"What can I tell you? She was terrified of Theodore. Once I assured her that we were watching his every move — and we are — she was able to fully open up about who she saw. And she saw Theodore Baskins, in a cloak, on the bridge, at the exact time the video showed him leaving."

"She told me it was a figure in a trench coat."

"She doesn't know you."

Siobhán felt like a drowning victim unsure of whether to grab on to the person in front of her. "I assume you're calling Catherine back in for questioning?"

"Of course. After I get his confession. Maybe if she confesses too, I won't charge her."

"I see."

"She wouldn't be the first woman to lie for a man," Cooley said. "And then there's the gold button."

Siobhán nodded. At least this piece of evidence she could agree with. "We found it by the bridge."

"You and Baskins," Garda Cooley said. "Did you find it, or did he?"

She stopped to think about it. "He did."

"Did you see it on the ground before he picked it up?"

She had to think about it. "No."

"What if he didn't find it at all? What if he had it in his pocket?"

"You're suggesting he wanted to implicate himself?"

"Of course not. He was getting rid of evidence."

"Evidence no one was looking for?"

Cooley was losing his patience. Instead of praising him, Siobhán was pushing back on what, no doubt, was his greatest professional accomplishment. Nailing Enda Elliot's murderer. She could imagine the pressure he was under. If it wasn't solved soon, no doubt a higher up from Dublin would descend on the village to take over the case. Garda Cooley was rushing against a ticking clock. And maybe Theodore Baskins was guilty. But there were too many other people who might have had reason to want Enda dead, and Siobhán did not like that Cooley seemed content to leave those threads hanging. "What about Enda's will? Or the decline in his mental health?"

"I misjudged you," Cooley said. "I thought you'd see we've done good work here. Let me be clear. This case will be closed in a matter of days. Go home. Tell Moira this will all soon be over."

"I see."

"One more thing."

She waited. He was drawing it out. "Yes?"

"If Theodore doesn't confess when we bring him in, we can't arrest him just yet. The higher-ups are waiting for forensics on the button and a few other bits and pieces. We may have to let him go. But with this storm coming in, he's not going anywhere. We're going to ask you and Detective Sergeant Flannery not only to keep this under wraps but also to keep an eye on him. The last thing we need is another murder on our hands."

"We don't have any authority here," Siobhán said. "We can keep an eye out, but any killer who is still free poses a risk."

"Now you see what we're up against," Cooley said, as if Siobhán had finally come around to his side. "When this storm passes, you might want to take your family and go home." Siobhán had no choice but to walk out of the garda station. The snow was now

251

nearly a foot deep. She didn't have much experience driving in it, but as long as she went slow, as she did on the way here, she should be fine. *Tell Moira this will all soon be over.* The words rung hollow in Siobhán O'Sullivan's ears. Far from being over, she couldn't shake the feeling that this case was just beginning.

CHAPTER 14

Given the busy schedule on Christmas Eve day with the concert, Elise insisted they open the Secret Santa gifts on December twenty-third. Tensions were high since Garda Cooley suddenly stopped questioning the witnesses. Only Siobhán and Macdara knew that they were waiting to arrest Theodore Baskins. They'd brought him in again for questioning, and he was there all day. He returned that evening and this morning went back to work. Apparently, despite Cooley's confidence, there had been no confession. If he had been alerted during that questioning that he was their top suspect, Siobhán hadn't heard about it. The snow had stopped falling, but the foot on the ground and the black ice were keeping them corralled. A little gift giving might just be the balm needed to soothe them.

Elise had arranged all the gifts in the center of Moira's living room. "I'll call you up one by one to find your gift," she said. "Search the tags for your name." James was the first name she called. He wandered up and found his on the third try. He tore off the paper and held up a snow globe of a miniature skating rink with a Christmas tree in the middle. It cranked up to play "White Christmas." Siobhán loved it. Given he wasn't the sentimental type, he would probably let her have it.

"I love it," Elise squealed.

James leaned over and kissed her on the cheek. "You can have it," he whispered. Siobhán felt like a fool. Of course he was going to give it to Elise. She would be number one in his life now. As it should be. James held the globe up. "Thank you, Secret Santa, it's lovely." Ciarán, Siobhán noted, was eyeing each guest as if keen to figure out which one of them was his Secret Santa. Siobhán was fine with that as long as it was the only thing he was trying to figure out. One garda in the family was enough.

Catherine was up next. She found her box after looking at nearly every single one of them. It was tiny and perched on top of Siobhán's snowman. Siobhán made sure not to glance at Ann, as she was pretty sure that Ann had drawn Catherine's name. The gift was a necklace made of blinking Christmas

bulbs. Catherine held it up. "How lovely."
She held it far away from her neck. She had
on a red scarf and did not make a move to
try on the necklace.

"That's not musical," Elise said.

"The lights beat out a rhythm," Ann said.
"Like a drum."

"Good point, Ann," Siobhán said. "It does
beat out a rhythm."

"Or music for a deaf person," Gráinne
said.

The moment was so awkward that when
Gráinne started to clap, everyone else joined
in. Theodore rushed into the middle of the
room and took a bow. "I can't help it," he
said. "I hear applause and I automatically
bow. It's like a tic."

Siobhán felt her stomach clench. He was
so arrogant. He'd made himself such an
easy target for the guards. Did he have any
idea how much trouble was coming his way?

"You're not far from being a tick yourself,"
Paul said. "But you're more of a leech, are
you not?"

Theodore pinned his gaze on Paul. "
might be a rock," Theodore said, pointin
at Paul. "But you're the glass house."

Paul opened his mouth as if to make
retort but seemed to realize too late that
had none. Instead, panic slowly took o

his facial muscles. A look passed between them. Paul dropped his head as if they had been conducting a silent battle and Theodore had won. *Theodore had something on Paul. What was it?*

"You might as well find your gift while you're up there," Elise said to Theodore. From the tone of her voice she was not happy her order had been breached.

Theodore Baskins made a big to-do over the size of the box the snowman was in. "Is it snowshoes?" he asked in a voice fit for an actor.

Snowshoes. Like that fit in the budget. If he didn't stop guessing he was going to hate it. Satisfaction, Siobhán always thought, was directly tied to one's expectations. That's why her new year's goal was going to be to lower all of hers.

"Snowshoes aren't musical," Elise said.

"They are if I can two-step in them," Theodore said, breaking into an impromptu tap dance.

"Just open it," Elise barked.

He opened the box slowly, looking up at the guests after every little rip.

"Get on with it," Paul said at last.

He revealed the box with the singing plastic snowman. He lifted it out. It was hideous.

"I think it sings," Siobhán squeaked.

Theodore stared at it for several seconds, then shook it. An off-key rendition of "Frosty the Snowman" began to play. His plastic eyes rolled up in his head.

"Deadly." Eoin laughed.

"Plastic," Theodore said. "Who cares about the environment, am I right?"

Siobhán felt herself shrink.

"So cool," Ciarán said.

Theodore turned his gaze on Ciarán. "You want him, little man?"

"No," Siobhán said. "Unless we're all trading gifts, Santy meant that for you."

Theodore stared at the snowman. "I guess I'm on Santa's naughty list this year." He looked as if he wanted to boot the snowman out the door.

Siobhán was relieved when they moved on. "Jason?" He walked up to the gifts, then held up a small box wrapped in green. Glitter fell from it. Green glitter. Like the elf in the woods. "Wait."

But he had ripped it open and was staring at the box. "Is this some kind of joke?" His gaze traveled from Paul to Orla to Elise. They stared back, unblinking.

"What is it?" Ciarán asked.

Jason held up the box with *"DNA"* splashed across the front. "A DNA test."

"What?" Faye screeched. She rolled her wheelchair forward. "Just what is someone insinuating?"

"That Enda wasn't my father," Jason said, looking at Moira.

"Me?" Moira said. "You think I would do such a thing?"

"You want the inheritance all to yourself, is that it?" Jason demanded.

"That's absurd," Moira said. "Of course you're Enda's son. Look at your nose."

"I won't play this sick game," Jason said. "My whole life I had to live in the shadows."

"This is an insult to me," Faye said, rolling next to Jason. "I won't stand for it. Let me speak directly to whoever sent this. Jason and I will not stand for this."

"I think you're overreacting," Theodore said. "Everyone is taking those tests now. It's miraculous what you can learn."

"Like what?" Jason said. "What does someone want me to learn?"

"Enda wasn't doing so well lately. Don't you wonder if you have the same genes?" Theodore said.

"Theodore!" Catherine stood. "That is unacceptable. Apologize."

"To these people?" Theodore looked around, dumbfounded. "They'll all think I'm a murderer."

"That's not true," Catherine said.

"You know it is. Who else was kept at the station for twelve hours? They think I did it." He turned to Moira. "I did not push Enda from the gallery. I was not in the mill. Frankly, I didn't care whether he lived or died."

"Get out," Moira said. "I want you out of my house right now."

"My pleasure." Theodore stalked out and slammed the door. A second later, the door flew open again. He darted across the floor and picked up the plastic snowman. "Frosty! What a perfect name. Just like all of you." One by one Theodore jabbed his finger at each of them. "Cold, cold, cold, cold." He got to Moira. "Ice cold. Freezing. Frigid!" He shook the snowman. "Looks like he's the only pal I have left in the world." He tucked the gift under his arm and strode out, slamming the door for the second time. Siobhán knew it was wrong, but she felt slightly gratified that he came back for Frosty. A thick silence settled over the group.

"These are stressful times," Siobhán said. "Will the person who gave Jason the DNA kit please confess?"

No one spoke up. Just like when Theodore was hit in the head with a rock. Was this one of the Elliot grandchildren, or Moira? Did they really think Enda was not Jason's father?

"Jason?" Catherine said. "I wouldn't mind the DNA kit. I can give you one of my paintings for it."

"You can have it." Jason tossed the kit to Catherine.

"No trades," Elise said.

"That wasn't part of the real Secret Santa," Catherine said. "It's not musical, and the giver wouldn't show themselves. Unless they want to do it now?" Nobody spoke. "It's settled," Catherine said, dropping the DNA kit into her purse and snapping it shut.

"Siobhán," Elise said.

"Yes?" Siobhán asked.

"I was just calling your name. It's your turn."

"Oh." Siobhán headed for the gifts and spotted it right away. Her gift was oddly shaped. And heavy. She ripped off the paper. At first she saw only rusted metal, and then the wooden handle was revealed. She could not believe what she was seeing. She didn't mean to gasp, but the sound escaped her mouth before she could stop it. Macdara was at her side in an instant.

"What is it?" Moira called from across the room.

The answer was unfathomable. A hatchet. Correction. Enda's hatchet. The crowd moved in. There was another gasp, and everyone began speaking at once.

"Is that Enda's?" Leah said. "Who did this?"

There was a piece of paper on top with a typewritten note:

Chop-in. Get it? (Chopin)

Harry Williams read the note out loud. He scanned the faces of the orchestra members. "I say there's very little doubt now. Between this and Mozart's *Requiem,* one of us is a killer."

"Tell that to the guards," Catherine said. "They're gunning for Theodore."

"Don't let paranoia get the best of you," Moira said. "They haven't arrested him, have they?"

"Not for lack of trying," Catherine said.

"Somebody call Garda Cooley right now," Macdara said. "And nobody touch that hatchet." He turned to Elise, Paul, and Orla. "I thought you said you buried it."

"We did," Orla said. "Someone must have dug it up."

"Who all knew where it was buried?" Siobhán asked.

"Buried?" Jason said. "I thought you were all joking!"

"You're the one who first saw Enda wandering around with it in the middle of the night," Paul said. "What were we supposed to do? Let him whack somebody with it? Maybe even you?"

"Why would he whack me with it?" Jason asked.

"I don't know," Paul said. "Because he was losing his mind?"

"Paul," Moira said. Her voice was strong, and the reprimand was clear. Face by face, Siobhán looked at all the suspects. Moira stood with her chin up, arms folded. Orla hovered in the doorway, her hands folded over her stomach, the dim kitchen light casting a shadow on her pale face. Paul, perched on the arm of the sofa, turned a harmonica round and round in his hands. Leah, hands over her mouth, stood staring down at the hatchet. Catherine was planted near the back door as if ready to bolt. Ruth was hiding behind her harp. Elise grasped James's hand. Faye pushed her wheelchair closer to the hatchet, Jason trailing after her.

"What in the name of heavens is going on?" Faye cried as she drew nearer.

And Harry Williams was staring at Leah from across the room with a look that said he wished he was anywhere but here. Elise went to call the guards, but just then there was a rap at the door, and she opened it to find they were already there.

Garda Cooley stood in the pasture with Siobhán. The burial spot was in the center of the field, between the main house and the guest house. If the hatchet had been buried there, whoever dug it up had done it long before the snow began to fall. There were no open holes in the ground, and Siobhán prayed Garda Cooley wasn't going to ask her to start shoveling snow. "Why do you think someone gave it to you?" It was the third time he'd tried to ask her that question.

"I don't know." It was the only answer she'd given him. But she'd been thinking about it. Why *would* someone give it to her? And did it mean the person who gave her the hatchet was the killer? Or someone else? Was there a message behind it? "Chopin. Choppin'." She shuddered. "Harry Williams is convinced it's an orchestra member."

"Theodore knows I'm onto him," Cooley said. "He's trying to point the finger at one of the musicians."

"Or," Siobhán said, "our killer is one of the musicians."

"Or," Garda Cooley said, "Theodore Baskins wants us to think the killer is one of the musicians."

Siobhán dropped her end of this losing tug-of-war. "We need to check the remaining gifts," Siobhán said. "See if my name is on another one." Garda Cooley followed her back inside the house. The remaining gifts were still piled in the center of Moira's living room. "I also want to see if there is another one for Jason."

"Jason?" Cooley asked. "Why?"

"Because someone gave him a DNA kit."

Cooley's face seemed to age in seconds. Was he finally realizing it was too soon to close this case? Siobhán found another gift with Jason's name on it. "He'll have to forgive me for opening it," she said. She tore open the wrapping paper to find a harmonica.

"Does he play?" Cooley asked.

"I don't know," Siobhán said. "But the gift is music related, which means it's probably from the real Secret Santa. Whoever gave him the DNA kit is trying to stir up trouble."

"How?"

"I don't know. Perhaps suggesting that

Enda wasn't his father."

"Of course he's his father," Cooley said. "Have you seen his nose?"

Siobhán finally spotted a small package and read the tag. "Here's another one for me." Siobhán opened it. It was Paul's CD. No doubt from Ruth. That hatchet wasn't from Siobhán's Secret Santa. It could be any of them. Was it the killer? Sending her a warning? *Was* it Theodore Baskins? After all, she was the one who had been at the station just before him. Did he think *she* pointed the finger at him? Did he now have his sights set on her? He was also the first to comment on Jason's DNA kit and make the horrible joke about Enda's failing health. Maybe Cooley was right. Maybe Theodore was after everyone in this town whom he felt had treated him poorly over the years. Maybe none of them were safe.

"Great gift if I do say so myself," Paul said, walking into the room.

She had been lost in thought, and his presence startled her. "Pardon?"

He pointed at his CD, still in her hand. "And tell you what. I shouldn't be doing this because it's really in demand, but I'll throw in a bottle of my award-winning Irish cream for you to sup on while you listen."

"Was your grandfather supportive of your

business?" Siobhán asked, trying to sound casual.

"Why wouldn't he be?" Paul's eyes blazed with suspicion.

"Sorry. I'm just trying to lighten the mood," Siobhán said. *Come on, Garda Cooley, pick up the thread. Ask him how his grandfather felt about his Irish cream business. Ask him if he's in over his head.*

Garda Cooley took the hatchet and left.

"I've had enough of this drama," Moira suddenly announced, sweeping into the room. Slowly all the suspects filed in behind her. Everyone was antsy after the discovery of the hatchet, but nobody seemed to want to be alone. There was safety in numbers, even if one of them was a killer. "We have a concert to put on," Moira said. "And I have a surprise." She left the room and returned holding a Santa costume. She approached Harry Williams. "Enda was going to delight everyone by wearing this at the concert," she said.

Faye rolled her wheelchair forward. "Was *that* his big announcement?"

"Yes, Faye," Moira said sarcastically. "Enda's big announcement was that he was Santa Claus." She rolled her eyes and turned back to Harry. "Since you will be conducting in his place, I thought you'd like

266

to wear it."

Harry gawped at the Santa outfit. "I appreciate it," he said politely. "But I don't think we're the same size." Moira looked crestfallen. "Tell you what." He picked up the Santa cap and put it on. "How about I just wear this?"

"Brilliant," Moira said. She handed him a pile of white fluff. "And the beard too?"

Harry Williams laughed. It nearly sounded like *Ho, Ho, Ho.* "And the beard too," he said, accepting it.

"Cool," Ciarán said. "Our first black Santy."

Harry looked startled for a moment and then laughed. "Hope I'm not the last." He winked and then fist-bumped Ciarán.

"Totally cool," Gráinne said. "And a black Santy is probably more historically accurate."

They were on their way back to the guest house, clomping through the snow and the wind, when Siobhán realized she'd left her scarf in Moira's house. It was too cold to go without one. "I'll catch up," she told the others as she headed back. As she neared the house, she could see Jason pushing Faye through the small patch of woods to Enda's house. They had their backs to her and must not have heard her. She caught part of their conversation.

"We have to go *now,*" Faye said, her voice in a panic. Siobhán crept closer. She really hated how it would look if she got caught, but she found a pile of firewood and crouched behind it.

"Home?" she heard Jason say. She peeked out. They had stopped.

Faye shook her head. "No. To a bank."

"Right now? Why?"

"First Enda stops the payments and now we're being harassed."

"But we don't even know who sent the kit." *The kit. He was talking about the DNA kit.* Jason stepped closer to his mother. "Do we?"

"Don't be ridiculous." She pulled her coat up and gestured for him to keep pushing her. He did. Siobhán crept forward, not wanting to miss the rest. "But it's not the last we'll hear from them."

"I don't understand. Are you worried Enda isn't my biological father?"

Faye laughed, a strangled sound. "Of course not."

"Then what are you so worried about?" *That was exactly what Siobhán wanted to know.* Faye said something Siobhán couldn't hear. Then Jason spoke again. "I won't let you do this."

They were past the wooded area now, and there was no way for Siobhán to keep following without giving herself away. She was going to have to find out what Faye was so worried about and why she thought she needed to go to a bank. She was obviously interpreting the DNA kit as some kind of blackmail. Given that everyone in the family joked that Jason had his father's nose, she wasn't sure what message was being sent. But Faye seemed to know. If only this group trusted her more, she might actually be able to help them.

By the time Siobhán fetched her scarf and returned to the guest house, her brood was already making hot cocoa and pulling out sweets and casseroles that Elise had kindly stuffed in their kitchen. Christmas music played overhead, and the lights on the tree sparkled. Ciarán was still talking about Harry Williams.

"I think someone has a crush on a certain violinist," Gráinne said with a wink.

"No," Ciarán said. "I just know a secret."

"You're one to talk," Ann said, wagging her finger at Gráinne.

Gráinne put her hands on her hips. "Me?"

Ann flung herself dramatically over the counter and flipped her hair. "Oh, Jason.

269

You're so funny." She threw her head back and laughed. Siobhán couldn't help but laugh with her.

"I think he's got his eye on Gráinne as well," Siobhán said.

Gráinne looked as if she was giving it some thought. "Just tell me he's not our killer."

"Don't tell her that," Ann said. "She'll want to marry him."

"Our family lines are complicated enough," Elise said. "I don't think we need to muddy them any more."

"Why do you think someone gave him a DNA kit?" Siobhán asked Elise.

Elise looked startled. "How would I know?"

"You're in charge of the Secret Santa. Just wondered if you had any thoughts on it."

Elise chewed her lip. "No, I don't."

"Doesn't anyone want to know my secret?" Ciarán asked.

"Of course, petal," Siobhán said, helping herself to an apple tart. "Tell us your secret."

"Tonight wasn't the first time I saw Mr. Williams in a Santa hat," he said in a singsong voice.

Siobhán had just taken a bite of what had to be the best apple tart on the planet. She sighed lovingly at what was left of it, afraid that Ciarán was about to ruin her appetite. "What do you mean?"

"At the town square," he said. "The night the carolers sang."

"I don't remember seeing him in a Santa hat then," Siobhán said. She snuck in another bite. She was going to have to ask Eoin if he could make these. They were superb.

"Because he was sneaking."

"Sneaking?" She dropped her fork. All that folks needed to avoid overeating was high drama all the time. She'd never finish the apple tart now. "Are you sure he was sneaking?"

"Yes," Ciarán said. "With Leah."

Siobhán shoved the apple tart away with a sigh and made eye contact with Ciarán. "What exactly are you saying?"

"I'm saying," he said, "I saw Leah kissing Santa Claus."

CHAPTER 15

Siobhán didn't get a chance to speak with Leah the next morning. The orchestra had headed off to the mill to rehearse for the concert, and interruptions would not be tolerated. Her brood had gone off with Elise and James to play in the snow. Macdara's mam had some secret shopping to do, and that left Macdara and Siobhán gloriously alone. They stood in the guest house with mugs of coffee — thanks to Macdara bringing her a bag of freshly ground heaven — and Macdara let her spill her thoughts about the case. How she'd already suspected that Leah and Harry were into each other. Had Enda found out about their affair? How long had it been going on? To be caught kissing days after your husband was dead was scandalous enough even if it was an accident. Then again, Siobhán couldn't be sure exactly what Ciarán saw. There were so many leads she would have followed up on if this were her case. Enda's will. His medical records. A possible affair. Faye's accident. She'd bring Elise, Paul, and Orla under the lights to find out more about that emergency meeting. Was there more to it? And what of the strange elf she saw in the woods? Not to mention the harp that Enda was crushed under. Was it valuable? What if Ruth had been up there trying to steal the harp?

"You're suggesting that Ruth was up there in the middle of the night?" Macdara said. "She was going to drag a ninety-pound harp down a set of stairs by herself?"

Siobhán sighed. "Probably not."

"I'd say the immediate family — current wives, daughters, grandchildren, ex-wives — stand to benefit more from Enda's death."

"I concur."

"But the guards are zeroing in on Theodore Baskins, and I don't think we can do much about that."

"There is one person we could speak with," Siobhán said. Macdara knew there was more and waited for her to continue. "Alison, the shopkeeper, did *not* identify Theodore Baskins as the hitchhiker. She very clearly said it was someone dressed in a dark coat — she called it a trench coat —

and she thought it could have been Enda. Not Theodore. I want to know why she changed her account." She had a feeling Garda Cooley had something to do with the troubling change in her story.

"I don't know about you, but I could do a little shopping," Macdara said. They clinked coffee mugs, had a bit of a cuddle, and then took off for Alison's shop.

Alison was in her usual perch behind the register, but she didn't recognize Siobhán at first. She was gazing out the window and fussing with the red bow in her hair. When Siobhán smiled, recognition dawned in Alison's eyes.

"Hello," she said when Siobhán approached. "Lovely to see you again." Alison glanced at Macdara, and her cheeks took on a rosier hue.

"You too," Siobhán said.

"How can I help you?" She fluttered her lashes and smiled at Macdara.

"I don't know if you remember speaking with me a few days ago . . ."

Alison smiled. "With that wonderful red hair? Of course I do." Beside Siobhán, Macdara chuckled.

Siobhan's hair, at least in her opinion, was auburn. But it was perceived differently depending on the light, many simply called it red. *A blessing and a curse.* "Thank you." She smiled. "You told me about encountering a hitchhiker the night Enda was killed. Near the bridge."

Alison began to blink rapidly, then began shuffling through receipts in a box as if she were suddenly very busy. "Yes," she said. "Theodore Baskins."

"That's just it," Siobhán said. "When we spoke, you weren't able to identify the man."

"You're not from here," Alison said. "I wasn't going to use names."

You're not from here . . . that was the exact phrasing Barry Cooley used. Had he coached her?

"You're sure then? It was Theodore Baskins you saw?"

"I'm sure."

"I thought it was dark. And that the figure was wearing dark clothing?"

"I'm afraid this is a matter for the guards."

Macdara stepped up. "We are guards. I'm Detective Sergeant Flannery. This is Garda O'Sullivan."

Alison stopped riffling through her receipts. "You're working Enda's case?"

Siobhán had been hoping she wouldn't ask that. "No," Macdara said. "We're friends of the family."

275

"I see." She pursed her lips and turned back to the receipts. "I'm sure Garda Cooley is doing his level best to put Theodore away."

He certainly was. And that's what they were afraid of.

"If it wasn't Theodore you saw . . . or if you're not sure —"

"I'm sure." She slammed the register shut. "I'm going to need extra time on these roads to get home. So unless you're buying something . . ."

The pair was silent on the first part of the ride home. The roads were still slow going with the ice and snow. Everything was so white they almost missed the lorry in front of them. It wasn't until they rounded the bend that Siobhán spotted the vehicle's tail-lights.

"That could be Theodore Baskins," Siobhán said.

"What's he doing?" The lorry seemed to be weaving. Just then it stopped in the middle of the wee bridge. Macdara reached over, placed his hand on top of Siobhán's head, and gently pushed down. "He'll see you. This hair is like a beacon."

"Who cares if he sees me?"

"He's stopping in the middle of a bridge.

He's up to no good."

She couldn't tell if he was playing protector or messing with her. She stayed down. "You'd better narrate."

"He's getting out of the lorry."

"Here?" Why? There wasn't much space to scrunch down into. Whatever Baskins was doing, she hoped he hurried.

"He's getting something out of the back."

"What is it?"

"A large black rubbish bag. Very large." Macdara leaned forward. Siobhán had enough and sat up slowly, ready to duck if he was looking. Indeed, Baskins had a large rubbish bag, and as they watched he heaved it over the bridge and into the river below. Siobhán imagined she could hear the splash.

"What in the world?"

"Call 999," Macdara said. "He could be getting rid of evidence."

Theodore Baskins sat in the garda station interview room across from two guards while Siobhán and Macdara watched from behind one-sided glass. On the table in front of Baskins loomed the rubbish bag the guards had fetched from the creek. They'd gone through it, but they hadn't told Macdara or Siobhán what they'd found. Apparently, they decided to put on a bit of a show

277

instead. They grilled Baskins about dumping a rubbish bag into the river. He looked straight at the window, and even though Siobhán knew he couldn't actually see her, his gaze weighed her down.

"I did no such thing," Baskins said. He sounded outraged.

"Maybe the town is right about him," Siobhán said. "He's a very good liar."

"Doesn't necessarily mean he's a killer," Macdara said.

"But it doesn't help his case."

"It certainly does not."

"Whose is this?" A guard rattled the rubbish bag.

"I've no idea," Theodore said. His upper lip started to sweat.

"No idea?" One guard turned to the other. "Can you see the headlines in the paper tomorrow?"

"I can," the other guard said. "The spirit of Christmas is dead in West Cork."

The other nodded. "Indeed."

"What in the world?" Macdara said.

They watched as the guard nearest the evidence put on a pair of plastic gloves, reach in, and pull a slip of paper from the bag. "It's odd you say this isn't yours. Any idea how your pay stub made it into someone else's rubbish?"

Theodore folded his arms and stared at the window as if he knew someone was watching him. "I haven't the faintest idea."

"Do you know what the fines are going to be for polluting the creek?"

"Mighty high," the other answered. "And can ye imagine the judge isn't going to be happy hearing this case during Christmas?" The guard ripped the rest of the rubbish bag clean off. Standing on the table, next to a banana peel and with goo dripping off him, was Frosty the plastic snowman.

"Frosty," Siobhán said. "He didn't."

Macdara started to cough and covered his mouth. He was trying to swallow a laugh. "Theodore Baskins wouldn't appreciate a good Secret Santa gift if it bit him in the arse," Siobhán said.

"Oh, I think it's done that alright," Macdara said. "It's the gift that keeps on giving."

Theodore Baskins slumped. "Catherine insisted I get it out of the house. I put it in the field, but she said she could still see his beady eyes watching her and hear the creepy song. She was nearly out of her mind. So, yes. I tossed it over the bridge. Fine me and let me go. Unless, of course, you're bringing me up on charges for murdering old Frosty."

This time when he looked at the window, he flashed a grin.

"I knew he saw you," Macdara said. "I told you to stay down."

"Me? You're the one who plastered your face to the windshield." She crossed her arms. "Poor Frosty."

"Do you want him?" Macdara asked. "I can ask the guards if we can have him."

"Not on your life," Siobhán said. "He was perfect for Theodore."

Macdara looked at the snowman, then moved his head left and right while staring at the plastic snowman. "His eyes do seem to follow me."

Siobhán elbowed him. "Theodore Baskins is a liar and a polluter. But you're right."

"I'm right?" Macdara said, straightening up and grinning. "What am I right about?"

"Just because he's a liar and a polluter doesn't mean he's a killer."

"No," Macdara said. "But it doesn't mean he's *not* a killer."

On the way back from the garda station, Siobhán asked Macdara to drop her off at the mill. He pulled into the car lot and stared at the building. "If it's Christmas shopping you're doing, I definitely don't need a cloak or a harp," Macdara teased.

"I'm only doing it so you can pop out and get me something," she teased back.

"Why do I get the feeling you want to spy on Santa Claus?"

"The guards are closing in on Baskins. I need to know if Leah and Harry are having an affair."

Macdara drummed his fingers on the steering wheel. "I don't like leaving you alone."

"I can handle myself."

"I never said you couldn't. How will you get home?"

"I'll either get a ride or hoof it."

"No hitchhiking." Macdara leaned over and kissed her. "Be careful."

"You too. Don't spend a fortune."

He laughed. "You'd be worth it."

"Flattery, Detective Flannery, will get you far. Very far indeed."

Harry and Leah were the last to exit the mill. Siobhán had been waiting for them just outside the front door, and although she didn't actually jump out, the pair reacted as if she had. Leah let out a cry and Harry a low-pitched exclamation.

"Sorry to frighten you," Siobhán said.

Leah placed her hand on her heart. "Is everything alright?"

"No. I'm afraid there's been a witness who

281

has come forward."

Leah edged in closer. "Did someone else see Theodore Baskins that night?" For a moment Siobhán was taken aback. Someone *else*. Leah knew a witness had come forward with information on Theodore Baskins. How? Was it simply that this village couldn't help but gossip, or was there something more to it? Was Leah friendly with Alison? Could she have persuaded her to say it was Theodore she saw that night?

"No," Siobhán said. "Someone saw the two of you."

Harry Williams stiffened. Leah twirled a strand of purple hair around her finger. "Whatever do you mean?" she said.

"If the two of you are having an affair, it's going to come out. I think it's best if you tell the guards yourselves."

Leah dropped her hand. "I don't know what someone thinks they saw. Harry and I are good friends. That's all."

Maybe Ciarán had seen a mere peck on the cheek. No. He wouldn't have called that *kissing*. "Secrets have a way of coming out," Siobhán said. "And I'd hate to see you go down for murder if all you're doing is having an affair."

"Murder?" Harry Williams said. "You're speaking to the best violinist on the planet.

You should show a bit of respect."

Leah gave a soft laugh. "You're not helping her suspicions."

No, he wasn't. Harry Williams adored Leah Elliot. It was obvious. Siobhán couldn't blame him. Unless that adoration had led him to kill Enda Elliot. He'd get the job and the woman in one shot. To Siobhán's surprise, Leah linked her arm in Siobhán's. "Come on. I think we all need a nice pint and a cozy peat fire."

"I'm not sure that's a good idea," Harry said.

"It's the only idea," Leah said. "If you haven't noticed, Miss O'Sullivan is like a hound after the fox." She shivered. "I don't watch the hunts anymore. Let's hope the fox gets away this year."

"My money is on the fox," Harry said.

"Siobhán isn't your average hound," Leah said. "I'm afraid our little hidey-hole is no longer big enough to burrow in."

Siobhán really didn't like being compared to a hound, even if Leah meant it as a partial compliment. But even if Leah was a killer, Siobhán couldn't help but like her.

They had their pints, and the roaring fire, and a cozy little table in the corner. It was the same pub they'd visited after they had been downtown for the carolers. The same night Ciarán had seen Leah and Harry kissing.

"He was wearing a Santa hat, was he?" Leah surprised Siobhán by asking. Her eyes flicked to Harry.

"He was."

"There was mistletoe," Leah said with a shrug and a smile.

"So much mistletoe," Harry said.

"You would have kissed anyone who was standing under it, is that what you're trying to tell me?" Siobhán asked.

"Yes," Harry Williams said.

"Enough," Leah said, placing her hand briefly on Harry's arm. "She knows."

Harry sighed and leaned back in his chair. He put his arm around Leah. "In some ways, it's a relief," he said.

"How long have you two been seeing each other?" Siobhán asked.

"It's not what you think." Leah played with a defect on the table, using her finger to trace the wood. "Enda and I had an agreement."

Harry shifted in his seat, looking uncomfortable. "This is really none of her business."

"We were married for five years. The last three have been little more than a friendship. Enda was no longer interested in romance."

"I see."

"He was in love with my playing." She smiled. "He said it often."

"Did you . . . love him? Romantically?"

Leah nodded. "At first. Enda was a towering talent. Five years ago he still had that spark, that vitality. I'm sorry you never knew him."

"He was a genius," Harry said.

"We came to an understanding. We would be companions. And I was free to love whomever I wanted. As long as I was discreet."

Siobhán didn't dare look at Harry Williams. Besides his looks, Harry was Enda's main competitor. That hardly fit the definition of discreet.

"Enda knew about the two of you?"

Leah shook her head. "No. Discreet, remember? Enda didn't want to know any particulars. And we've always been on the down-low."

"Until the hound sniffed us out," Harry said, smiling at Siobhán. She really wished they'd stop calling her a hound.

"I don't suppose you have any proof?" Siobhán kept her voice light.

Leah laughed. "What? Like a contract

285

where Enda states in writing that his wife can take lovers as long as she's discreet?" She shook her head. "No. It was a verbal agreement."

"There was no reason for me to kill him," Harry said. "Leah and I have been together for two years. It may not be proper in the eyes of others, but it's worked for us."

"Exactly," Leah said. "Besides, we weren't even in town the night he was killed."

"Where were you?" Siobhán asked.

Leah tilted her head. "Are you officially on this case?" Siobhán wished people would stop asking her that.

"Are you officially going to tell the guards about your relationship?"

"We stayed at an inn about an hour away. We knew once we arrived we'd have to keep our distance."

Everyone seemed to be playing that game this year. Did any of them want to be together?

Leah took Harry's hand again, and this time she held it. "Looks like we failed miserably."

"The name of the inn?" Siobhán asked.

"We don't recall," Leah said.

Siobhán stared at them. They stared back. "We were in Kinsale," Harry said. "It was a private home they rent out."

Kinsale wouldn't take an hour from here. But was it likely they'd drive back and forth?

"If you ever need a getaway, I'd recommend it," Leah said.

"I thought you couldn't recall where you stayed?" Siobhán was going to have to put her like for Leah to the side. Just like Garda Cooley couldn't see beyond Theodore Baskins, Siobhán had to treat all of them like suspects. Being a friend and a fan wasn't going to help Siobhán find a killer.

"Harry's always had a better memory than me," Leah said, holding her hands out à la *What can you do?*

"Except when it comes to musical scores," Harry teased.

"True," Leah said, beaming. "Those I never forget." She leaned forward. "Speaking of scores. If you want to suspect someone — that is, besides Theodore, who if you ask me is our killer — why don't you take a closer look at Moira Elliot?"

CHAPTER 16

"Moira?" It certainly didn't take long before Leah pointed the finger at someone else. Her stepdaughter. The absurdity of calling Moira a stepdaughter wasn't lost on Siobhán. "Why should I be looking at Moira?"

Leah swallowed. "A week before Enda was murdered, he phoned me in the middle of night. He had just arrived in West Cork, and I was still in Dublin. At the time, I thought he was mistaken. He was rambling. Almost incoherent. He said, 'Can you believe it? Can you believe me own daughter wants to have me declared mentally unfit?' "

"I've heard rumors," Siobhán said, "that he was on a mental decline."

"It's nonsense," Leah said. "He was as sharp as ever. Who do you think started those rumors?" Leah mouthed the answer. *Moira.*

"Garda Cooley himself told me your

husband had been wandering about in the middle of the night. Jason added that sometimes he was wandering around with a hatchet. Are you telling me they're all lying?"

Leah sighed. "Enda liked to walk while composing in his head. That could explain walks in the middle of the night. Artists don't always get to choose. Inspiration often strikes at inconvenient times. I don't know about the hatchet. That might very well be a lie."

"You think his wandering around in the middle of the night could be explained by Enda composing?"

"Absolutely," Leah said. "Remember, he was close to retiring."

His swan song. "Do you have access to your husband's medical records?"

"I suppose. I've never tried to get ahold of them."

"Could you try?"

Leah leaned back in her chair and contemplated it. "What will it prove?"

"If there's no evidence of dementia, it will prove Moira was planting the seeds long before Enda died." The autopsy should show whether Moira was right about his declining health.

"I'll see what I can do." Leah's tone

289

conveyed she wasn't going to get it done in any kind of hurry.

"What about Enda's will?" Siobhán asked.

Leah folded her arms. "Last I heard, Enda's solicitor wanted to wait on the official cause of death to probate the will. I believe since he said that it's been ruled a homicide, but I haven't contacted the solicitor since then. I'd like to get the concert over with, and I suppose the solicitors don't want me to touch my inheritance if I'm suspected of killing him."

"It may be their preference, but I don't think they can hold up the will. Some cases never get solved," Siobhán said.

"I still want to deal with it after the concert," Leah said. "I can't even grieve yet."

"I'd like to get some rest now," Harry said, pushing back from the little table. "I'm going to go back to my room at the inn."

"I should get home too," Leah said. "Before someone wonders what we're all up to."

They stood and began bundling up in their coats, hats, and scarves. Harry held the door open for them.

"Are you going to tell everyone?" Harry asked as they stood outside the pub. "About our relationship?"

"No," Siobhán said. "Not at the moment." *Not unless she had to.* But no matter the spin they'd tried to put on it, the information about Leah and Harry having an affair was damaging. Was anyone really going to believe that Enda didn't mind if his wife was in love with another man? It seemed more likely that these two world-class musicians were trying to play a worn-out tune.

"I've heard so many things about Enda, I feel like I knew him personally," Siobhán said. She was standing in Catherine's kitchen, looking out the window to the field. Soon women from the village would gather to help make cookies for the Polar Bear Swim. Catherine was setting up stations with various equipment: rolling pins, cookie cutters, icing. Siobhán was early and hoped to get some info out of Catherine. She was especially interested in any local gossip concerning Enda and Leah's romance. Or were they chin-wagging about Leah and Harry? So far, Catherine hadn't taken the bait to gossip. Given she and Theodore were often the recipients of it, maybe she refused to stoop to that level. Good on her, but it made it difficult to investigate. Siobhán turned her attention to the view out the window. From here, Siobhán could see

Moira's backyard. She found herself staring at the spot where the Elliot grandchildren said they had buried the hatchet. The question was, Who had gone to the trouble to dig it up?

"None of us really knew Enda," Catherine said. "Although many thought they did."

What a thing to say. Then again, everyone else had plenty of things to say about Catherine and who she had decided to share her life with. Siobhán was trying to find a way of validating Leah's claim that Enda was no longer amorous, or jealous of his wife taking another lover. "Three wives. Sounds like Enda loved the ladies." She gave a little smile as if she was inviting Catherine into a secret.

"Enda was a passionate man. I do feel sorry for anyone that never saw him conduct. A man with that kind of fire, well, it catches onto everything else around him. And yes, he did like the ladies." Catherine shook her head as if trying to jostle the memory away.

"There was quite the age difference with Leah," Siobhán said lightly.

"I don't think that's why Enda married her. He connected with people, not ages. Look at Faye. She was his contemporary."

"Things didn't end well between them, I hear."

"There was a time I thought Enda and Faye would be together forever."

"Did the accident change their relationship?"

"I'm sure it did. But I think it started to change the moment Faye realized she wouldn't be able to carry his children."

"I imagine it must have been shocking for those times," Siobhán said. "When they decided to use a surrogate."

If Catherine had anything to offer on that subject, it was going to have to wait. The door opened and women filed in. Catherine began to assign stations, and Siobhán was delighted to be assigned to the icing. It wasn't long before the sweet scent of fresh-baked cookies filled the air. It was a grand thing to do for the brave souls who wanted to take on the challenge of the Polar Bear Swim on Christmas morning. Siobhán did not think any cookie incentive enough to dip into that frigid water, but she was happy to help make them. Soon Siobhán was icing reindeer, Santas, gift boxes, penguins, and of course polar bears. "These are adorable," Siobhán said, tempted to bite the head off a reindeer.

"They were a big hit last year," Catherine

said. "Don't be shy with the icing now. I think it's always the favorite bit."

Siobhán settled into a rhythm, following Catherine's very detailed photos of what color was supposed to go where on the cookies. Catherine was an artist, and it seemed she saw these cookies as an extension of her work. Siobhán would have been happy to eat penguins of any color icing, but she wasn't here to start a row. Every hobby had its control freaks, even the cookie-baking variety. As she worked, Siobhán couldn't keep her mind from returning to the case, going over each moment of the last few days beginning with their arrival at the mill.

"Woah," Catherine said. "Not that much icing." Siobhán looked down to see a huge clump of the sugary white stuff nearly suffocating a poor penguin.

"I'll take the hit." Siobhán shoved the penguin in her mouth before Catherine could deny her.

"Where's Paul and Orla?" Moira suddenly asked from where she stood rolling out the dough with precise, harsh strokes.

"He's bringing Irish cream to the mill," Elise said. "Orla tagged along." Elise was in charge of the sprinkles and seemed to be painstakingly dropping them onto the cookies bit by bit.

"I hope they're coming straight home," Moira said. "We have that meeting with the solicitor, and I want all the family members to be present."

This was news. "What meeting is that?" Siobhán asked.

Moira's face flushed as if she hadn't meant to blurt it out. "Just getting some of my father's affairs in orders." *Affairs.* She probably wasn't referring to Leah and Harry. Would she suspect Leah of murder if she knew?

"He's coming this close to Christmas?" Siobhán said. That was very unusual, everyone was quiet at Christmas.

Moira raised an eyebrow, and an amusement played out on her face. "He plans on coming to the Christmas concert," she said.

The concert. Their golden ticket. Would Enda be pleased or horrified that his death was drawing so much interest? "What exactly are you discussing in this meeting?" Siobhán knew she was pushing her luck asking such personal questions, but just because this wasn't her case didn't mean she wasn't going to keep her ears open.

Moira didn't answer. Instead she removed a mobile phone from her apron pocket and dialed. A few seconds later she shoved it back in. "Paul is not answering." She bit her lip. She seemed nervous, but there was no subtle way for Siobhán to find out why.

"Woah," Catherine said. "Now you're being a little grinchy with the icing."

Siobhán glanced down at her sparsely iced cookie, sighed, and put down her spatula. "Should I go and collect Paul and Orla from the mill instead?"

Catherine smiled, her right hand flexing as if ready to pounce on the spatula in Siobhán's hand. "That's a lovely idea."

Siobhán pulled her scarf up around her mouth, trying to shield herself from the bitter wind. She was out of breath and nearly frozen when she finally reached the mill. The large wooden door opened with a creak. From within the building, she heard voices raised in anger. Although she hadn't come here to spy on anyone, she made sure to shut the door as quietly as possible. She ventured forth toward the voices, one male and one female.

"He was a horrible, horrible man!" It was Orla and Paul. Siobhán froze. *Horrible, horrible man.* Was she talking about Enda? She crept forward. Paul and Orla stood face-to-face in the middle of a sea of wooden crates. He had certainly purchased enough bottles of Irish cream to get all of West Cork langered. Orla turned from her brother, crouched down, and slipped a sheet of paper into one of the crates. What was that? Siobhán had little choice but to step forward. If she turned back they might see her, but if they caught her spying, that would be worse.

"Hey there," Siobhán said, stepping into the light.

"Jaysus," Paul said with a shriek. He placed his hand over his heart. "You put the heart in me crossways."

"Sorry," Siobhán said. She wasn't sorry at all. She paused. "I heard arguing." There was no use pretending otherwise. "Is everything alright?" Orla still hadn't turned around, and Siobhán could see her shoulders heaving. Either she'd gotten into the bottles of Irish cream or she was crying about something else.

"We were discussing private sibling matters," Paul said. "You know yourself."

"I certainly do." She held up six fingers. "Imagine the sibling tiffs we go through?" She laughed. They did not. "Anything I can do to help?"

Paul Elliot looked at her intensely. The dim light of the mill cast a shadow across half his chubby face. "Whose side are you on?" It was more of an accusation than a question.

"Pardon?"

He took another step. "I know we're not family yet. But we will be." He glanced back at Orla as if to get her approval. She chewed on her lip and looked away.

"Yes." *Unless James and Elise break things off before they are wed, which isn't out of the realm of possibility.* "We are practically family." And one of my new family members may be a cold-blooded killer.

"I hope you're not conflicted."

"I'm not sure what you mean."

"You're a guard. But you're also family. And the family members of the victim tend to be the prime suspects, do they not?" He tilted his head. "I imagine that makes you a little conflicted."

"I don't take sides in investigations. I'm only interested in the truth."

He laughed, a sound that sent a chill through Siobhán. "Do you mean to tell me that when your brother James was accused of murder, you didn't take his side?"

She felt her jaw clench and realized her fists had curled in. *Don't let him bait you.* "That was years ago before I was a guard."

"Is he now an equal suspect?" Paul's questioning seemed to infuse him with energy. He pushed his shoulders back and cracked his knuckles.

Siobhán winced at the sound, having always hated the loud popping of joints. "Excuse me?"

"Elise was with us that evening. As you've already found that out."

"Yes, your emergency family meeting."

"At least we can verify one another's alibis. Who can verify James's?"

"Why would anyone need to verify his alibi?" *Don't let him get to you. Stay calm.*

"You're saying we're suspects but your brother is not?"

"My brother hadn't ever met your grandfather, nor could he have possibly known about the whiskey mill, let alone figure out how to lure him there."

"You say you're only interested in the truth."

"That's right."

"Sometimes the truth is murky." Orla ran past Siobhán, tears streaming down her face. A few moments later, a door slammed shut, leaving Siobhán alone with Paul.

"Why is your sister so upset?"

He glanced in the direction she ran as if she had left a shadowy trial in her wake. "She's grieving the death of her grandfather."

There was more to it than that and they both knew it, but Siobhán had yet to find a way to force the truth out of people. "I almost forgot why I'm here."

"Yes," Paul said. "Why are you here?"

"Your mother. She wanted to make sure you were home for the meeting with your solicitor."

"Say no more." He started off, then stopped when he realized she wasn't following. "Are you coming?" He glanced at his crates.

Don't worry, your Irish cream is safe with me. She wouldn't drink the sour potion again if he paid her. "No. I have other business to attend to here." Paul Elliot wasn't the only one who could keep secrets.

"Oh?" He lifted an eyebrow and waited to see if she would supply any more information.

She flashed a grin, if only to show him she wasn't afraid of him. "See you later." Paul kept his gaze on her for a minute, then turned and headed for the exit. She waited until she heard the old door shut behind him. She headed for the stairs up to the gallery. She'd return and figure out how to find the piece of paper Orla had slipped through one of the crates, but only when she was sure he was really gone.

The upstairs was jammed with boxes and discarded items, all covered in layers of dust. The building still smelled like oak barrels and whiskey. A large piece of plywood had been nailed across the section where Enda fell to his death. Siobhán peeked over and gave a shudder. Hitting one's head on the cement floor from this height would have been a frightening way to go. He landed on his back, and unless the pathologist had reason to believe his body flipped during the fall, that meant he had been standing with his back to the railing. The harp was now in the evidence room at the garda station. She doubted that anyone would pick it up, unless they gave Ruth permission to take it. If the fall was enough to kill Enda, why had the killer pushed the harp on top of him? Was he or she hoping the death would be ruled an accident?

She nosed around a few boxes, but nothing jumped out at her. She had just turned to go when something sparkly caught her eye. She bent down to get a closer look. *Green glitter.* Just like the kind she found in the patch of trees between Moira's and Enda's houses, where she'd glimpsed a person in an elf costume. Two questions jumped out at her. Was the elf a Peeping Tom? And was the Peeping Tom a killer? She gazed again at the place where Enda had fallen to his death. It looked directly down on the spot where the orchestra was to play. That's why, when the lights in the mill were flipped on, there had been a spotlight on Enda's body. Siobhán crouched. The plywood board blocked her view. But whoever had been up here would have been able to see below. Why here? Why this exact spot? What if it wasn't just Enda the killer was after, but what if the killer had a much more sinister plot, this time against the entire orchestra?

Chapter 17

Siobhán took photos of the glitter with her mobile phone and immediately called Barry Cooley. His voice mail picked up after the first ring. She sent him a text to give her a call. Glitter wasn't hard-and-fast evidence — the guards would be laughed out of court if they tried to claim it was — but if the same elf-peeper dropped it, and they ever caught the person, no doubt the guards would want to question him or her, and Siobhán hoped they could use the glitter to exert maximum pressure during the interrogation.

The problem with Christmas was that glitter was everywhere. Siobhán highly doubted that there were any tests they could conduct to match up particles of glitter, but the beauty of interrogations was that slight truth-bending when questioning suspects was allowed.

Are you aware that we can trace glitter? Yes,

it's true. Amazing what technology can do these days and all that glitters is not gold. . . .

Siobhán headed down to the crates. Her second problem was how to answer Garda Cooley when he inevitably asked her what she was doing up in the gallery. She sighed. The truth would have to do: She had come to fetch Paul and Orla and observed a piece of paper being slipped into one of the crates, so she concocted a cover story in order to hang around and find it for the guards.

He'd want them to do the searching, but then she may never get to see what's on it. She had to know. She reached the sea of crates and stared at them, trying to remember exactly where Orla had been standing.

What were her chances of finding the one with the errant slip of paper? She couldn't break into every crate. She had a feeling Paul Elliot would blow up when he realized that even one of his crates had been messed with. She wished she had a proper torch, but the flashlight function on her smartphone would have to do. She headed for the area where she'd seen Orla standing, then knelt and began shining the light through the small cracks in the crates. It wasn't until the fourth crate that she saw a flash of white amongst the bottles. It took her another twenty minutes to find a long piece of steel. She used it as pry bar, and on her third attempt the wood splintered. Siobhán looked down at the damaged box. She hoped that whatever was in there was worth incurring Paul's wrath. She pulled at the broken pieces of wood until she could finally stick her hand into the crate. She pawed around until she felt a piece of paper, then lifted it out. She hurried and opened it. The top was embossed in gold.

ENDA ELLIOT

It was on Enda's official letterhead. The letter was handwritten, in neat black cursive:

To Orla Elliot:
As per our agreement, you must maintain high marks at Trinity College if you wish me to continue to fund your education. I have yet to receive your marks for the fall. Until I receive them, your funding is on hold. I will leave it to you to tell your mother. As you are probably aware, if you do not, I certainly will.

Sincerely,
Enda Elliot

This was how a grandfather spoke to a granddaughter? Even though that's not the part the guards would be interested in, it was the first thing that struck Siobhán. How sad. Where was the love, the support, the kisses and hugs? No wonder Orla was crying. Moira was so proud of her daughter's attendance at Trinity, no doubt making the secret torture for Orla to keep. Unfortunately, it also gave Orla strong motive to kill her grandfather. From everything Siobhán could tell, Moira certainly did not know that her father was not going to pay the next tuition installment. Did he tell anyone else? Would they all soon learn this at the meeting with the solicitor? How Siobhán wished she could be in that meeting. She shoved the letter in her pocket and checked the phone. There was no message from Barry Cooley. Perhaps he was in the middle of an interrogation. Her phone rang the minute she was outside. It was a local West Cork number.

"Hello?"

"It's Theodore." He sounded strange. He was whispering.

"Yes?" She barely had reception, and it was a struggle to hear him.

"A guard car just pulled up our drive. I think Barry Cooley is here to arrest me."

"I'm sorry. Don't resist. Ask for a solicitor."

"You have to help me. I didn't do this. I swear." The phone clicked off. Siobhán texted Dara to meet her at Catherine's house and hoped he'd get the message.

Catherine stood outside of her home covered in flour and crying. Others stood around her, trying to coax her back into the warmth of the kitchen. Theodore Baskins had indeed just been arrested for the murder of Enda Elliot.

"They said they have a witness who saw Theodore hitchhiking on the bridge," Catherine said. "Whoever it is, he's lying."

Or she. Alison. Macdara and Siobhán exchanged a look. "He'll need a solicitor," Macdara said. "There's nothing anyone else can do."

"We need to find out who this witness is," Catherine said. She was still wielding a rolling pin. Macdara gently took it out of her hand, and then others encouraged her to get inside. Macdara and Siobhán remained outdoors. She filled him in on the glitter, Orla's letter, and her fear that the killer had something in store for the Christmas Eve concert. *Tomorrow.* If it was all building toward a crescendo until they knew the exact master plan, everyone was in immediate danger. Could she convince the others

307

to cancel the concert? Leah would be the linchpin. If the widow canceled it, everyone would respect her wishes. Siobhán had a feeling that Leah would no more cancel the concert than Siobhán would stop looking into this case.

"We need to get back to that shop and talk to Alison once more," Macdara said.

"Right with you." Siobhán checked in with her brood. They were happily playing board games in the guest cottage.

Siobhán eyed the deck of cards and the Scrabble and Monopoly boards. "Where did you get those?"

"Catherine Healy," Ciarán piped up. "She gave them to us so we wouldn't linger in her kitchen eating all the Polar Bear cookies."

Siobhán laughed. "Lucky you."

Ciarán shrugged. "Personally, I would have gone for the cookies." Siobhán kissed him on the head before he could shove her off, announced that she and Macdara were going into town, and slipped out.

Alison waited until she rang up a customer and he was out the door before turning to them. "You two. Again."

"What can we say," Siobhán said. "We just love shopping."

"Do we love anything in particular?" Macdara asked.

Siobhán laughed. "I'm sure anything you get me will be fine."

"Fine," Macdara muttered. " 'Fine' has me shaking in me boots."

"Cut it out," Alison said. "You're not here to shop. I consider this harassment."

"Lying to the guards is a lot worse," Macdara said.

"It's not lying if . . ." She clamped her mouth shut. Siobhán and Macdara stepped forward together.

"If?"

"Can I really get in trouble? If someone — with authority — is the one who told me what to say?" Her voice squeaked.

Siobhán shut her eyes for a second. It was worse than she thought. Barry Cooley had convinced Alison to lie. Even if Theodore Baskins *was* guilty, Barry had just blown it. "It's very serious to lie," Macdara said. "Especially if a guard asked you to do it."

Alison swallowed. "I wouldn't have done it, except Garda Cooley said they knew that Theodore was guilty. They knew it for a fact and I would be helping put a murderer behind bars."

"He doesn't know it for a fact," Siobhán said. "And he'll be taken off the case."

309

"Because of me?"

"You're going to need to put the Closed sign on the shop and come with us," Macdara said.

"Where?"

"To the station. You have one chance to make this right. We'll ask a judge for leniency."

"I saw *someone* hitchhiking on that bridge. It wasn't all a lie."

"I'm going to ask this once," Siobhán said. "Did you without a doubt see Theodore Baskins hitchhiking on the bridge?"

"No," Alison said. "Just a dark figure." She slumped. "I don't even know if it was a cloak. I thought it was a trench coat at the time."

"We can make a case that you felt unduly pressured and intimidated," Macdara said. "Garda Cooley shouldn't have manipulated you. But if we walk out this door without you, then our next stop is the garda station and you're on your own."

Alison gave it two beats. She shut and locked the register. "Let's go."

Thirty minutes later, at the garda station, Barry Cooley was being led away in handcuffs. It wasn't something Siobhán ever wished to see. They would transfer Barry

Cooley to the garda station in Cork City. Barry Cooley caught sight of Siobhán as he was about to exit the main door. He glared at her. "He's guilty you know." Siobhán did not reply. "I did what I had to do. To protect this village." The guard holding him seemed inclined to let him have his say. They were being forced to take Garda Cooley away, but that didn't mean any of them liked it. He rattled his handcuffs. "If Theodore Baskins kills again, it's on *you*." The words rang in her ears as Cooley was finally taken out, and the door slammed shut behind him.

Macdara had been on the phone with a superintendent, and he was now officially heading up the Enda Elliot case. Because of the weather and the proximity to Christmas, it would have been impossible to get another Detective Sergeant to West Cork. They were grateful to have him. Macdara sat at the desk in the main office across from Siobhán. Orla's letter was in front of him. Siobhán quickly jotted down a list:

Find the elf — glitter
Protect the Christmas Eve concert
Check into Paul Elliot's finances
Question Orla about the letter. Check with
* Trinity College about her tuition*
Get Enda Elliot's hospital records

311

Macdara glanced at the list and sighed. "Any chance we'll get this all done before Christmas?"

Siobhán shook her head. "Not without a sleigh and a load of reindeer."

He sighed and glanced at the list again. "The concert is nigh. We'd better get cracking."

"What's going on?" Why are you trying to bring Orla in for questioning?" Elise stood in the doorway to the guest house. Siobhán had just returned and showered, and she had planned on finding Macdara's mam along with her own brood to catch up on what was going on and maybe spend some time with them, hoping against logic that Nancy Flannery wouldn't be too upset that her son was now heading up Enda Elliot's murder probe. Macdara was still at the garda station and had just sent word that he'd like to speak with Orla. Siobhán noted Elise's excited state and realized she needed to play it cool. Unfortunately, she'd learned through many years of experience that yelling at someone to "Calm down!" would do the exact opposite.

"It's normal procedure to reinterview all parties when a new Detective Sergeant is on the case."

"Your fiancé," Elise said in a scathing tone. She and Paul were apparently on the same sleigh, careening downhill straight at this investigation. "Garda Cooley arrested the murderer. It's bad enough you let him go. Now you want to drag my siblings into this?" Elise's face was nearly purple with rage.

"Garda Cooley coerced a witnesses into lying," Siobhán said. "There's no hard evidence that Theodore Baskins did anything to your grandfather. The case is far from closed."

Elise shook her head. "He did it. Everyone knows it but you."

"Even if he did," Siobhán said, doing her best to keep her voice level, "Garda Cooley broke the law. Justice doesn't work that way."

"What about justice and peace for us?"

"Orla will be fine," Siobhán said. "Everyone is going to have to answer questions." James appeared and stood next to Elise. He put his arm around her waist but remained quiet.

"Orla is not fine," Elise said. "She's crying."

Perhaps she's crying because her tuition to college isn't going to be paid. "Macdara will need to start at the beginning, and that involves calling in witnesses." Siobhán wasn't going to let Elise bully her.

Elise barged in, put the kettle on, and began rummaging through cupboards. Soon Siobhán wondered if it was just to slam them. Siobhán stepped into the small family room to gaze at the tree, hoping the twinkling lights would bring her some comfort. "I haven't been called in, nor has Paul, and Orla is freaking out."

"I see." Elise was the one freaking out. "She will soon find it to be a nonthreatening experience. They'll even offer her tea and biscuits." Siobhán made a mental note to text Macdara and suggest that he offer Orla tea and biscuits. "There is no reason whatsoever for *anyone* to freak out." *Unless of course Orla pushed her grandfather from a gallery because he threatened to stop paying her college tuition.* Then perhaps a bit of freaking out was in order.

"Why don't you just speak to her here?" Elise checked her phone, then headed for the door to the guest house. She threw it open to reveal Orla on the doorstep. She was hunched over, her hair was in disarray, and perspiration dribbled down her cheek. Perhaps Elise had been correct in her estimation.

"Orla," Siobhán said. She tried to touch

her hand, but Orla yanked it away. "Would you like a cuppa?"

"I've already made it," Elise said, pushing Siobhán aside and handing Orla a cup of tea. She maneuvered her to the sofa. Orla began to cry, her shoulders heaving and a mourning noise pouring out of her. Siobhán tried to make eye contact with James, but he was counting specks of dust on the windowsill.

"There's nothing to worry about," Siobhán said gently. "I can accompany you to the station if you'd like."

Orla sniffed and didn't reply.

"I can save you loads of time," Elise said. "And James can confirm it. None of us did it." She put her hands on her hips. "There." In her mind, that settled the matter.

"It's fine," Orla said, gathering strength from somewhere. She straightened up, finished her tea as if it were a shot of Jameson, and plunked it on the coffee table. "You can take me in. Ask me anything you'd like." She stuck her hands out as if she expected Siobhán to cuff them.

Orla's lip quivered as the letter from Enda slid across the table. Siobhán watched from the room behind the window. Macdara had indeed offered her tea and biscuits, but Orla

315

refused. Now she locked eyes with Macdara, then stared at the window. "You went through the crates?"

Macdara gave her a kind smile. "Does it matter?" Orla shrugged, sniffled, and wiped her nose with the back of her sleeve. "If I've learned anything from my years of investigating, it's that secrets always come out," Macdara said.

"I suppose they do." Orla remained hunched over. It was startling how she could go from a perky twentysomething to a little old lady with just the hunch of her shoulders.

Macdara gave it a beat. "When did you receive the letter?"

"The night we buried the hatchet." She seemed to startle herself with the phrase, then laughed.

"I want to get back to that," Macdara said. "But first, tell me about the letter."

"What do you want to know?" Orla's posture changed. She sat back, folded her arms, and stared without blinking.

Macdara, of course, wasn't thrown. "Take me back to the beginning. How and when did you receive it?"

Orla dropped her hands. "It was shortly after I arrived home. I went over to see my grandfather."

She seemed content to answer the question but not elaborate. That was more sophisticated of her than Siobhán would have imagined. "What day did you arrive?"

"Wednesday morning. He barely said hello before he strode to his desk, removed the letter, and presented it to me." She shook her head and wiped a tear from her cheek. "I thought it was a Christmas gift."

"How did the letter make you feel?"

"I know what you want me to say." She folded her arms again.

"I don't have any preconceived notions of what you're going to say."

"Of course you do."

"Then tell me what you think I want you to say." Orla was getting defensive, which was often when witnesses would blurt out unintended statements.

"I say it made me angry, then you say, 'Angry enough to kill?' "

"And then what do you say?" Siobhán had to hand it to Macdara, he was keeping steady.

"I say, 'Don't be ridiculous.' "

Macdara nodded, then circled back to an earlier question. "How did the letter make you feel?"

Orla sighed, then ran her hand through her long blond hair. "It made me feel bad, but not for the reasons you think."

"Oh?"

"I'm taking a break from Trinity."

"Because your grandfather was no longer going to pay your tuition?"

She shook her head. "That had nothing to do with it. I swear."

"You're saying this letter isn't the reason you're taking a break from Trinity?"

Orla ran her index finger along the table. "I knew my secret would come out. You don't need to be a guard to know that. I just hoped I would make it through Christmas."

Even though she could not be seen through the window, Siobhán found herself leaning forward. Macdara stayed still. "What secret is that, Orla?"

She shoved the letter back across the table as if the very proximity of it was offensive. "I didn't send him my grades because, as I've already told you, I didn't intend to continue at Trinity."

"Did something happen?"

She drummed her fingers on the table. "Do I have to tell you? I haven't even told Mam yet."

"I'm afraid you'll need to be as forthcoming as possible for us to eliminate you as a suspect."

318

"Why? My grandfather didn't know either."

"He knew you hadn't sent your grades in yet."

"Call the school, then. You'll see I got the high marks needed to keep my tuition funded."

"I can do that. I probably will do that. I still need the entire story."

"I've told my siblings."

"Was this secret the reason for the family meeting the night Enda was murdered?"

Orla's eyes widened as she realized how it was all starting to piece together. "Which one of them said something? Was it Paul?"

Macdara leaned forward. "Were you really worried about your grandfather and that hatchet?"

She sighed. "We saw him wandering around with it."

Macdara looked down at his notes. "It says here that Jason saw him wandering around with it."

"Jason was first to see him, he told us, then we stood watch and we saw him."

"That night?"

She gulped. "Yes. That night."

"Despite telling us you did *not* see him that night. Paul said you left to take Elise back to the inn and you must have just missed him."

Thank goodness Macdara had all of Siobhán's notes in front of him. It was hard to keep track of the story with witnesses who constantly lied and switched the narrative.

"You weren't on the case then," Orla pointed out. "We didn't officially lie to the guards. Just you and Siobhán."

Siobhán hated to admit it, but Orla had a point there. However, Macdara was now officially on the case and Orla was stalling.

"Why did you lie in the first place?"

"Because Elise said it would make us look guilty."

Macdara took a note. "You saw your grandfather with the hatchet. What time was this?"

"I wasn't paying attention. It was dark and cold, and we were just about to take Elise back to the inn." Orla glanced at the window as if she knew Siobhán was in there. "She wanted to get back to James before he woke up."

Once again Macdara looked at his notes. "Paul stated that you took Elise back to the inn just before midnight."

"It must have been, so."

"Did you approach him?"

"No. I wanted to, but Paul said he might

320

be sleepwalking and we shouldn't startle him."

"How good of a look did you get at him?"

"A glimpse."

"Just a glimpse?"

"It was dark. He was in his coat in his back garden. We could clearly see the hatchet because he was standing near his back light." This was more to the story than they'd previously known. That is, if Orla was telling the truth.

"You're positive it was your grandfather?"

"It was definitely his coat. Who else would be wearing it?" She gasped. "Could it have been Jason?" She ran her fingers through her hair. "He lied about his alibi, right? Maybe he never left West Cork."

"Did you enter your grandfather's house that night?" Orla bit her lip and shook her head. "Then how did you get the hatchet?"

"He'd dropped it right where he was standing. Or Jason was standing." She folded her hands across her stomach and pressed, as if hugging herself.

"After he dropped it, where did he go?"

"He went toward his lorry." *Was that when he noticed his flat tire?* "That's when Paul dashed over, grabbed the hatchet, and came back."

"Did you see him after that?"

321

"No. Paul brought the hatchet back and we discussed Grandfather's wanderings, and Paul decided it wasn't safe to let him take to the night with a hatchet, so Paul grabbed a shovel from Mam's shed and we buried it. As you know."

"And you called this family meeting just to tell them you were taking a break from Trinity."

"No," she said, placing her hands over her stomach. "I called the family meeting to tell them *why* I was taking a break from Trinity."

"And why is that?"

Orla nodded to the window. "Ask her. I'm sure she's already figured it out."

Cheeky. But she was correct. Siobhán had caught Orla's subtle movements. Her hands constantly going to her stomach. Macdara, from the look on his handsome face, had yet to put it together.

Orla Elliot was carrying a little bundle. Only this Christmas she feared the news might not bring everyone joy.

CHAPTER 18

Siobhán and Macdara walked the rocky coast along the ocean's edge. The water was turbulent, which matched Siobhán's mood exactly. The Christmas Eve concert was this evening, less than twelve hours away, and they were no closer to nabbing a killer.

"Maybe Barry Cooley was right," Siobhán said, kicking a rock out of her way. "Maybe it's as simple as Theodore Baskins is our killer." After all, just because he went about proving it in the wrong way didn't mean he had the wrong killer.

"Is that what you really believe?" Macdara asked.

"No."

"Walk me through it."

"Theodore Baskins doesn't have a motive as far as I can see. He's just annoying. And if being a total eejit was a crime, we'd run out of jail cells."

"Maybe he was in love with Leah," Macdara tossed out.

"I can see him getting a crush on Leah, but he really wasn't around her much. Moira said her visits were sparse. Enda usually came here alone."

"And if being in love with Leah is a motive, then we have to give equal consideration to Harry Williams," Macdara said.

Siobhán stopped to wave at a fisherman in a Santa cap. He waved back. They continued walking. "If it's one of the Elliot grandchildren, then I'd say they're all in it together." It was a horrifying thought.

Macdara raised an eyebrow. "Because?"

"They're all together for this emergency family meeting. They see Enda that evening, and if they aren't the killers, they could very well have been the last ones to see him alive. But instead of giving us this information, they lie to us about it. Why pretend they didn't even see him? All three of them have been tight-lipped, the *Musketeers*. Given the way they're sticking to one another like superglue, it doesn't seem likely that one of them would wander off to the mill without the other two knowing and sanctioning it."

"I see your logic," Macdara said. "I can only imagine how difficult this could turn out to be for you."

"Especially James," Siobhán said. "But

before we make the same mistake Garda Cooley did, we have to look at all our suspects. After all, Jason and Faye lied about their alibis as well."

"Let's not forget Leah and Harry," Macdara added. "'Tis the season for lying."

"Given that, I think we need to dig into the *reason* each of them lied. Because all of them lied to cover *something* up, but only one of them lied because that something was a murder."

"Only one of them, unless it's our Three Musketeers."

"Correct." They stopped to gaze out at the ocean. "Let's hope it's not one of the Elliot grandchildren," Siobhán said. "And let's hope a baby will be seen as welcome news."

"One life taken and another coming into the world," Macdara said. "But Orla is so young."

"Yes. She is." Siobhán hesitated. "I don't think she's our killer."

"Unless Enda Elliot did know about the baby and threatened to cut her out of the will," Macdara mused.

"If you say raging hormones . . .'"

"I wouldn't dare."

A voice rang out, the sound of someone calling their names. Elise ran toward them,

James trailing in her wake. Her fringe was matted to her forehead by sweat. She had a wild look in her eyes. "Look," she said. "I've solved the case."

Macdara arched an eyebrow. "Oh?"

Elise waved her hands. "It's not too difficult. All you have to do is bit of poking around."

"What exactly have you been poking?" Siobhán asked before she realized how that sounded. She did not dare look at James.

"I found this." Elise shoved a business card at her.

HARRY WILLIAMS
CONDUCTOR
RTÈ NATIONAL SYMPHONY

"So?" Macdara said. "What does that prove?"

"He didn't have these printed in town. I've asked every printer. Which means they were printed before he arrived. When my *grandfather* was still conductor. The only way he could have thought to have these made prior to arriving was if he knew something horrible was going to happen to my grandfather."

Macdara took the card. "Where did you find it?" Elise shrugged, looked at her feet.

"It's not ethical to go through people's things," Macdara informed her. "Or safe."

Elise's head shot up. "Somebody had to. You're wasting all your time going after my sister."

"Don't say a word about this to anyone, and no more poking around," Macdara said. "I mean it."

Elise shrugged, then grabbed James's hand and took off. Macdara turned to Siobhán, flashing the business card. "What do you think?"

"Leah was convinced that Enda's big announcement was that he was retiring. Maybe Harry made these in anticipation."

"What if it was more sinister?"

"We can take a highly suspicious tact when we question him. See what he reveals," Siobhán said.

"He's a conductor. He's used to performing under pressure."

"Let's put that to the test."

"So much for a peaceful walk on the beach."

"We can be in peace when this case is closed."

Macdara grabbed her hand and kissed it. "If you believe dat, you might as well believe in Santy."

"Macdara Flannery. Are you saying you don't believe in Santy?"

Harry Williams stared at the business card. They'd met him in town at a café, where Harry sat at a two-seater with a pot of tea and the newspaper. He leaned back and straightened his tie.

"I believe Leah already told you that Enda was retiring."

"She told us she *thought* that's what his announcement would be," Siobhán said. "Both of you insisted you didn't know for sure."

"I met with the symphony last week. It was all very unofficial, but they wanted to know if I would be willing to take the position in the event of Enda's retirement."

Macdara tapped the business card. "I'd say you're willing."

"One might even say eager," Siobhán added. "I don't know many people who get their business cards made up *before* the job offer is official."

"I can't imagine Enda would have reacted well to that had he seen one of these cards," Macdara said.

"He would have thrown a fit, maybe even made threats," Siobhán said.

Harry Williams folded his newspaper.

"Enda didn't see my cards. Nobody saw my cards. I demand to know how you got this. I've kept them tucked into my wallet." He looked startled, then pulled out his wallet and started to go through it.

"Is anything else missing?" Macdara asked.

"No." He held his wallet, then lightly tapped it on the table. "When did I have this out of my possession? Only at the inn." He stared at Siobhán. "Where Elise is staying with her fiancé. James O'Sullivan, isn't it?"

Siobhán felt heat crawl up her neck. Elise had snuck into Harry Williams's room at the inn? That was way over the line. Elise was turning herself inside and out. Because she was trying to protect her siblings. But why was she going to such lengths? Because she knew they had secrets that were damaging enough to make one of them want to kill?

"That's it, isn't it?"

They did not answer. But Siobhán was furious with Elise.

"Can anyone else verify this news?" Macdara asked.

"We can call the symphony," Siobhán said.

Harry bowed his head. "Please don't do that."

"Why ever not?" Siobhán asked.

Harry sighed. "There's another bit of news that I didn't want Leah to find out. If you call the symphony and they reveal it, I only hope you'll have the good sense to keep it to yourself."

"This I've got to hear," Macdara said. "From you," he added when Harry did not answer.

"Before he retired, Enda confided in me that he planned on demoting Leah to second chair."

Siobhán gasped. "Why? She's brilliant."

"She is. And I don't know yet if it's reversible. But if it is, I intend to keep her first chair." He spread out his hands. "I hope you can see my dilemma. Why upset her with this if I can make it go away instead?"

What if Leah had found out? It would have driven her mad. Mad enough to kill? Siobhán flashed back to Leah crying while playing the violin for a donkey. She assumed she was grieving over her husband's death. But what if the tears were another kind? What if she had been raging against her demotion instead? Siobhán hated to admit it, but the facts were clear. Leah and Enda were no longer romantically involved. She said it herself — he'd lost that fire that first attracted her to him. He was on a mental decline. And he was retiring from the orchestra. If on top of all that she found out one of his last acts would be to have her demoted to second chair? Siobhán couldn't imagine the wound a betrayal like that would have inflicted. She could even imagine Leah pushing Enda to his death. Siobhán didn't want to admit it, but she could imagine it.

"You're positive you and Leah were in Kinsale during the murder?" Siobhán asked.

"Yes, quite positive."

"Kinsale isn't a far drive," Macdara said.

"It's very close," Siobhán agreed.

"What you're suggesting is impossible," Harry said. "Leah did not drive here behind my back."

"How do you know?" Macdara asked. "Were you not sleeping?"

"If she knew about the demotion, I think I would have known. She couldn't have kept that bottled up. She's a violinist, not an actress."

"You'd be surprised what people keep bottled up," Siobhán said. "That's why it's best not to shake them." And news such as this would have been like an earthquake.

"It's not what you think," Harry said. "Not exactly."

"How is it, then?" Macdara said. "Because

half the time I don't even know what I'm thinking."

"Is that why you let me do most of the thinking?" Siobhán quipped.

"That's probably why, boss," Macdara said. He turned back to Harry. "Why isn't it what we're thinking?"

"Enda wasn't trying to seek some revenge against Leah. He called me the day before the murder. He was worried about Leah. He thought she was too stressed by the orchestra but would never give herself a break. Unless she was forced to."

"You actually think a demotion would calm Leah down?" Siobhán asked.

"Of course not. But that's what Enda thought. I tried everything I could to reason with him." He folded his arms. "He did not sound like himself. He was rambling about all the mistakes he'd made, how everyone in his orbit was falling apart and he didn't want to leave them like that and he didn't know how to put them back together."

"Was that all?"

"Just one more thing. I don't know what he meant. And before you ask, I didn't get the chance to ask him. He hung up on me. It was the last thing Enda Elliot ever said to me." They waited. Harry Williams gave it a dramatic pause. "He said he knew what was wrong with him. He said taking your secrets to the grave was the worst advice he'd ever heard. He said his secrets were killing him."

Siobhán leaned in. "What secrets?"

"That's what I asked," Harry said. "He said I'd have to wait and see."

Macdara seemed to grow impatient with the dramatic pauses. "Wait for what?"

"Why the Christmas Eve concert, what else? Enda told me that's where he planned on letting all of his secrets come out, in front of a captive Christmas Eve audience. His last words to me were, 'Every last one of them.' "

CHAPTER 19

"What did the pair of yous do?" Moira stood, hands on hips on the footpath, blocking Macdara and Siobhán from the sweetest little gift shop filled to the rim with chocolates. From the look on Moira's face, the woman could use a few herself. They had left Harry about an ago and had spent precious little time trying to gauge what to get each other for Christmas by popping into shops and eyeballing each other for reactions. It yielded very little results, except Siobhán had a feeling they were giving each other chocolates. Gazing at Moira, Siobhán put it together. *Orla.* Did Moira know about the baby?

"We simply had a few questions for her," Siobhán said. "Orla did fine. I'm sure everything is going to be grand."

"Orla?" Moira said. "I'm not talking about Orla." She narrowed her eyes. "What do you mean everything is going to be grand?"

"What can we do for you, Moira?" Macdara asked.

The distraction worked. Moira stopped glaring at Siobhán and turned to Macdara. "Leah says the concert is off. Something about the two of you riling everyone up has put her in a sour state."

Getting demoted to second chair more likely. Or was it because they were just grilling her secret lover?

"I'm running an investigation into who murdered your father," Macdara pointed out. "Can't the concert go on without Leah?"

"Without the *widow*?" Moira said. "No. It cannot go on without the widow."

"I would speak to her, but I don't know if it would do any good," Siobhán said.

"You'll have better luck than any of us," Moira said. "We have to go on with the concert. It's what my father would have wanted."

Siobhán nodded. "Very well, I'll have a word with her now."

"There's something else you have to do now," Moira said. "There's another reason I'm here."

"And that is?" Macdara prompted when she didn't come out with it right away.

"Catherine came over in a state. Apparently, Theodore didn't show up at the fish market. His boss is livid. And Catherine insists that Theodore would never miss work."

Had he left town? What if he was the killer? If he was and they let him go, Siobhán didn't know how she'd ever make peace with it.

"I'm only assigned to the one case," Macdara said. "But maybe we can stop by and speak to his boss."

"I'm sure Catherine would appreciate that."

"While we're still here," Siobhán said, hoping Moira would take her question in stride, "how far did you go in checking out your father's health scare?"

Moira began to blink. "What health scare?"

"His mental state. The night wanderings. Roaming around with a hatchet. I'm sure it alarmed you. Did you try to get him to a doctor?"

Moira lifted her chin. "Of course I tried. But he said he was fine, and so far I'd left it at that. I was waiting until after the concert to see if I could get Jason to help convince my father that he needed to have some tests done."

"Did Jason agree?"

"Of course. We were going to have a family meeting after the holidays."

Another family meeting. Only for this one they were too late.

Just pulling up to the fish market gave Siobhán an unpleasant flashback. The boss was waiting for them in front of the warehouse, and he looked browned off. "Barry had to go accusing him of murder and now he's done a runner."

"Do you know that's what happened?" Siobhán asked. "Or are you making assumptions?"

The man sighed. "I don't care what they say about him. He's arrived a little late, hungover, and cranky as all get-out, but he always shows up."

"When was he expected?"

The boss glanced at his watch. "Three hours ago."

"And you've tried calling him?"

"Of course I gave him a bell. His phone is going straight to voice mail."

"Do you mind if we have a look around?" Macdara asked.

"Look at what?"

"Does Theodore Baskins have a locker?"

The boss squinted, then shrugged, then nodded, all in the span of a few seconds.

337

"I'll take you to it. You," he said, pointing to Siobhán. "Would you like another shift?"

She shuddered. "Definitely not."

He sighed. "Christmas should have been canceled this year."

"Siobhán," Macdara said. "Would you try calling Catherine while I have a poke around?"

"Not a bother." She didn't want to enter the warehouse again. She didn't trust the boss not to suit her up in gloves and an apron and start flinging salmon at her head. She stepped away from the warehouse to place the call.

Catherine's phone also went to voice mail. Siobhán left a message that they were at Theodore's place of work and for Catherine to give her a call back. If she was so worried about Theodore, why wasn't she answering her phone? Siobhán didn't think she'd ever get used to living in a place where it was difficult to get a signal.

Macdara emerged from inside the warehouse a few minutes later. "Catherine?" he asked.

"No answer."

"Come have a look at this." Macdara led her into an office and pointed to another room that was lined with gray lockers. He lifted up a small silver key. "He's number 104."

"You waited for me," Siobhán said.

"It's Christmas, isn't it? I know how much you like opening things." Macdara handed her the key. She stepped up and opened the locker. An avalanche of items rained out. Coats, wellies, hats, aprons, gloves, all coated in shiny green specks. Platform shoes and an elf costume were the last items to fall. Macdara locked eyes with Siobhán, then stooped and lifted the outfit. "At least we know you weren't losing your marbles."

"Didn't realize that was under consideration," Siobhán said.

Macdara grinned. "It's always under consideration."

"Noted." She tried to calm the worry tumbling inside her. She knelt next to the items. "The platform shoes are here, but not the cloak."

"This is the same green glitter and elf costume you saw spying on the houses?"

Siobhán nodded. And they'd found it in Theodore's locker. And it looked like Theodore had just done a runner. If Garda Cooley had been right all along, they'd never be able to show their faces in West Cork again, even if he did go about it the wrong way. Especially when the deceased was Enda Elliot. "Did we just let a killer go?"

"We outed a corrupt guard. Don't get distracted." Macdara was trying to sound confident, but Siobhán could hear the same doubt in his voice.

If Theodore was guilty, so be it. They'd get him again. Garda Cooley's arrest never would have stood up in court. This time they would do it by the book. She went back through the events she'd encountered ever since they'd arrived. "Not only did I see this green glitter in the woods, I also saw it in the mill. And up in the gallery where the killer was waiting to push Enda over the balcony."

Macdara snapped photos of the items with his smartphone. "I'll get some guards out to process the locker. If Theodore is doing a runner, he's got a three-hour head start, so there's no use setting up checkpoints on the roads. I better get to the station and get some balls rolling, see what shakes out."

"You can drop me off at Catherine's and I'll see what I can suss out on that end."

Macdara nodded, then took her hand. "Don't let this get to you. If Theodore is our guy, we're going to get him."

"Do we need to cancel the concert?" she asked.

"I don't know if I have it in me to deal with the wrath that would generate. Unless you work on Leah. If the widow is still insisting she doesn't want it to take place, we're home free."

"If the concert does go on, you're going to need a lot of guards stationed at the mill. I can't help worry that our killer isn't quite done yet."

"If it's Theodore, this may be a trap. He wants it to look as if he's skipped town."

"Only to return in the middle of the concert," Siobhán said. "Maybe that's why the cloak isn't here."

"How much time do we have before the concert?"

Siobhán checked the time on her phone. "Seven hours."

"Then we have seven hours to catch a killer."

"If that's the case, I need to make a list of things we need to do." She reached into her handbag and brought out her notebook. "We're going to have to divide to conquer."

"Isn't it 'Divide and conquer'?"

"I like my way better."

"Of course you do."

She jotted down the items on her list:

Check in with Enda's doctors
Talk to Enda's solicitor. Get info on Enda's will
Get more information on the harp
Talk to the RTÈ National Symphony
Re-examine Enda's lorry
Talk to the owner of the mill
Questions for Jeanie Brady

"Seven hours, seven items," Macdara said. "Very efficient."

"Some of them may require follow-up. We'd better get cracking."

"How do you want to divide, Ms. Conqueror?"

"I want to talk to Enda's doctors if you can get that permission going. I want to have a look at Enda's lorry."

"It's in the police lot. That's an easy ask. But I don't suppose you're going to tell me why."

"I also want to talk to the owner of the mill. If you could ask the solicitor, did Enda plan on any changes to his will, and who benefits the most?"

"Gotcha. What else?"

"Call the symphony. I want to know if Harry Williams is telling the truth."

"About Leah being demoted to second chair?"

"Yes. And whether Enda knew about the affair."

"You think the symphony would know?"

"Yes, I do. They're one big family."

"Got it."

"And if you have time, give Jeanie Brady a bell. I want to know if the fall killed him or the harp."

"When we're done with all this, should we just deliver gifts to all the children of the world?"

Siobhán laughed and gave him a quick kiss. "No. Just a few O'Sullivans will do."

"Let's go back to the garda station. I can get a sanctioned garda car and you can take mine."

"Darn," Siobhán said. "I was hoping for a sled pulled by reindeer."

Enda's doctor's office was off the main street in town and occupied the first floor of an old house. The floorboards creaked as Siobhán entered. A nurse was behind the counter, going through files.

"Garda O'Sullivan, is it?" she said when Siobhán walked in.

"Yes," Siobhán said with a silent nod to Macdara for being so quick with her list.

"I have Enda's file right here. But you can't take it out of the office."

343

"I'm not a medical practitioner," Siobhán said. "Can I just ask the doctor a few questions?"

"He's not in. But I know everything that goes on here. If you follow me, I'll answer whatever I can."

They entered a small office outside the reception area. The nurse took a seat behind a large desk and opened the file. "What would you like to know?"

"I've heard that family members of Enda Elliot were concerned about his mental decline."

"That's true. Moira tried to bring him in several times for us to determine the causes."

"Tried?"

The nurse nodded. "It was very obvious that Enda did not want to be here. They had terrible rows in the lobby.

"In your professional opinion, was Enda suffering from a mental decline?"

"Yes. I believe he was showing signs of trouble, but without tests I cannot decisively say."

"And what did you observe that concerned you?"

The nurse hesitated. "This isn't an official diagnosis."

"I understand that. I would still like to know."

"He often didn't know what day or even year it was. He had a touch of paranoia. He would get people confused."

"People?"

She nodded. "Catherine Healy picked him up after a few appointments when Moira needed help. He thought she was his wife."

"Did Leah ever pick him up?"

The nurse shook her head. "I don't think she was in town." At least that backed up Moira's claim that Enda more often stayed here alone.

"Anything else? Anything at all?" Siobhán asked.

The nurse bowed her head. "He was often angry with the grandchildren, and his son. He kept telling me he was going to cut everyone out of the will. Threatened to leave it all to charity." She straightened in her chair. "I don't think that would be a bad thing, but I have a feeling it's not what the family wanted to hear."

"Did Moira Elliot succeed in getting power over Enda's medical decisions?"

The nurse shook her head. "The next step would have been court."

"But Enda died before they could go to court."

"Correct."

"But he was aware? That Moira was trying to do this?"

The nurse nodded. "Every time I saw him, he was not only aware, he was ranting about it." She sighed. "I felt for him. It's not easy to admit you're suffering from memory gaps. But he wasn't helping his case. The more he ranted, the more likely I thought that a judge would side with Moira."

"Thank you very much."

The nurse closed the folder. "I didn't do anything."

"You did," Siobhán said. "And I appreciate it." On her way out she texted an update to Macdara. She asked him to make speaking with the solicitor a priority. Did Enda make last-minute changes to the will before Moira could have power of attorney? He'd made threats to cut them all out. How seriously had anyone in the Elliot family taken those threats?

CHAPTER 20

Siobhán's mobile rang on her way to the garda station. She was stopped on the road, waiting for a trio of fat sheep to waddle across. She glanced at the screen before picking it up. "Hey, Dara." The first two sheep made it across, but the third stood in the middle of the road, his little face turned up to the sky. Siobhán lightly honked her horn. The sheep looked at her, then went back to looking at the sky. *Are you joking me?*

"Do you remember Cooley questioning a lad who came forward about Theodore? Said he was at his party the night of the murder?" he asked.

The lanky man rose in Siobhán's mind. "Yes."

"He just contacted the station. Said he found a picture from the night of the party that we might find interesting."

"Interesting how?" The sheep was still

blocking the road. She laid on the horn.

"He didn't say. Where are you now?"

"I've got a stubborn sheep blocking the road."

Macdara laughed. "Do you want me to send backup?"

"Definitely send shears, because this guy is going to get it." She swerved the car around the sheep, nearly diving her front end into a ditch but straightening it at the last minute. "I'm actually headed to the garda station to have a look at Enda's lorry."

"I hope the picture will have been e-mailed by then. I'll grant you permission to look at it."

"Thanks." She paused. "I really don't see Baskins for this. What's his motive?"

"Let's discuss when you've seen the picture."

"Got it." She filled him in on the visit with the nurse.

He whistled. "I get why you're focused on motive. Money is always a big one."

"And family," she said. It was sad but true. "What about your end?"

"I'm waiting for a call back from the symphony and having trouble getting ahold of Enda's solicitor." He sighed. "I feel as if he's avoiding my call."

"Moira said he'll be at the concert this

evening. If all else fails."

"He'd better hope he calls me back before then."

"If you're not at the garda station, where are you?"

Macdara chuckled. "My to-do list consisted of mostly phone calls. I can do that while shopping now, can't I?"

Siobhán laughed. "I suppose you can." Siobhán O'Sullivan would never say this to a soul, but Macdara Flannery wasn't the best gift-giver in the world. They were often very practical: slippers, shawls, something she might need for the bistro. He tried a few times with perfume, but they were never her style. Sometimes they booked weekends away — those were her favorites. Truthfully, she never put much stock in gifts. It was indeed the intention behind them that warmed her. He could never miss with chocolates and a good book. Then again, he knocked it out of the park with her engagement ring. It was so beautiful she never wore it out in public, and it rested in its box in her nightstand at home. That drove Dara a bit nuts, but she just couldn't go flashing it around. A gorgeous emerald surrounded by diamonds. No way did she want to lose it. She realized, as she ran through all this in her mind, that she had yet to buy him anything for Christmas either. But he liked to get what he gave — practical gifts. She was pretty sure a pair of socks would suit him just fine, but she was hoping for something with a little more spark. If only there was time for shopping. It would have to wait just a little longer.

"Call me after you see the picture," Macdara said. "He's being a bit sneaky about it."

"Got it." Another witness trying to take the reins. It would have saved them all time had the lad simply told them what the picture showed. At least she was near the station and had planned on heading there anyway. Siobhán concentrated on the road. It was a gray day, and snow had started to fall again, making the visibility poor. A car crept up on her, the headlights blaring into her space. She tapped her brakes and beeped the horn, hoping the person would get the message to back off and turn down the brights. She tried to see the car model or who was driving, but between the snow and their glaring lights it was impossible to tell. The roads were curvy, and she wasn't as familiar with them as someone who lived in this area. She would not let the driver bully her into speeding up. She was coming into a curve, and she slowed down. The car in back of her bumped her.

She cried out as the back of her car began to slide to the right, sending the front of her car into the curve. If a vehicle was approaching from the other direction, it would collide with her head-on. She laid on the horn again as she tried to keep calm and let the car finish its trajectory before slowly pumping the brakes. She had just straightened out when she was bumped from behind again. This was no accident or annoyed driver. She was being deliberately assaulted.

She pulled the car to the right, driving up on pasture as she fumbled for her mobile and hit redial. The car followed her onto the grassy field. She hadn't realized exactly where she was until now. Theodore had taken her this way when they drove to the ocean. The cliff was just ahead. Was someone trying to push her into driving near it? Hoping she'd go over it? If she got out of her vehicle, was she in more danger or less? Would someone be waiting with a hatchet? She locked all the doors in the car as she idled. The headlights were still blaring into her car. She inched forward in the opposite direction of the cliff but not quite on the road. She couldn't allow this person to force her into an accident with another vehicle.

"If you're calling to find out what Santy

got you, you can forget it."

"Dara," she said. That was all she needed to say, the panic in her voice was clear.

"What's wrong?"

"Someone ran me off the road."

"Where are you?"

She gave her best description. "I was headed for the garda station, I just went around a curve, I'm in a field and the cliff is to my right."

"Can you get back on the road?"

"When I do, they ram me from behind. Visibility is poor. I think they're trying to cause an accident."

"Can you go forward into the field?"

"I can try, but it's snowing and I can't see."

"I've got a guard car on the way. I'm going to stay on the phone. Try to go forward."

Siobhán slowly pushed forward, her car jutted along the field. "I'm going to get stuck."

"We just need to buy time until the guards are there."

The car behind her kept pace inch for inch. It rammed into her again. She cried out.

"What?"

"He just rammed into me. Or she. I can't see a thing." Macdara let out a string of curses and promises of what he'd do when he found out who it was. His panic actually helped her stay calm. "Next Christmas let's go somewhere tropical," she said.

"You're paying," he said. He was trying to lighten the mood, but she could hear the anger and fear in his voice. Siobhán inched forward again, and she felt the front tires sink into mud. They started to spin.

"I'm stuck."

The car rammed her once more, sending the front of her car in deeper. Her chest hit the steering wheel. She tried not to cry out but couldn't help it.

"Siobhán!"

"They're going to keep ramming me. I'm stuck. I'm stuck in the mud."

"Blow the horn." She laid on the horn. "Don't stop." She kept on the horn, wondering how long until the driver got out of the car. She heard a car door slam shut behind her. Whoever it was, he was coming. She had no weapon in the car, just the family iPad, and unless forcing them to watch black-and-white Christmas movies would scare him away, she had no idea what to do. She was rummaging through the glove compartment, trying to think of what to say to Macdara's repeated pleas, when she heard sirens.

"Is that the guards?" Dara yelled.

"Yes." She let out a breath, tears falling that she wished she could tamp down. She heard the door slam again as the car or lorry behind her roared to life. It screeched back onto the road. "It's probably a lorry. Something with winter tires and four-wheel drive."

The guard car pulled up to her. She opened her door as a guard was getting out.

"It went that way," she said, pointing to the road. "Did you see him?"

The guard turned in the direction that the vehicle had taken. "I saw the taillights."

Siobhán jumped into the passenger side of the guard car. "Let's go." The guard got in but didn't start the car. "What are you doing?" She pointed up ahead. "Let's follow him."

The guard shook his head. "We've got a second guard car positioned ahead. If a lorry speeds by, they'll be on it."

"If?"

"He knows we're here. He could have pulled off in any of these farms, might try and wait us out."

She exhaled. "Siobhán?" She stared at her phone. She had no idea Macdara was still on the line until she heard him speak.

"I'm okay. I think whoever it was got away.

And my car will need a tow. But I'm okay." Her chest was a little sore and her blood pressure was probably through the roof. Her heart still beat out a panicked rhythm in her chest. But she was okay.

"Have him drive you to the hospital," Macdara said.

"Don't be ridiculous. I'm fine. I'm going to the garda station."

"Don't drive by yourself again."

She glanced at Dara's sunken car, snow already covering it as if Mother Nature had just decided it was time for Siobhán's car to go to sleep and had laid a soft blanket over it. "That won't be an issue."

The clerk at the garda station was expecting her. He set her up in the interview room with a laptop and insisted on bringing her a mug of tea and biscuits. Being stalked by an unknown driver had been a terribly close call, and the tea and biscuits were an instant salve. She opened her e-mail and clicked on the attachment sent via the garda station. A photograph jumped on the screen. A holiday party, people jammed into the living room. Someone had drawn a red arrow and circled a person. He was standing to the side near the door. It was Theodore Baskins standing near the door in a brown trench coat. The time and date appeared in the corner. Friday, or technically nearly Saturday morning, the day of the murder. Close to midnight, just like the witness had said.

Siobhán leaned back in her chair and pondered this. Alison had seen Theodore hitchhiking. Did he have time to go to the mill? If so, where was the cloak? Why would he change from a trench coat to a cloak and back to the trench coat? And where was the cloak?

Had he thrown it into the creek? After all, he'd thrown things into the creek before. *Poor Frosty.*

"Thank God." Siobhán turned to find Macdara in the doorway, out of breath. She stood and he ambushed her in a hug. She winced a little, and he pulled back.

"I'm grand," she said. "Mug of tea and some biscuits, I'm good as new."

"You're not good as new. Let's go to hospital."

"Not on your life. Just a few bruises."

He ran his fingers through his hair. "Take some headache tablets, and if you're still sore we're going." He reached into his pocket and handed her the tablets and a bottle of water.

"You think of everything."

"My car is being towed."

"Grand. Did they ever catch him?"

"No. He or she must have pulled in somewhere to wait us out. I might send guards farm to farm."

"You might want to send them to the creek first."

"Why is that?"

She showed him the photograph. He rubbed his eyes. "It's not going to look good if we turned Garda Cooley in and he had nabbed the murderer after all." Siobhán once again pointed out. As the new Detective Sergeant on the case, Macdara would take the most heat if they screwed this up.

"Hitchhiking is not the crime we're interested in," Macdara said. "This photo could actually exonerate him."

"How?"

"It proves that Alison saw a trench coat, not a cloak."

"But there's a gap of time between the party and hitchhiking. If Theodore didn't go to the mill and kill Enda, what was he doing during those few hours?"

"It's an excellent question, and we'll have to find out. But unless we find a cloak in the creek, I'm still not convinced Theodore is our killer."

Siobhán agreed with him but felt it was her job to play devil's advocate. This case had been mishandled once before, and she didn't want to make the same mistake. "It's been a week since the murder. If Theodore did throw the cloak into the creek, who knows where it could have washed up. What we do know is that Theodore Baskins has thrown items into the creek before," Siobhán said.

"Don't bring up poor Frosty. It's still a touchy subject," he said with a wink. She looked around to make sure no one was watching, then stuck her tongue out at him.

"You know there are cameras everywhere," he said with a grin. Before she could reply, his mobile phone rang. He glanced at the screen. "It's the symphony."

"Don't keep them waiting." While Macdara took the call, Siobhán headed for the clerk's desk and returned the laptop.

"Do you have the keys and report for Enda's lorry?"

"Right here," he said. He slid a set of keys over to her, then opened a folder. "We processed the lorry for fingerprints, fibers, blood, etcetera. Nothing unusual, but that's because the lorry was cleaned."

"You're sure?"

He nodded. "It seems to have been vacuumed on the inside, washed on the outside, and some kind of cleaning fluid found on the inside, as if Enda wiped it down with one of those wet cloths you find at the shops. Kills germs and whatnot."

"Any glitter found?"

He glanced at the report, then arched an eyebrow. "A few green specks. On the floorboard in the driver's seat. How did you know?"

She didn't answer. "And the flat tire?"

"No objects found inside the tire. Puncture wound made by anything sharp enough — most likely a knife."

Someone took a knife to the tire but cleaned the lorry? Or Enda had it cleaned, ready to pick Leah up at the airport, but afterward someone punctured his tire? Why? To stop him from going to the airport, or to force him to walk to the mill? If the killer had lured Enda to the mill, why did he or she care whether he walked or drove? Was he or she afraid of someone hearing Enda's lorry leave the drive? Would it have been loud enough to wake people up?

Siobhán headed out to the car lot. Enda's lorry was parked in a back corner. She headed for it, opened the vehicle, and slid into the driver's seat. Enda was shorter than Siobhán, and the seat seemed appropriately positioned for his height. Siobhán would have needed to push it back. She started the lorry. Its engine purred. Quiet. It wouldn't have disturbed Moira or anyone in the house. Unless of course they were up, and in the backyard, and could have seen the lorry pulling out.

Did the killer know that the Elliot grandchildren were in the backyard? How was this possible? Did someone other than the killer puncture the tire? She turned off the car and removed the key. It didn't make sense. When was the tire punctured and why? She had a feeling that the answer to that was important. Siobhán had made an assumption earlier, one that she was now starting to question. It was an assumption that, if it turned out to be false, left a new trail to follow. It wasn't a question of whether the tire had been slashed. It was a question of when. And if Siobhán followed this new trail carefully, she had a feeling it would lead her straight to the killer.

CHAPTER 21

"It's not like it's a John Egan," Ruth said. She sat primly in front of the harp that had fallen on Enda. It was in a small storage room in the garda station. Now that it wasn't covering a body, Siobhán had a new appreciation for the beauty of the instrument. Sturdy, curvy, and gorgeous. Ebony wood and gold inlay with ornate carvings. It was a real showpiece. It also wasn't covered in dust, which meant it hadn't been up on the second-floor gallery for long, or it had been protected by a cover. They didn't find a cover, so strangely the killer must have taken it with him or her. Ruth seemed to be purposefully trying *not* to look at it, which completely gave her away.

"John Egan?" Siobhán asked. From the way Ruth said the name, it was apparent she thought Siobhán should recognize it.

"The most famous Irish harp maker, 1801 to 1841. They were three feet high. Ideal for society ladies. One of those wouldn't have killed poor Enda. They were similar to the pedal harps of Sébastien Érard. French, of course. 1752 to 1831."

Siobhán looked at the harp again. The craftsmanship seemed spot-on. "I don't know much about harps, but this one seems nice."

"Nice?" Ruth said. "Nice? It's a premium Salvi! Look at those curves."

"You pretended you knew nothing of the harp that landed on Enda. It's becoming apparent that was a lie."

"I didn't kill Enda over a harp. In fact, I think it was going to be a present for me. A surprise. That's why I was so distraught."

"Tell me about this particular harp."

Her eyes flicked over the instrument, and her tongue darted out for a second. "It's an Aurora pedal harp by Salvi. He chose the ebony. It's stunning, isn't it?"

"'Tis."

"What else do you want to know?"

"What makes it special?"

"It's a forty-seven-string concert grand, for heaven's sake. Timeless. Unmatched quality of sound. I'm dying to play it." She stopped as a horrified expression overtook her face. "It was just an expression."

"I understand." Siobhán gave it a beat. "Is it old?"

Ruth shook her head. "No. Victor Salvi originated in the mid-nineteen hundreds in Italy, but this is a recent production. Salvi has showrooms all over the world. Enda either rented it or purchased it. Perhaps it was Enda's big announcement."

"Where would he have rented or purchased it?"

Ruth shrugged. "London. Berlin. Italy?"

Siobhán wondered if they would find the paperwork for it in time to catch a killer.

"What is it worth?"

"It's very dear. Around twenty-two thousand euro."

"And you knew nothing about this harp until that Saturday morning?"

Ruth violently shook her head. "Nothing! It was such a shock. First I didn't even notice the harp, I was looking at poor Enda. But when I saw what it was, that's when I had to run to the ladies' room."

"Why didn't you tell me the truth at the time?"

Ruth's lip quivered. "I'm a coward. I didn't want anyone to associate me with his death. Even if it was just an accident. If he got killed by a harp he bought for me?" She shook her head. "I just couldn't face it."

When was it purchased and why? Who moved it up to the second-floor gallery? Where was the cover? They had questions to ask now, which was better than having no questions, but who could answer them? It would have taken two people to haul it up to the gallery. She needed to speak with the owner of the mill. They needed to speak with Moira, see if they could track when and where Enda purchased it. Ruth had lied to her, but from the way she was practically vibrating near the harp, she couldn't imagine her shoving it on top of Enda. Ironically, the harp hadn't suffered any damage. She was waiting to hear back from Jeanie Brady to ask if the harp had played any part in Enda's death. The pun was not intentional; it certainly wasn't the type of "playing" for which this beauty had been crafted.

"Do you think?" Ruth asked, her hands flexing.

"What?" Siobhán asked.

"Enda obviously wanted me to play this at the concert. I'd have to check that it's in tune and all . . . but it doesn't look damaged. Do you think I might, please, just once, please may I play it for Enda?"

"I'll let you take that up with Detective Sergeant Flannery," Siobhán said. "But I don't see why not." Given the fact that they were still holding the concert in the mill, she didn't think anyone would find it offensive. They all seemed to agree that the music came first and that's what Enda would have wanted.

Ruth clasped her hands. "Thank you," she whispered. She lifted her head. "Thank you, Enda. I won't let you down."

Siobhán had just stepped outside after the interview with Ruth when a car pulled in the lot behind the station and Jeanie Brady emerged. Siobhán was shocked, but thrilled to see her. Jeanie trudged toward her, then surprised Siobhán a second time with a hug. Siobhán towered over the short woman as they embraced. Jeanie stepped back.

"Jaysus, that was some drive in the snow." Her full cheeks were rosy from the cold, but her hazel eyes were bright and cheerful.

"I can't believe you're here!"

"Detective Sergeant Flannery made me an offer I couldn't refuse."

"The concert?"

"I'm a big fan of classical music. I like to listen to it while I work."

"I'm starting to become a fan myself."

"Is there anywhere we can sit and have a chat? A mug of tea, perhaps?"

"Let's go into town."

"Call that handsome man of yours. I promised him a briefing."

The trio sat at an adorable café downtown with mugs of tea and coffee and a small selection of pastries. White lights twinkled from the ceiling, and Christmas music played overhead. Siobhán allowed a few seconds to enjoy it. At a nearby table sat her brood, entertaining Nancy Flannery and equally happy with hot cocoa and a plateful of pastries. Once in a while she heard them erupt in laughter, or sing along with a carol, and it filled her with joy. She hadn't quite kept her promise to them, but they seemed to be making the best of it and one another.

Eoin was the only one who heard about her close call with whomever was stalking her in the car. He was really stepping up and keeping the others blissfully ignorant. She hadn't even told James, as he had enough to deal with when it came to Elise. Siobhán asked Eoin to be on the lookout for anyone or anything strange and to make sure none of them went anywhere alone. Apparently, Gráinne was always trying to be near Jason, which made Siobhán nervous on several fronts. Luckily, he was always with his mam. Elise and James walked in a few minutes late (as usual) and barely threw a glance at their table before joining her siblings. Siobhán felt a pang of jealousy, then realized it was for the best. As soon as they caught the killer, she could focus on trying to improve her relationship with her soon-to-be sister-in-law.

Siobhán had decided she would make as many batches of brown bread on Christmas morning that she could to share with the musicians and guests. She'd rise early and surprise everyone. If time permitted, maybe she would be able to make enough for the folks who braved the Polar Bear Swim that morning. She never underestimated the power of a little brown bread to go a long way.

"Don't keep us in suspense," Macdara said to Jeanie Brady when the pastries had disappeared from the plates. "Did the fall kill him, or was he crushed by the harp?"

"The fall killed him," Jeanie said. The waitress came around to wet the tea, and Jeanie topped hers up with milk as she spoke. "He hit the back of his head on the cement floor."

"Could you tell if it was an accidental fall or he was pushed?" Siobhán asked. She knew Jeanie had already ruled it a homicide, but she wanted to hear the details firsthand. She also stirred milk and a wee bit of sugar into her second cup of tea. She had a feeling she needed all the fortification she could get for the tasks ahead.

"The force needed to hit his head to that degree, and break through the railings, tells me he either was shoved or ran backward at high speed. Common sense tells me he was given a shove."

It was just as Siobhán thought, but she wanted to be sure. "There was a theory he was dragging the harp out from storage and misjudged how close he was to the railing."

Jeanie shook her head. "His hands were not on the harp, and we tested the harp for fingerprints, which I must admit is a first. With the evidence of the video on the iPad, it's my professional opinion the harp was pushed over *after* he was already lying on the floor."

"Did the harp deliver any damage?"

"None. Nor did it suffer any damage. Remarkable, actually."

"Then it played no part in his death." Siobhán understood the strange looks coming at her from Jeanie and Macdara, but she was still disappointed. Her comedic delivery must have been off. "Sorry," she said. "Pun intended." Maybe she should just keep her gob shut for a while. Forever might be a good start.

"Definitely not the role Enda expected the harp to play," Macdara said.

"Speaking of which, Ruth is going to ask if she can play this particular harp at the concert."

"The one that fell on him?" Macdara exclaimed.

Siobhán nodded. "Supposedly it's a very special harp. She believes he meant to surprise her with it, and she wants to do it in honor of Enda."

"I don't see why not," Macdara said. "Given everyone insists the concert must go on in his honor. I just hope she isn't the killer."

"I don't see her harming the harp under any circumstances," Siobhán said. "She's over the moon about harps." She turned back to Jeanie. "Did you find any objects in his pockets?"

"He was wearing pajamas. Nothing in his coat pockets."

"Keys?"

Jeanie shook her head. "Nothing."

Siobhán turned to Macdara. "Did the guards turn up anything in the mill? A torch?"

Macdara shook his head. "There are so many boxes stored up in the gallery. The owner has been charging folks for storage.

It's possible an item such as a torch could have been dropped into one of the boxes, but Cooley didn't continue the search."

Siobhán had one more question for Jeanie Brady. "Did you find any green glitter on Enda?"

Jeanie raised an eyebrow. "Is the glitter a clue?"

"Yes. Green glitter."

Jeanie nodded. "There was some green glitter on his front side." No keys, but there was glitter. It meant something.

"I'm working on a theory that the killer accidentally came into contact with the glitter when he or she was lying in wait."

"Glitter in an old whiskey mill?" Macdara asked. "Have they held hen parties there?"

"I'm sure they would if they could," Siobhán said. "I think the glitter is from a box of Christmas items that had been stored up there, waiting to decorate for the concert."

"If your theory holds true," Jeanie Brady said, "then the killer may have had glitter on his gloves when he shoved Enda's chest."

"That's one complication the killer probably didn't see coming," Macdara said.

"Indeed," Siobhán said. "And we've found it in quite a few places. Lucky for us, once glitter gets out, it's almost impossible to clean it all up."

"Does this point to any particular killer?"

Siobhán mulled it over. She had her theories, but nothing she could prove, and she wasn't going to follow in Garda Cooley's footsteps of drawing unnecessary focus to one suspect before evidence could bear it out. "Not yet."

"The harp would have required at least two people to move it into the balcony," Macdara said.

Siobhán nodded. "It also would have been protected by a cover. There was no dust on it, and I highly doubt Garda Cooley had it polished."

"I didn't see mention of a harp cover being discovered," Jeanie Brady said.

"Me neither," Siobhán said. "But there had to have been one."

"You're thinking the killer took it off and then what?" Macdara asked.

"I suppose it could have been hiding under that dark cloak."

"The cloak we can't find."

"Correct." She paused.

Macdara asked the obvious question. "Why would the killer have removed the cover and taken it with them?"

"I can think of only one reason the killer would have removed the cover." Jeanie and

Macdara waited, allowing Siobhán the dramatic pause. "Showmanship."

Jeanie Brady let her spoon fall to her plate with a clink. "This I've got to hear."

"Me too," Macdara said.

"Someone wanted us to know they didn't approve of the harp. Ruth said it was worth around twenty-two thousand euro. Maybe the killer was disgusted that kind of money was spent on a harp."

"But Enda's a renowned conductor. Isn't that exactly the type of thing he should have spent his money on?" Jeanie asked.

"I'm not begrudging him the purchase — and there's a chance it could be a rental. But it's some kind of message from the killer. The harp. The requiem on the phone. Enda's big announcement." She leaned forward. "Either the killer is one of our musicians *or* the killer wants us to think it's one of the musicians."

"That's just another way of saying the killer could be anyone," Macdara said.

"True. But it does tell us something. Musician or not, the killer was conducting a performance of his or her own. The killer is communicating. We just needed to figure out the message from the misdirection before the killer can surprise us with an encore."

CHAPTER 22

Time was fleeing, and here it was, only three hours until the concert. Siobhán had donned a little black dress that she'd packed in her luggage and was at the entrance to the mill waiting to speak with the owner. She almost didn't recognize the older man in a tuxedo when he approached. "You wanted to speak with me, Garda?"

"My. You look handsome."

He blushed. "Tanks. And no worries about me tree. I mean it."

His tune had changed slightly since he'd apparently learned she was a guard. She had more than made up for the tree incident with the monies paid and did not care to prolong the conversation. "Grand. I did want to speak with you about the mill."

"Let's go inside before it's a madhouse." He opened the door, then entered and reached to his left. Soon the place was lit around the sides.

"What about the center light?" she asked.

He reached to another set of switches on the right wall, and soon the center was lit up. Chairs were set up for the orchestra. Villagers could bring their own chairs or stand. It was only an hour in length, shorter than a traditional concert, but afterward the musicians would mingle with the guests and they would all have a Christmas celebration. No doubt at some point the musicians would break out in song long after the official concert had ended. All nights with Irish musicians ended in song.

Feeling the pressure of the clock ticking, Siobhán got down to business. "I'd like to know about the items stored in the gallery, and I'd like to know who all had keys to the mill."

The old man rubbed his chin as he looked around. "The night of the murder, the door was locked, but the figure easily enters. You can see on that video that the guards showed me. That suggests they had a key. But as to how many keys to this mill are floating out there? I'm afraid I was too trusting. Anyone could have made a key. There was a set given to Moira Elliot, and then Moira gave them to Catherine, who needed earlier access to paint her mural, and Ruth, dats our harpist, was in and out at one point, Enda of course had a set of keys . . . and Paul El-liot has a set of keys. Come to think of it, so does Leah Elliot. At least, she could get them off Enda if she wanted them."

"Is there anyone who *didn't* have a set of keys?" She hadn't meant to turn sour, but she couldn't help it. A man might be alive if he'd kept better track of the keys.

"I suppose you're blaming me for what happened to poor Enda, is dat right?"

"Of course not. But I am trying to catch a killer. What about the harp. Who brought that in?"

"Enda must have arranged that. Once he rented the space for the concert, I wasn't involved."

"You weren't here when the harp was delivered?"

"I was not."

She sighed. Most likely deliverymen had followed Enda's instructions and brought it to the second-floor gallery. Why didn't he just keep it downstairs? Was he trying to hide it as a surprise? Or did the killer instruct that the harp be stored up there? If only Enda had stayed on the first floor. Would the killer still have done the cowardly deed? Enda was facing his killer when he was pushed. His last view would have been of his murderer. What an awful revelation to have at the end. Betrayal of a family member, or colleague, or neighbor.

"When did Enda have those security cameras installed?"

"He didn't tell me about that, but I'm guessing it was before he brought that fancy harp in."

"He installed security cameras without your permission?"

"He gave me enough money for me to let him be. I told him the space was his but if he wanted security he'd have to deal with it himself. I guess that was his way of dealing with it."

"Did you ever have trouble with theft or break-ins before this event?"

"Not that I'm aware. But when anyone rented space up there, I made them sign a waiver that I'm not responsible for such tings."

"Smart."

He tapped his head. "Up here for thinking." He pointed to his waist. "Down there for dancing."

"Basically the Elliot family and anyone who had things stored here could easily get access."

"I'm afraid so. This is a small village. The mill is empty now. As for storage, I told you, that was at the renter's own risk. Never had a problem, big or small, before this. Of course I didn't know anyone was plotting a murder."

"Of course." Most of this conversation had been a waste. But not all of it. Siobhán tucked the nugget in the back of her mind. She needed to get ahold of Moira. A story was forming in her mind, but she needed to check on a few more bits before she could declare it the end.

Macdara was waiting outside the mill to give Siobhán a ride to Moira's. She'd try to ask her questions as everyone was getting ready to leave for the concert. Maybe under pressure, someone would let something slip. Macdara had plenty of guards posted at the concert, and they'd already done a sweep-through. If earlier the killer had been planning something for the concert, they would soon realize their plans would be foiled. "Learn anything?" Macdara asked when she stepped into the car.

"Maybe," Siobhán said. "But I'm still turning it over. What about you. Any updates?"

"I just got off the phone with the solicitor," Macdara said. "He said there had been some interesting developments related to Enda's financing but that it was better to discuss it in person. I got the feeling he was worried about someone listening in."

"Someone in the room?"

"It's possible. He's going to meet us at Enda's house. Leah said we could have a private discussion in Enda's office."

Everything was coming down to the wire. Siobhán had an awful feeling the killer was going to slip away. "What about Theodore Baskins or the car that ran me off the road?"

"Nothing on either. Theodore hasn't returned home, or to work, and guard cars have been out on the roads but they haven't spotted anything unusual."

The solicitor was an older man with a shock of white hair, standing tall in a gorgeous blue suit. From the way he smoothed down his jacket, his hands shaking slightly, Siobhán picked up that this man's nerves were frayed. *Join the club.* The solicitor gestured to two chairs across the large desk, and they all sat. If it was odd for this solicitor to be sitting in Enda's seat, he didn't mention it, but his eyes widened every time Leah darted by the door, and so far that had happened three times. She was wearing a white silk dress that shimmered like snow. The fourth time Siobhán caught sight of Leah, she waved.

Leah stopped, waved back, then looked down at her dress. "I know, I know," she said. "You expected me to be in black."

"No. You look stunning."

Leah blinked back tears. "Enda bought this for me. He said it made me look like an angel."

"Angels wish they looked like you."

Leah laughed, then covered her mouth with her hands as if she needed to stop the sound. "I can't believe the concert is almost here. And he's not here."

"No tears," Harry Williams said, coming up from behind. He was dashing in a tuxedo. In his hand he clutched the Santa cap. "You can cry after the concert."

Leah took a breath and straightened up. "You're right, you're right." She leaned in the doorway. "And thank you." She addressed this to Macdara.

"Me?" he said.

Leah nodded. "The symphony called me. They assured me that Enda was never going to demote me to second chair. It's the best Christmas present I could have asked for. You know, bar a miracle that Enda would still be alive."

"Wonderful," Siobhán said. "We can't wait to see you play."

Leah laughed, then twirled in the doorway

379

before vanishing from sight.

Macdara turned his attention back to the solicitor. "Did Enda cut anyone out of the will?"

The solicitor shook his head. "It's primarily what you would expect."

"Did he punish Paul, or Jason, or Orla?" Macdara asked.

"No. I'm sure he threatened to, but this is all above board. However, Detective Sergeant, you asked me to look for any changes or monies that had started or stopped."

Macdara leaned forward. "Yes?"

"Faye Elliot and the surrogate had been receiving payments. Those stopped this year when Jason turned twenty-one."

"Twenty-one," Siobhán said. He was a good age for Gráinne. If he wasn't a killer.

Macdara raised an eyebrow. "That's your takeaway?"

"No. Sorry." She mulled it over. "I can't believe he paid the surrogate until Jason turned twenty-one."

"He was quite insistent on that," the solicitor said. "And he wanted to take care of it solo."

Someone's golden goose had just laid its last egg. Was that reason enough to kill? "Did Faye or this surrogate ever reach out to Enda after the payments stopped?"

"That I wouldn't know. There are rumors that Jason was trying to convince his father to keep up the payments to Faye. But Enda could be a stubborn man. Then again, I think it was more than generous paying Faye and the surrogate until Jason was twenty-one."

"Do you have contact information for this surrogate?" Macdara asked.

The solicitor shook his head. "As I said, Enda handled those payments himself. I don't know anyone in the family who has any information at all on her. That's the way Enda wanted it."

Siobhán thought back to the argument between Faye and Jason. Something about getting to the bank. *I won't let you do this.* This happened right after the Secret Santa gift exchange.

"What?" Macdara said. "You have that look. What am I missing?"

"We need to talk to Faye. Right now." Siobhán thanked the solicitor and hurried out of the room. Leah and Harry were headed out the door. Siobhán stopped them.

"Do you know where Jason and Faye are?"

"They left early for the concert," Leah said. "They wanted extra time for Faye."

Jason was very protective of his mother. And attentive. He couldn't be happy that

Enda had stopped her payments. Didn't he say there was so much she still needed? Given she'd be in the wheelchair the rest of her life, it didn't seem fair that Enda put a cap on her treatment. Then again, Siobhán didn't know the ins and outs of the agreement. But whatever went down, it seems to have rattled Jason and his mother. She turned to Macdara. "Find out how many banks are downtown. I'd like to know why Faye needed to go so urgently."

"I don't think it will be easy to get the banks to give up that kind of information," Macdara pointed out.

Siobhán smiled. "Use your charm."

"That's your suggestion? Use my charm? I don't think I have an unlimited supply. What are you going to do?"

"I need to talk to Moira and Catherine. Use my charm on them."

"Are you going to tell me what's going on here?"

"I haven't proved it yet. But I'm close."

"I don't like leaving you alone," Macdara said quietly.

"I'm capable." If someone had stalked and rammed Macdara's car, she would feel the exact same way. They were both capable guards, but that didn't stop a loved one from worrying.

"I know. I still don't like it."

"I need to check in with James and Eoin, make sure they don't leave Gráinne, Ciarán, or Ann alone. Let's worry about the civilians, not the guards."

"Yes, boss. See you at the concert?"

"Not if I see you first." She smiled and planted a kiss on his cheek.

"Now? You have to see them now?" Moira, dressed in black with her fur coat and hat, was poised to go out the door.

"Yes, please, I need to look at those rental records again." Moira sighed, then left the room and returned with the folder. There was a pounding on the door.

"What now?" Moira hurried to the door. Jason stood on the other side, out of breath. "You're as pale as a ghost." She pulled Jason inside. He nodded at Siobhán. "I'm looking for Detective Sergeant Flannery."

"He's got a few meetings scheduled before the concert," Siobhán said. "What's wrong?"

"Mam's wheelchair is missing," Jason said. "I loaded it into the van. Then Paul and I carried Mam to the van. I didn't even look for the chair, why wouldn't it be there? But when we arrived at the mill, it was gone." He sighed. "I returned because she insisted I must have forgotten it. But I did not. I loaded it into the van."

"Your mam is at the concert now?"

Jason nodded. "She has a seat. But she can't be expected not to need mobility."

"Of course not. Moira, do you have any idea where we can get her a chair at this late hour?"

"I'll call the hospital. Someone should be able to bring one."

"Thank you," Jason said. "I can't believe someone is doing this to us."

"Jason, may I speak with you?" Siobhán asked.

Before he could reply, Moira's phone rang again. She looked at the screen and picked it up. "Catherine?" She held the phone away from her ear, and Siobhán could hear a woeful voice on the other end. "Calm down, please," Moira begged. "I'm sorry, and that's horrible, but it's too late to worry about it now. We can deal with it after the concert." From the sounds of it, that didn't calm Catherine down. "I have Garda O'Sullivan here, would you like to speak with her?" Moira nodded. "Stay put. I'll send her over." She clicked off the phone.

"Someone broke into her painting shed and destroyed her Christmas mural. She's having a total breakdown."

Great. "Isn't a mural something that's

384

painted on a wall?"

"The owner of the mill didn't want anything painted on the wall. And the town wanted to be able to use it again. She was supposed to paint it on plywood and bring it in. She's behind. I suppose that's because of what's been going on with Theodore."

Theodore Baskins. Siobhán had almost forgotten about him. "Has there been any word?"

"You're a guard and you're asking me?" Moira said.

"Yes."

Moira shook her head. "There's been no sign of him. I say good riddance, but Catherine's always been so attached." She paused. "Unless . . ."

"Yes?"

"Do you think it's Theodore who broke into her shed? Maybe he's signaling her."

Signaling her. That was certainly one interpretation. "What's the message?"

Moira straightened up. "That's for you to figure out."

"I'm going with you," Jason said.

"I'm going to ask that you stay back," Siobhán said. "This is official police business."

"And yet you're not officially on the case," Jason said.

Siobhán loathed when people tried to use logic on her. "I've been granted permissions by the Detective Sergeant."

Jason held his hands up. "I've no doubt. But something is going on and it's silly to go it alone." He sighed, then took her in as if trying to figure her out. "I would be offering the same help if you were a male guard."

"And would you call them silly?"

He had the decency to flush. "Probably not. Apologies."

"Two conditions."

"Go on."

"You do as I say at all times. And when we're finished with Catherine I have a few questions for you."

He pulled his scarf tight. "Got it." He trudged behind her toward Catherine's. "I think one would have covered it all."

"What?" The snow was falling again, the wind biting.

"You said you had two conditions. But one — do as I say at all times — would have covered it all."

"Noted." *Cheeky.*

They arrived at the shed. It was set back in the pasture, near Siob hán's guest cottage.

"I need you to stay out here," Siobhán said.

"Why? Are you worried about me or Catherine?"

"Just give me a minute."

"Got it." He folded his arms and leaned against the painting shed.

"Why was your mother so upset about the DNA kit you received as a Secret Santa gift that she wanted to immediately go to a bank?"

Jason's eyes widened. "How did you know that?"

"I might be silly, but I do keep me ears open."

"I offended you. I'm terribly sorry. Again."

"Not a bother. Can you try answering the question?"

He shrugged. "She never went to the bank. I talked her out of it."

"Evasive."

"Fine. She thought someone was trying to send a message and would be contacting us again. I thought she was overreacting. But now it's obvious she was right. What do they always say? A mother is always right?"

"What does she have to hide?"

His face only took seconds to morph into anger. "Excuse me?"

"Going to the bank implies she thought she would have to pay someone off. You can be blackmailed only if there's something you don't want anyone to know."

He chewed on his lip. "I don't know. She wouldn't say."

"I see." He knew something. She gave it a beat. "I'm trying to help. Secrets get people killed."

"There's only one secret I know my mother's been keeping. But I don't know how someone could have found out, or why it even matters at this point."

"Go on."

"My mother's accident. The one that landed her in a wheelchair."

"Yes?" Siobhán waited. "Your parents had been to a holiday party. The roads were slick. Had your father been drinking?"

"Yes," he said. "My father had been drinking."

"I see. I'm sorry."

"You don't understand."

"Tell me."

"Because my father had been drinking . . . my mother drove home."

"Your mother?"

"Yes." He lowered his head. "My mother was driving. Given she was thrown from the vehicle, despite being drunk, my father slid over from the passenger seat. He thought she was dead. He wanted to be punished. He pretended he was driving."

"Even after he found out she was still alive?"

Jason nodded. "She had enough to deal with. And my father was just becoming a celebrity around town. He thought he could make a drunk-driving charge go away."

"I see." He'd been right about that, Enda Elliot had never been charged. Nor, of course, had Faye. She'd paid a heavy price. They should be grateful no other cars were involved.

"You think someone found out and is blackmailing your mother?"

"It's the only thing I can think of," Jason said. "My mother is very rattled."

"Are there people with your mother right now?"

He nodded. "The mill is crawling with guards."

"Good. Now give me a minute to speak with Catherine and then we can all head over there together."

"I took a taxi back here. I told him not to wait."

"We'll figure it out. Don't move."

He reached into his pocket and pulled out a pack of cigarettes. Siobhán sighed. It was a strike against him in her eyes; she'd prefer Gráinne date a nonsmoker. But she had less control over her family than she did murder probes. She turned away from the sharp scent of cigarette smoke and knocked on the door to the painting shed.

Catherine stood inside the shed sobbing at broken pieces of painted plywood spread out across the floor of the small building. They looked as if they'd been sawed into as many pieces as possible. Colors bled together, so it was impossible to tell what the mural had been. Catherine stood, tears streaming down her face.

Siobhán's number one goal was to keep her calm and get her to the concert. "Tell me what happened."

Catherine looked even more ragged than when Siobhán first saw her. "This village happened. Even if Theodore never comes back, I'll always be a target. A murderer's lover." She shivered. "I don't think I can stay here."

"When did you discover this?"

"Just now. I was supposed to call a few lads to come pick it up."

"Listen to me carefully. This is not an accusation. But have you heard from Theodore at all?"

Catherine shook her head. "Do you think something's happened to him?"

"Do you lock this shed?"

"Not usually. But because of the mural,

yes, I've been locking it." She shook her head. "But it's just a normal lock. Very easy to get in if one is determined."

"Who else has keys?"

Catherine's eyes widened. "You think Theodore did this."

"Did anyone else know where you kept the keys?"

"Why? Why would he do this?"

"Maybe he's angry."

"Can you blame him? Look how everyone treats him. Now they're saying he's a killer."

"Do you think he could have done this?"

Catherine stared at the chopped-up pieces on the floor of the shed. "I don't see why he would punish me."

Siobhán noted that Catherine left open the possibility that it was Theodore. That's when her eyes landed on the corner of the shed. There sat a wheelchair. On top of it, heaps of fabric. Something thick and gray, then something black, and on top of it all a torch. Siobhán didn't have to touch it to know what it was. Faye's wheelchair. The cover to the harp. The Grim Reaper cloak and the torch. That must have been the object in Enda's hand. He didn't enter the mill expecting a fight. He carried a torch to light his way. *He knew.* He knew who was sneaking into the mill. The outfit hadn't fooled him. No way was Siobhán going to touch it. The killer's fingerprints were all over it. Which is why she needed Catherine to step away without touching it as well. "Catherine. Step forward." Catherine tilted her head in confusion but she did as she was told.

"What's wrong? You're scaring me."

"When was the last time you were in here?"

"A few days. Since Theodore's been missing."

"We need to get out. Now."

"What on earth is the matter?" Catherine turned. She yelped when she saw what was in the corner. Mouth open, she turned back to Siobhán. "Someone's framing him. It's not Theodore. It's not."

"Is that Mam's wheelchair?" Jason stood in the doorway, openmouthed. He turned to Catherine. She held up her hands and shook her head.

"It wasn't me."

"Theodore," he said.

"Let's get out of here. Don't touch it. I'm afraid your shed is a crime scene now." Siobhán managed to coerce Catherine out of the shed. Macdara was at the concert. Nearly all the guards in the village were at the concert.

Siobhán turned to Catherine. "Come on. I need you to get ready."

"Ready for what?"

"We're going to the mill."

"What?" Catherine was dumbfounded. "No. I'm not going. I never want to see anyone in this village again."

"I need you to go. We all need to be there."

"Aren't we bringing Mam her wheelchair?" Jason asked.

"I'm afraid it's evidence now," Siobhán said.

"That's exasperating," Jason said. "I'm sure whoever took it wore gloves."

"We still have to follow procedure. I hope Moira was able to get your mam another wheelchair until we can clear this one."

"I guess it doesn't matter. I was surprising her tomorrow morning with a new chair."

Tomorrow morning. *Christmas*. Siobhán had nearly forgotten. It was Christmas Eve. "Let's go," Siobhán said to Catherine. "Maybe we can all try to enjoy the concert."

"Why?" Catherine shook her head. "It will be worse if I go."

"No," Jason said. "It won't. You've been so good to my family over the years."

Tears came to Catherine's eyes. "Thank you for saying that. If you must know . . . you've always been my favorite."

"That's settled then," Siobhán said. "We're all going. There's safety in numbers."

"You think I'm in danger?" Catherine put her hand over her heart.

"Until we catch the killer, everyone's in danger." Siobhán stepped forward. "I can have Detective Sergeant Flannery stay by your side the entire evening. I promise, no one will bother you." Catherine looked down at herself, as if just now realizing she wasn't dressed for the occasion. Siobhán looped her arm through Catherine's. "Come on. I'll help you pick something out."

Catherine found a pretty yellow dress, and Siobhán was about to give her privacy to change when she stopped. "Moira suggested you wear the fur coat Enda bought you, what was it, last Christmas?"

Catherine looked startled for a moment. "I don't like to wear it," she said.

"I'm just passing it along."

"Moira mentioned me specifically?" Catherine stared intently at Siobhán.

"I thought so, but I've been totally absorbed in other things. Perhaps I'm mistaken."

"No worries, I'll wear it."

Twenty minutes later, they were outside, and Catherine indeed had on a fur coat. "Should I call a taxi?" Siobhán glanced at a black lorry in the drive, caked in mud.

"It's a rental," Catherine said. "I've been driving all over looking for Theodore. I'm afraid it's out of gas."

"You can come with us, we need a ride as well." Siobhán turned to find Paul Elliot standing in the pasture. He stood next to the green lorry with the Irish Cream logo and painting of a deliriously happy cow.

"Any chance you can give the three of us a lift to the concert," Siobhán called out.

Paul studied them. He was wearing a suit underneath his coat. He finally nodded. "Not a bother. But one of you will have to stand in the back with the crates."

"More crates?" Siobhán said. "You don't think there's enough at the mill?"

Paul glared. "There's nowhere else to store them."

"Fine," Siobhán said. "I'll get in the back. Let's go."

It wasn't possible to perch on a crate, so Siobhán was stuck hunched over in the back. Paul seemed to go over every bump in the road. When Siobhán's mobile rang, she fumbled so much she accidentally hung up twice before finally connecting with Macdara.

"Faye's wheelchair has been stolen," he said.

"I just called it in," Siobhán said. "It is in Catherine's painting shed."

"Catherine?"

Siobhán glanced up at the passenger seat. Catherine stared out the window. She was probably listening to every word. "Yes. Catherine's shed was broken into. Someone smashed the mural she was working on for the concert. And in the corner of the shed we found Faye's wheelchair, the cover for the harp, a cloak, and a torch." She let that settle in.

"Catherine is with you right now?"

"Yes."

"Did you ask about Theodore?"

"I did. The answer remains the same."

"She's protecting him?"

"Or she believes it isn't him."

"How could someone steal a wheelchair out from under a woman?"

"Apparently, Jason loaded it into the van, then he and Paul went to carry Faye out. He didn't notice the wheelchair was gone until they got to the mill."

"Is the painting shed in close proximity to where the van would have been parked?"

"As close as neighbors." She glanced at Jason. "I need you to stay with Faye,"

Siobhán said. "Don't leave her side."

"I'm trying to coordinate getting another wheelchair for her."

"Don't."

"Don't?" He sounded exasperated. "You're telling me *not* to help a disabled woman at Christmas?"

"Yes. I'm sorry. I think someone is trying to distract us. I don't want you leaving the concert venue."

"Where are you?"

"I'm in the back of Paul Elliot's van," she said loudly. Paul glanced back at this.

"Watch out," Catherine yelled, gripping the dashboard. Paul swerved again to straighten the van.

"Those blasted sheep," Paul said. The crates rattled next to Siobhán. Her heart leapt into her throat.

"What was that?" Macdara said. "Is someone after you again?"

"No," Siobhán said. "Just a few sheep crossing the road. Be there soon." She hung up before Macdara could work himself into a state.

They were almost to the bridge. Siobhán just wanted to get to the concert. She'd bring Macdara in on her theory of the killer, see if they had enough to get a confession. She was too close to make any sudden moves. Paul swerved again, then slammed on the brakes and cried out, "Is someone following me?"

CHAPTER 23

Siobhán braced herself for a hit from behind. "Everyone hold on." Seconds later it came. The van lurched forward.

Catherine cried out. "Watch out." Paul turned the keys in the ignition, and they all listened to whines of a flooded engine. He glanced into his rearview mirror.

"Don't," Siobhán said, a second too late.

"I can't see," Paul yelled, his hand flying up to his eyes.

"What's going on?" Catherine asked.

"Someone is behind me," Paul said. "With his brights on."

"I've been through this before," Siobhán said. She placed a call to Macdara. "We're by the bridge. There's someone behind us blinding us again and trying to run us off the road."

The second bump came. The van lurched forward again. "What do I do?" Paul yelled.

"Don't let him drive you off the bridge,"

Siobhán said. "I have a solution, but you're not going to like it."

"What?"

"Is there a pry bar for these crates?"

Paul reached down to his left, picked up a pry bar, and handed it back. Another thud to the back of the van. "He's crazy."

"He wants us in the creek."

"What good is the pry bar going to do?"

"This can't be Theodore," Catherine said. "It can't be."

"Of course it's Theodore," Siobhán said as she began prying the tops off the crates. "He doesn't realize you're in here with us."

"Stick your head out the window," Paul said. "Show him it's you."

Surprisingly Catherine did as she was told.

"It's him!" Paul said. "He turned off the brights."

They were in the middle of the small bridge. It was too small for Theodore to turn around. Siobhán had to keep him here. She opened the back doors, careful not to get too close. "What are you doing?" Paul yelled.

"Keep idling," Siobhán said. She looked out at the lorry behind them. It was dirty. And white. Theodore was the one who stalked and rammed her vehicle. This made doing what she had to do a little easier. She

400

overturned the first crate of Irish cream. Bottles rolled out and rattled as they hit the hood of the lorry, then smashed to the road below. The scent of alcohol filled the air.

"My Irish cream!" Paul yelled.

Theodore's tires spun as he tried to get away. She heard a hiss. His front tire was eaten up by glass and was on its way to deflating.

"Your Irish cream is saving the day," Siobhán said. "Think of the good publicity."

Paul stopped yelling. The dirty white lorry was still trying to spin out despite its flat front tire. Catherine was out of the van, running toward Theodore. Siobhán jumped out to stop her. Finally, in the distance she heard the sound she'd been waiting for. A siren. Then two. And three. Macdara was sending the calvary. The door to the lorry flew open. Theodore jumped out. The only place to go was over the bridge and into the creek.

"You won't get far," Siobhán said. "Don't move. You're under arrest for assault with a deadly weapon."

He held up his hands. "I'm not holding a weapon."

"Your lorry is a deadly weapon when you

use it to run people off the road," Siobhán said.

Theodore looked over the bridge and down at the water. "Don't do it," Siobhán said. "The guards are here."

Catherine was still circling him, trying to get his attention. "Theodore!"

He turned, staring at her with a panicked look. "You did this," he said. Another glance back at the water. There were only a few railings to climb before one could jump into the creek.

"Me?" Catherine yelled. "What do you mean I did this?"

"I wouldn't add resisting arrest to your list," Siobhán said.

Theodore took her in, bouncing like a wild animal as he debated whether he could get away. "What's that compared to murder?"

"We won't be charging you with murder."

"What?" Paul and Jason yelled at the same time.

His eyes practically glowed. "Liar."

Guard cars pulled in from either direction. Macdara got out of one, approaching slowly with a firearm.

"Hands up," Macdara said. Theodore slowly put his hands up.

"She said she's not arresting me for murder," he yelled.

"Assault with a deadly weapon is the charge," Siobhán said. "Twice."

"Twice?" Catherine said, her head zipping from Siobhán to Theodore.

"He ran me off the road the other day," Siobhán said.

"Why?" Catherine cried. "Why did you do it?"

Theodore spat on the ground just before he was cuffed. "You know why. They all deserve it. They think I'm a killer."

"I don't," Siobhán said.

"Why do you keep saying that?" Jason asked. "You saw the wheelchair, and the cloak, and all that other stuff in the shed."

"What?" Theodore said. "I have no idea what you're talking about."

"The painting shed," Siobhán said. "Where Catherine claimed to be working on a mural."

"Claimed?" Catherine said as the guards holding Theodore led him to the nearest guard car.

Macdara fell in beside Siobhán. "What are you thinking here, boss?" From his tone, he was worried that their killer was Theodore. And even though they'd done it by the book, it wasn't going to look good — having hoisted out Garda Cooley only to arrest the same exact man for murder. Thank heavens there wouldn't be a second one. She turned to Catherine Healy.

"Catherine Healy, you are under arrest for the murder of Enda Elliot."

"What?" Jason and Macdara said at the same time. Theodore stared out the window of the guard car. Catherine didn't move or blink.

"You are not obliged to say anything unless you wish to do so, but anything you say will be taken down in writing and may be given as evidence," Siobhán continued.

Catherine stared at Siobhán, then ran her hand along her fur coat. "Moira didn't ask me to wear this, did she?"

"No," Siobhán said. "I don't believe she even realizes you have one."

"Then how did you know?"

"Because Enda gave the same present to all the women in his life."

"How is Catherine considered a woman in my father's life?" Paul asked.

"You can't convict Theodore, so you're arresting me?" Catherine said.

"We can convict Theodore for attempting to assault me *twice* with his vehicle. But you are Enda's killer."

"Prove it," Catherine said even as guards placed cuffs on her. "What do you think you know?"

"I wouldn't mind a heads-up myself," Macdara said.

Siobhán made eye contact with Catherine. "Do you want to tell him, or are you going to make me do it?" Siobhán said.

"Jason," Catherine said.

Jason jerked back, surprised to be mentioned. "Yes?"

"Everything I did, I did for you."

"Me?"

"I'm sorry you have to find out this way," Siobhán said.

Jason stepped forward. "Find out what?"

"Tell him," Siobhán urged. "Or I will."

"I carried you," Catherine said. "I gave birth to you." The words spilled out. And given they'd been simmering for the past twenty-one years, they sounded heavy on Catherine's tongue.

"You're my surrogate?" Jason asked.

"Yes," Catherine said. *And your father's killer.*

"Catherine isn't *just* a surrogate," Siobhán said. She had given Catherine a chance. It was time for the truth.

"Jason," Catherine said. "I didn't want you to find out like this."

"Surrogate?" Paul said, whipping around to face her. "You?"

"Moira's records will show that Catherine

was 'out of the country' for a little over a year," Siobhán said. "She came back a few months after Jason was born."

"My word," Paul said.

"That's hardly proof," Catherine said.

"It was a big piece of the puzzle though," Siobhán said. "Given you never traveled that long before or after."

"Catherine?" Jason said. "What does she mean you weren't *just* a surrogate?"

Siobhán knew the pieces were clicking into place for Jason the way they had for her. The DNA test. Everyone was so focused on it pointing to paternity that they never considered it was all about the mother.

Not just a surrogate. A biological mother.

Catherine refused to make eye contact, but that didn't stop Siobhán. "You and Enda had an affair while he was married to Faye."

"It was hard to resist Enda Elliot when he turned all that passion on you," Catherine said.

"I'll have to take your word for it," Siobhán said. She turned to Macdara. "Enda wasn't driving in that car accident. Faye was." She gave a nod to Jason. "There's something about that story you don't know. Enda did blame himself for the accident. He's the one who confessed his sins to her that night. And it almost killed both of them."

"News that he was having an affair," Jason said. "And that Catherine was pregnant. *With me.*" He put his hands on his head as if the pressure of the news was too great to bear.

"It's not your fault," Catherine said. "It's not your fault."

"You knew," Jason said. "All these years, you knew."

"I wanted you to have a better life." Tears poured down Catherine's face. "He promised me you'd have everything. The best education. Travel. Family. I couldn't give you what he could. What they could. I knew Faye would be a good mother. It was either go along with your father's plan or lose everything."

"What plan?" Jason said.

"The surrogacy story," Siobhán said. "Enda didn't want to humiliate Faye by admitting he fathered a child with another woman. They convinced Catherine to pretend to be a surrogate, and he paid her well for it over the years."

"It wasn't just about the money," Catherine said. She tried to make eye contact with Jason. "I didn't give Jason that DNA test."

"No," Siobhán said. "Theodore did."

Catherine chewed on her lip and looked away. "Theodore figured it out, didn't he? Was he pressuring you to ask for more money?"

"I deserved that money."

"Was that when you knew Theodore was finally too much of a problem to keep around?" The guard car housing Theodore had already left. Siobhán had no doubt Theodore would back up Siobhán's story, once he realized Catherine had tried to set him up. "Not only did you kill Enda, but you were very close to having it all blamed on your lover." The cloak that used to belong to Theodore. The made-up alibi. Theodore's reputation. Catherine Healy not only planned this murder but also picked out the one who would take the blame. The village had been wrong about one thing: Catherine Healy no longer adored Theodore Baskins. He had worn out his welcome.

"That's absurd," Catherine said.

"Then why did you stuff his locker with the elf costume and Enda's torch?" Catherine folded her arms and chewed on her lip. "What were you doing in that elf costume anyway? Was that when you dug up the hatchet?"

"If you hadn't been so nosy I wouldn't

have had to create distractions," Catherine said.

"That's my lass," Macdara said. "Nosy as can be."

Siobhán kept her focus on Catherine. She'd give out to Dara for his cheeky comment later. "Not a bad plan considering everyone in this town so wanted to believe the devil they knew." Siobhán turned back to Macdara. "The DNA kit wasn't a present for Jason. It was a warning to Faye. You see, Enda's payments to both women had recently stopped. Moira mentioned how hard it was for Catherine to keep up payments on her house."

"Theodore tried to blackmail my mother?" Jason said.

"He never knew when to stop," Catherine said. "That's when I knew Theodore had to go. I chose my son over my lover." She held her arms open to Jason as if she actually expected him to run into them. He turned away in disgust.

"I guess Theodore's lucky he trusted his instincts and ran," Siobhán said.

"Did you ever care about me, or was it all about the money?" Jason asked.

"I loved you," Catherine said. "Always."

"You had a funny way of showing it." Jason was shocked and hurt. This was going to take time to process.

"Lay out the case for me, will you, boss?" Macdara asked. "From the beginning?"

"Of course." She almost forgot Dara wasn't here from the beginning. "Catherine was late the morning we were supposed to decorate the mill. She had flecks of paint on her face — at least that's what I assumed, because she said she'd been up all night working on a mural. But it wasn't paint. It was glitter. Catherine knew that Enda planned on spilling all his secrets at the concert, including that she was Jason's biological mother. This way she'd have no power over him anymore. Her golden goose was on his deathbed. Catherine didn't have the lorry that evening, because Theodore drove it to a party. She was on foot. She knew Enda had cameras on the mill, which is why she dressed in costume. She must have grabbed it from the mill on one of her earlier scouting expeditions for the mural. Her trap worked, and Enda was lured to the mill. Did you try to talk him out of it once more?"

Catherine folded her arms. "He was a stubborn man."

"After she pushed him and exited — with his torch and the cover to the harp stuffed in her cloak — she realized that Enda had

410

driven his lorry to the mill." Siobhán stopped to gaze at Catherine, who she could tell was listening intently. "She could have just left his lorry there. But she thought maybe it would cause more confusion if she brought it back and slashed the tire. Only you didn't realize you were covered in glitter from hiding up in the gallery. And you spread glitter all over the lorry."

"All that glitters is not gold," Catherine said dryly.

"Indeed. You had to clean it. But that was actually the first big clue you left. Why on earth would Enda's lorry be spotless when it's nothing but mud out here?"

"Glitter," Catherine said, shaking her head. "Brought down by glitter."

"Then I realized she was Jason's biological mother. The DNA kit, the logs Moira kept showing that Catherine was out of town for an entire year. And your checks were about to be cut off. You had to stage a break-in in your painting shed because otherwise you were going to have a tough time explaining why there was no mural." She'd been too busy trying to get away with murder.

"You should have stayed out of it," Catherine said.

"It's not in my nature," Siobhán said.

411

"Please. He was probably dying anyway. I won't hurt anyone ever again."

"You can't be serious," Jason said. "We're not going to let you get away with this."

Siobhán was almost finished. Jason needed to hear it all. "She had it all planned. This was her performance. Everything under a spotlight." She turned back to Catherine. "I heard your phone playing 'Jingle Bells,' which is when I realized you at least knew how to change the ringtone. And of course Enda made you play classical music while you were pregnant, didn't he?"

"All day, every day," Catherine said. "And this is the thanks I get."

"I'd say it wasn't successful," Jason said. "I never did fit in with the rest of the Elliot family."

"You're perfect," Catherine said. "Just the way you are."

"I wish I could say the same thing about you," Jason said.

"I'm sorry," Catherine said. "Not about your father. His time had come. I'm sorry I'll never have the chance to be your mother."

"I already have a mother," Jason said. "You're right about one thing. I'd take Faye as my mother any day. And my father didn't deserve this. I'll never forgive you." Catherine hung her head. "But I will have just the tiniest bit of respect if you give a full confession and own up to everything you've done."

"She's already been read her rights," Macdara said. "Everything she just said has been written down and can be used in court." He hoisted his notebook in case they were in doubt.

Catherine stared at her son. "I did it," she said. "I pushed Enda Elliot from the balcony."

He stared at her, then nodded. "At least you've confessed."

"We'd better get her to the station," one of the guards said. "We'll have her in the holding cell until you're finished with the concert." Catherine thrashed as the guards tried to seat her in the car.

"You did it," Macdara said. "And now the musicians can honor Enda in peace." Paul grabbed a bottle of Irish cream from his lorry, opened it, and started to drink. He stopped, then offered the bottle to Jason, who took it, drank, and handed it back. Perhaps there was a right time to drink Elliot's Irish Cream after all, and maybe, just maybe, Jason could become closer with the rest of the family. The wind picked up and snow began to fall as the guard car pulled away. Catherine stared out the window at

Jason. Once again, he turned away.

"Come on," Siobhán said, gesturing to Jason and Paul and taking Macdara by the arm. "It's Christmas Eve. And the holiday concert is about to begin."

CHAPTER 24

The mill was finally what it was once envisioned to be — cheery and bright, sparkling with Christmas. Harry Williams stood in front of the orchestra, smiling broadly in his Santa cap. After the local priest gave a quick blessing for Enda Elliot, the music swelled and washed over the villagers. The notes infused everyone from head to toe, filling them with joy. Siobhán felt tears come to her eyes, that is until several of her siblings poked her. She wiped her face and grabbed Ann and Ciarán's hands, and soon they held on to Gráinne, and James, and Eoin, and Elise, and Macdara. The hand holding started to spread, to Orla, and Paul, and Moira, and so on down the line. By the time the orchestra was playing "Jingle Bells," the crowd was all linked, swaying to the beat, and singing. It was a true gift, the power of music. It connected people. It pulsed through one's heartbeat, and breath, and blood, even vibrated the earth beneath one's feet. No wonder she wanted her family to be more musical; its power to transform was nothing short of miraculous.

After the concert, the open bar made sure that the cheer continued. People avoided the Irish cream, but there were plenty of other libations. Siobhán hoped that Paul Elliot would learn how to improve his product. And find a new use for the ones that were already bottled. Perhaps it could replace coal in one's stocking for everyone on Santa's naughty list. Siobhán stuck to champagne. But not too much — she didn't want to be tipsy for Midnight Mass.

The O'Sullivans agreed they would do a private gift opening Christmas morning in the guest cottage, with Elise, Macdara, and Nancy Flannery joining the family. Later, everyone would gather at Moira's for Christmas dinner. News of Catherine's arrest did begin to leak out during the reception, but Siobhán purposefully kept away from all the chin-wagging. As far as she was concerned, it was Christmas and she was all-in. Moira had given her permission to use her kitchen, and Siobhán planned on making heaps and heaps of brown bread for Christmas morning. People would beg her for the recipe, as they always did, but she'd have to parrot her Mam: *"Recipes are handed down, not out."* She was lucky to be the recipient of it.

Siobhán stood in Moira's kitchen, watching snow fall out the back window. She was sliding her seventh pan of brown bread into the cooker when Moira entered.

"Nollaig shona duit," Moira said.

Siobhán hoisted up her mug of tea. "Happy Christmas to you as well, Moira."

Moira smiled. "There's nothing like the scent of fresh-baked bread in the morning. Especially Christmas morning."

"It feels good to get a few batches in."

"Perfect timing," Moira said. "You might need a loaf yourself."

Something in Moira's tone was putting Siobhán on edge. "Why is that?"

"Now that Theodore and Catherine are not available, we need another person to take the Polar Bear plunge. How about you and that handsome Detective Sergeant of yours?"

"The Polar Bear Swim?" Siobhán said. "Me? And Dara?"

"Yes, the pair of ye's."

"Now?"

Moira grinned. "Right now. You're young. Think of how refreshing it will be."

"A shock of cold can do wonders for one's

perspective, is that it?" Siobhán asked.

"Mind like a steel trap, I see." Moira laughed. "Why don't you try it and you can tell me?"

"How about James and Elise? Aren't they eager to take the plunge?"

"No worries," Moira said. "I just thought you were brave."

"No worries. I just thought you were brave." That little manipulator.

"Why do you always get me into these things?" Macdara shivered in his swim trunks beside Siobhán. Her own teeth rattled so hard she suddenly felt musical.

"We can do this." Siobhán squeezed his hand, then dropped it lest he decided to give her a shove. They stood on a fat rock above the ocean, listening to the guttural yells of those who felt the frigid waters before them. *Eejit. She was a right eejit.* Perhaps this was the best ending to her stay in West Cork, and she knew when she emerged, the warmth that waited for her. Her siblings. Presents to open around the tree adorned from nature. Chocolates. A nice big feed: turkey, and ham, and mashed potatoes, and carrots and parsnips. Champagne. An apple tart with real cream. A fat mug of coffee, or cocoa, or tea. And of course Christmas wouldn't be complete without a cuddle with the blue-eyed, messy-haired man. "Happy Christmas, Dara."

"Happy Christmas, boss."

"Ready?" She squeezed Macdara's hand. He squeezed back.

"On three," Macdara said. "One . . ." When he reached two, she pushed him in.

SIOBHÁN'S BROWN BREAD RECIPE

HAPPY CHRISTMAS

Author introduction: Brown bread is a delicious staple in Ireland, good with butter and jam on its own, or to complement a meal or a soup (seafood chowder or potato leek soup!). I get asked for this recipe a lot, which is a challenge because I do not cook or bake extensively. But I did fall in love with the brown bread in Ireland, and I've learned that although there are variations on it, the recipes are pretty simple. There are even entire kits you can buy if you are so inclined. The Irish will recommend you buy only Irish flour. There are several varieties. King Arthur, Odlums, and Irish-Style Flour are a few.

Ingredients
2 1/2 cups stone ground whole wheat flour
1 1/2 cups white flour (some bakers use whole wheat again)

1/2 cup rolled oats
1 1/2 teaspoon salt
1 teaspoon baking soda
1 3/4 cups buttermilk
2 tablespoons molasses or treacle (optional, but Siobhán uses it)
Siobhán even splashes in some Guinness for luck.

In a large bowl, combine all flour, oats, salt, and baking soda. In a separate bowl, whisk together the buttermilk and molasses.

Make a well in the center of the dry ingredients and pour in the buttermilk mixture. (Add a drop of Guinness for good luck.) Stir with a fork or spatula until combined.

Cover your hands with flour and knead the dough into a ball. Place the dough ball on a lined baking sheet and press it flat, a few inches thick. With a knife, make a cross on top of the loaf.

Bake at 450°F for 15 minutes. Then reduce to 400°F and bake an additional 20 to 25 minutes, until the bottom of the bread sounds hollow when tapped.

Note: I once asked an Irish woman for her brown bread recipe. She let me know that recipes are handed down, not out. So I pushed my luck and asked how hers was so soft. She relented on this and suggested longer baking times at lower heat, that is, 180 degrees for one hour.

ABOUT THE AUTHOR

Carlene O'Connor is the *USA Today* bestselling author of the acclaimed Irish Village Mysteries and the Home to Ireland Mysteries. She comes from a long line of Irish storytellers. Her great-grandmother emigrated from Ireland filled with tales in 1897 and the stories have been flowing ever since. Of all the places across the pond she's wandered, she fell most in love with a walled town in County Limerick and was inspired to create the town of Kilbane, County Cork. Carlene currently divides her time between Chicago and the Emerald Isle. Please visit her online at CarleneOConnor.net.

The employees of Thorndike Press hope you have enjoyed this Large Print book. All our Thorndike, Wheeler, and Kennebec Large Print titles are designed for easy reading, and all our books are made to last. Other Thorndike Press Large Print books are available at your library, through selected bookstores, or directly from us.

For information about titles, please call:
  (800) 223-1244

or visit our website at:
  gale.com/thorndike

To share your comments, please write:
  Publisher
  Thorndike Press
  10 Water St., Suite 310
  Waterville, ME 04901

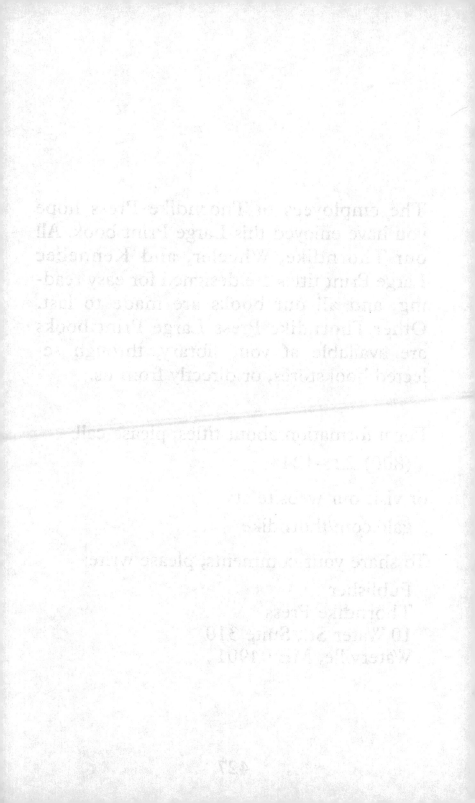